er's CREATURES

Case #1: BOG GONE!

P. Knuckle Jones

Penguin Workshop

For K.K. and R.K. Thank you for
finally letting me out —P.K.J.

W

PENGUIN WORKSHOP
An imprint of Penguin Random House LLC, New York

First published in the United States of America by Penguin Workshop,
an imprint of Penguin Random House LLC, New York, 2023

Visit us online at penguinrandomhouse.com.

Library of Congress Cataloging-in-Publication Data is available.

Manufactured in China

ISBN 9780593519851   10 9 8 7 6 5 4 3 2 1 HH

Design and lettering by Jamie Alloy

Chapter 1: Mystery Monday

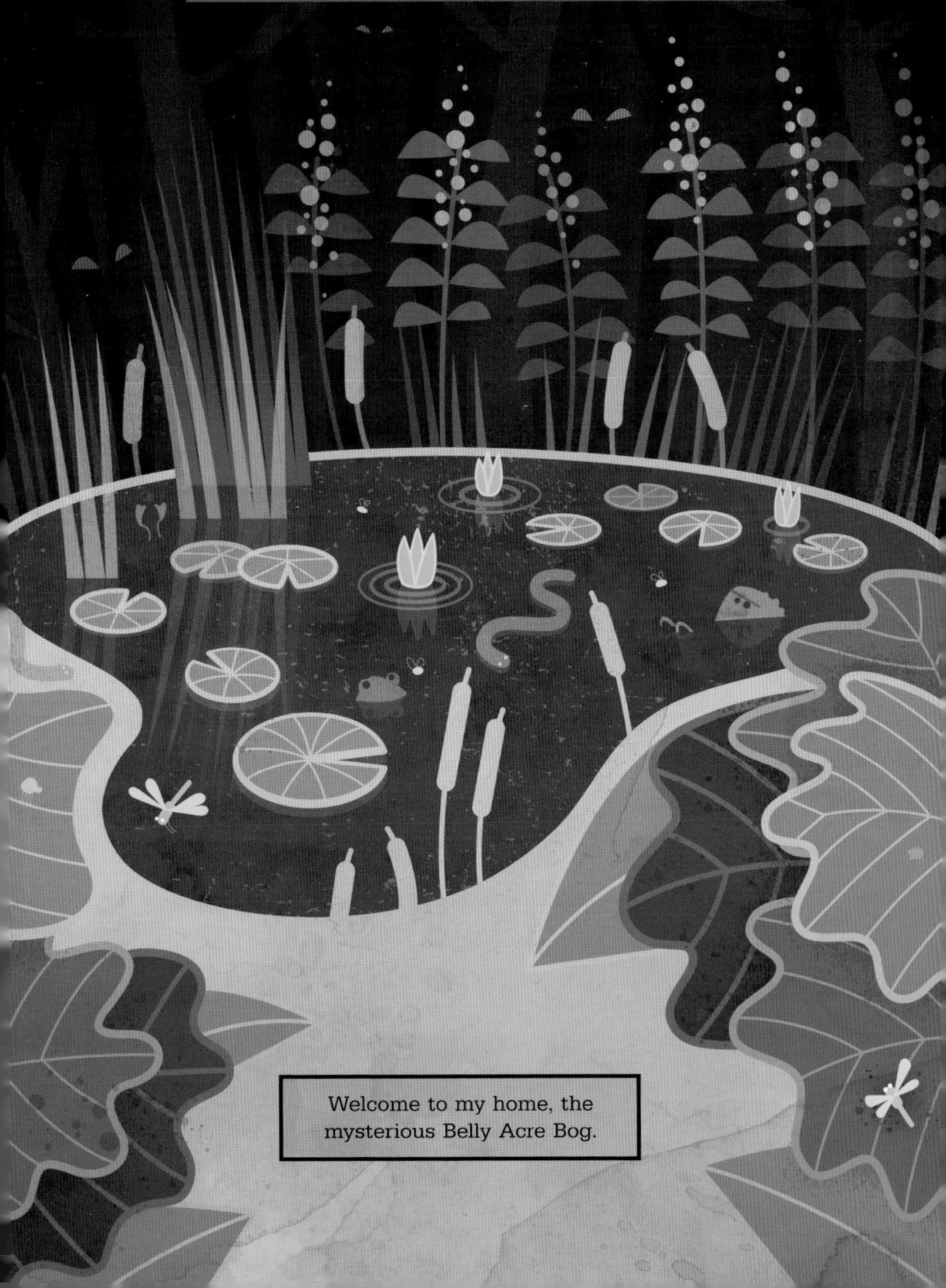
Welcome to my home, the mysterious Belly Acre Bog.

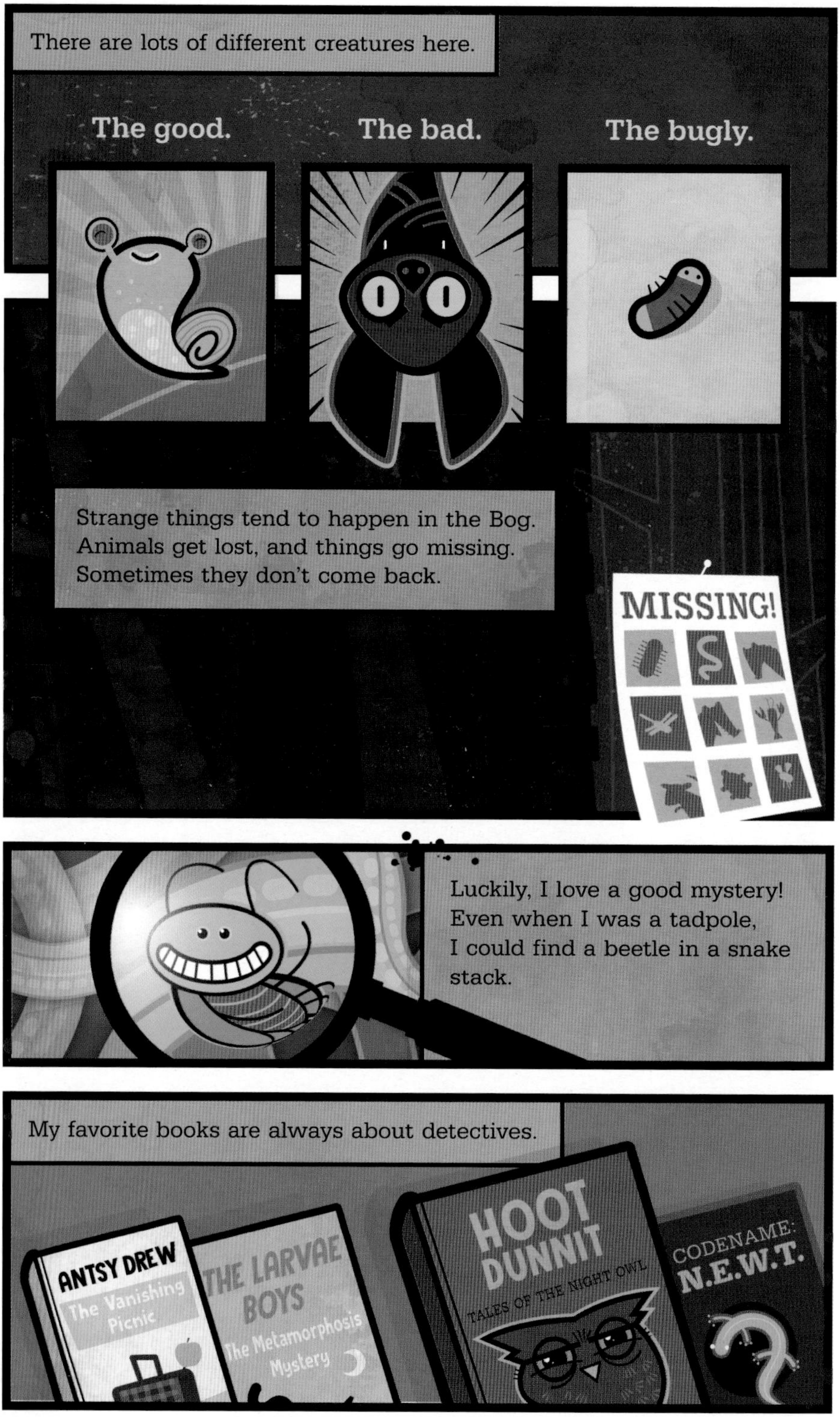
There are lots of different creatures here.
The good.
The bad.
The bugly.
Strange things tend to happen in the Bog. Animals get lost, and things go missing. Sometimes they don't come back.
MISSING!
Luckily, I love a good mystery! Even when I was a tadpole, I could find a beetle in a snake stack.
My favorite books are always about detectives.
ANTSY DREW
The Vanishing Picnic
THE LARVAE BOYS
The Metamorphosis Mystery
HOOT DUNNIT
TALES OF THE NIGHT OWL
CODENAME: N.E.W.T.

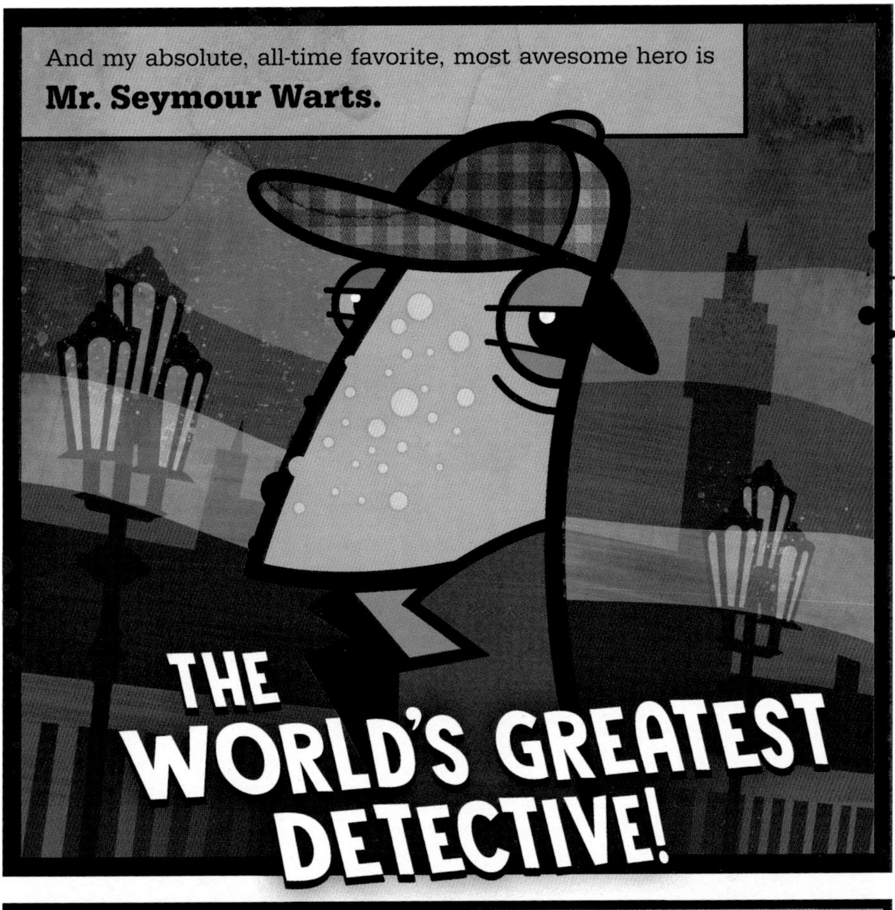
And my absolute, all-time favorite, most awesome hero is **Mr. Seymour Warts.**
THE WORLD'S GREATEST DETECTIVE!

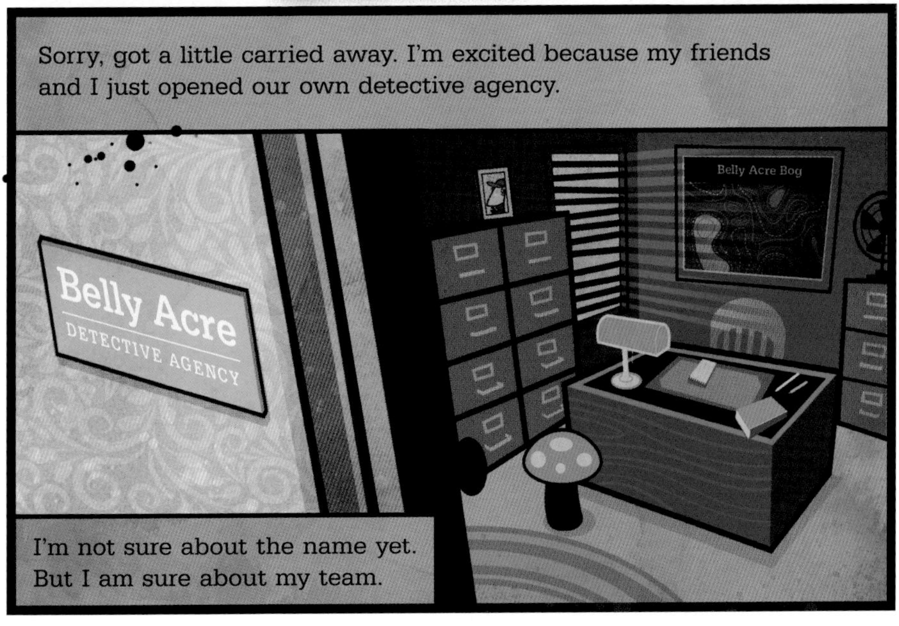
Sorry, got a little carried away. I'm excited because my friends and I just opened our own detective agency.
Belly Acre Bog
Belly Acre DETECTIVE AGENCY
I'm not sure about the name yet. But I am sure about my team.

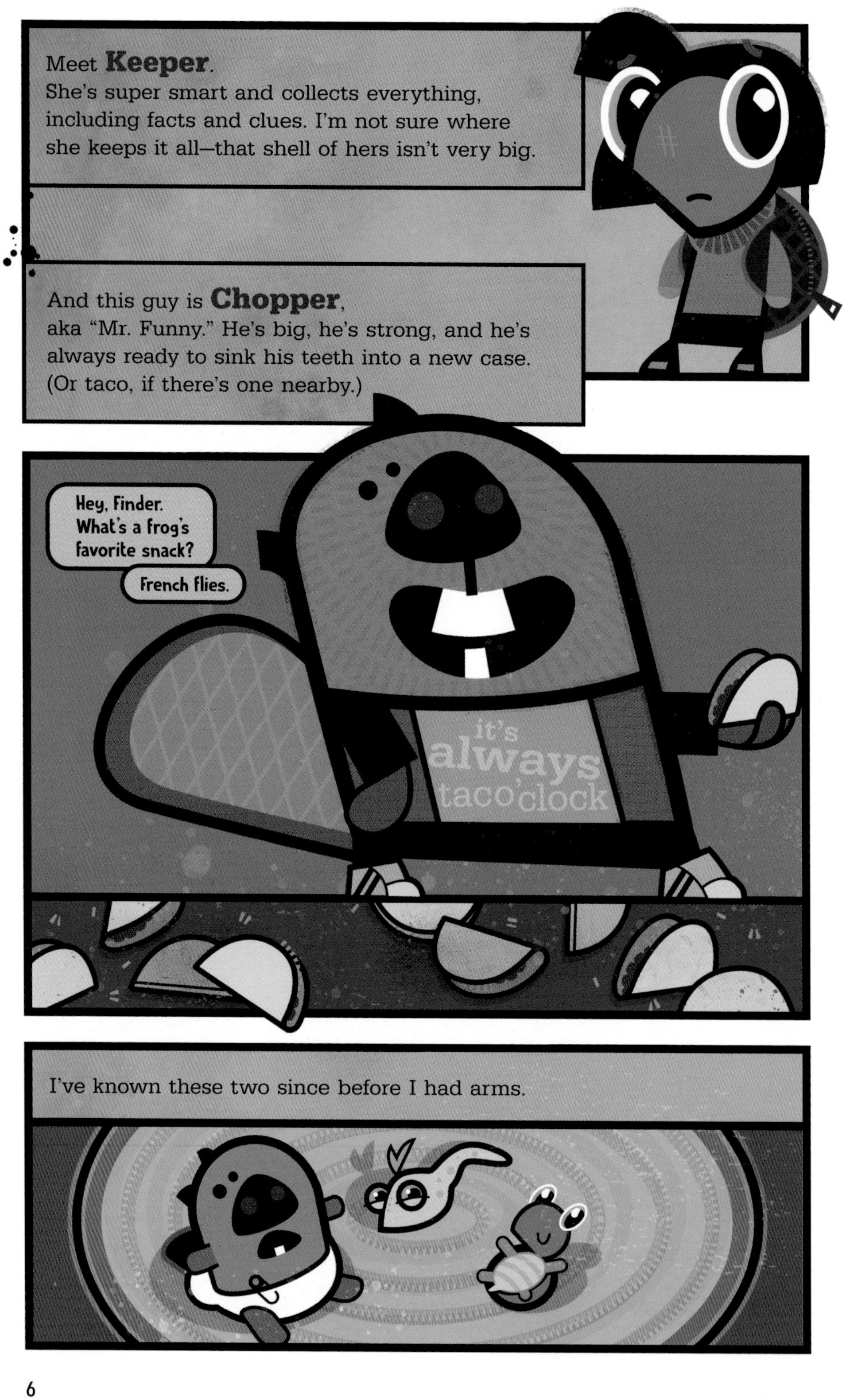
Meet **Keeper**.
She's super smart and collects everything, including facts and clues. I'm not sure where she keeps it all—that shell of hers isn't very big.
And this guy is **Chopper**,
aka "Mr. Funny." He's big, he's strong, and he's always ready to sink his teeth into a new case. (Or taco, if there's one nearby.)
Hey, Finder. What's a frog's favorite snack?
French flies.
it's always taco'clock
I've known these two since before I had arms.

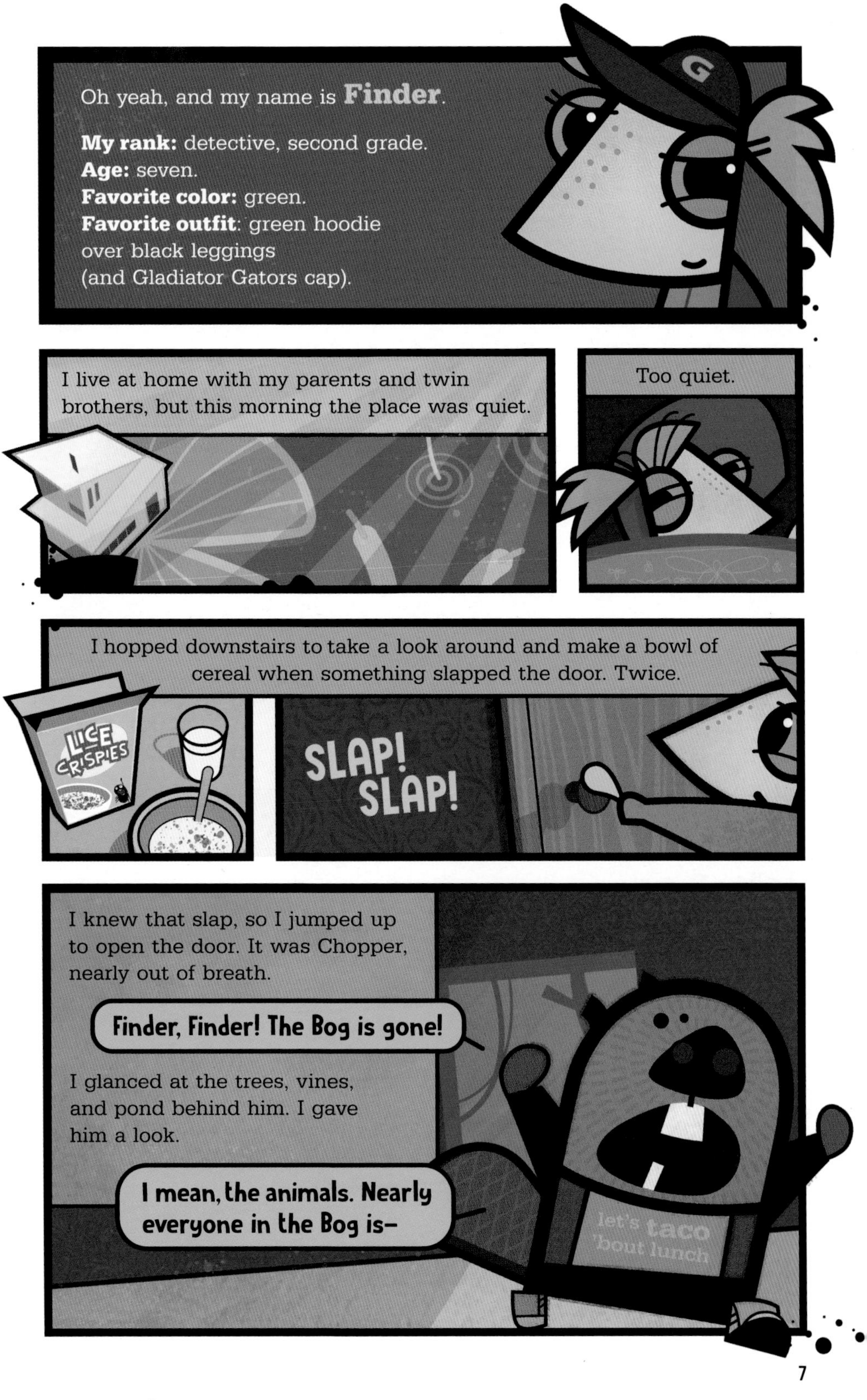

Oh yeah, and my name is **Finder**.
My rank: detective, second grade.
Age: seven.
Favorite color: green.
Favorite outfit: green hoodie over black leggings (and Gladiator Gators cap).
G
I live at home with my parents and twin brothers, but this morning the place was quiet.
Too quiet.
I hopped downstairs to take a look around and make a bowl of cereal when something slapped the door. Twice.
LICE CRISPIES
SLAP! SLAP!
I knew that slap, so I jumped up to open the door. It was Chopper, nearly out of breath.
Finder, Finder! The Bog is gone!
I glanced at the trees, vines, and pond behind him. I gave him a look.
I mean, the animals. Nearly everyone in the Bog is–
let's taco 'bout lunch

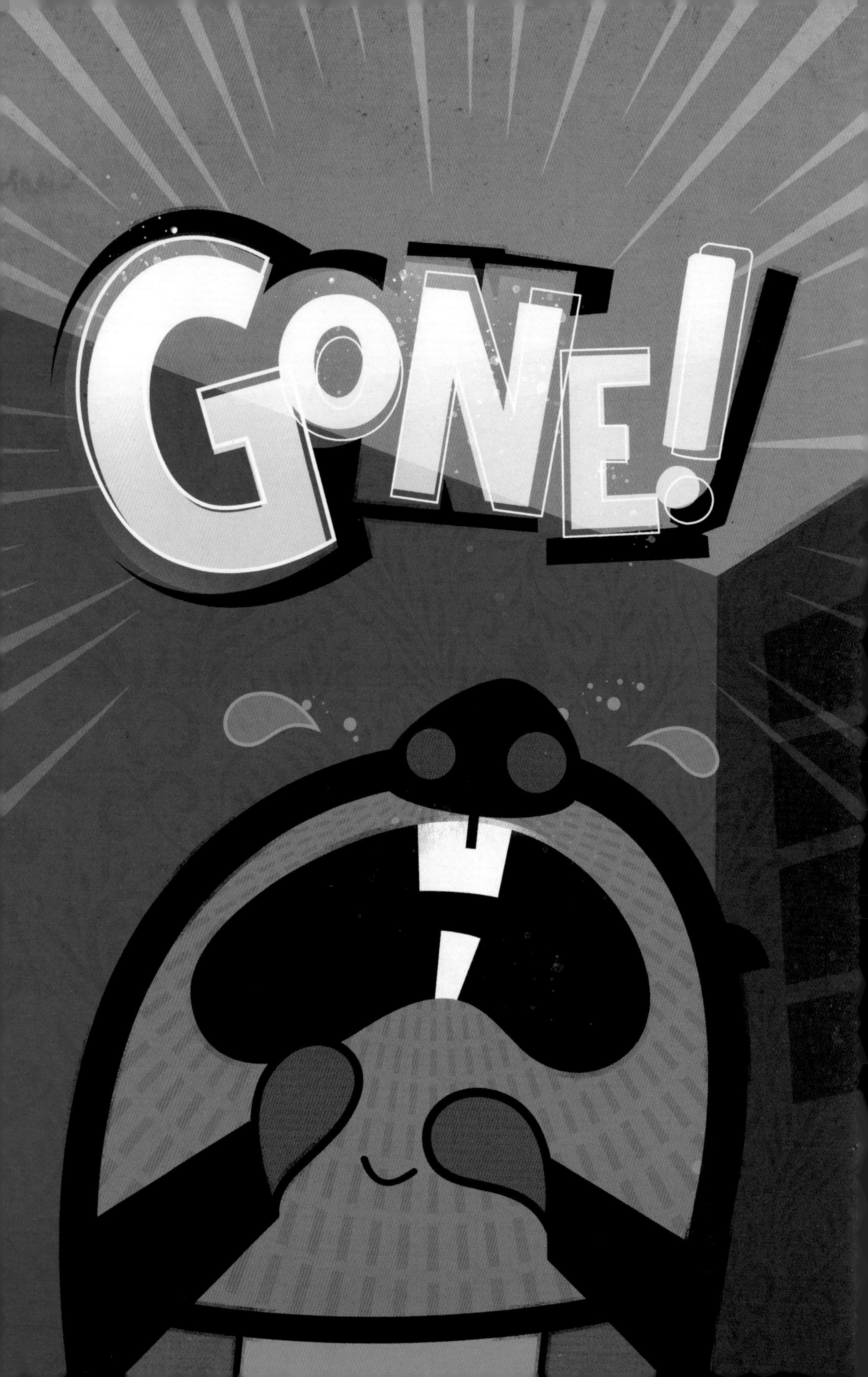
GONE!

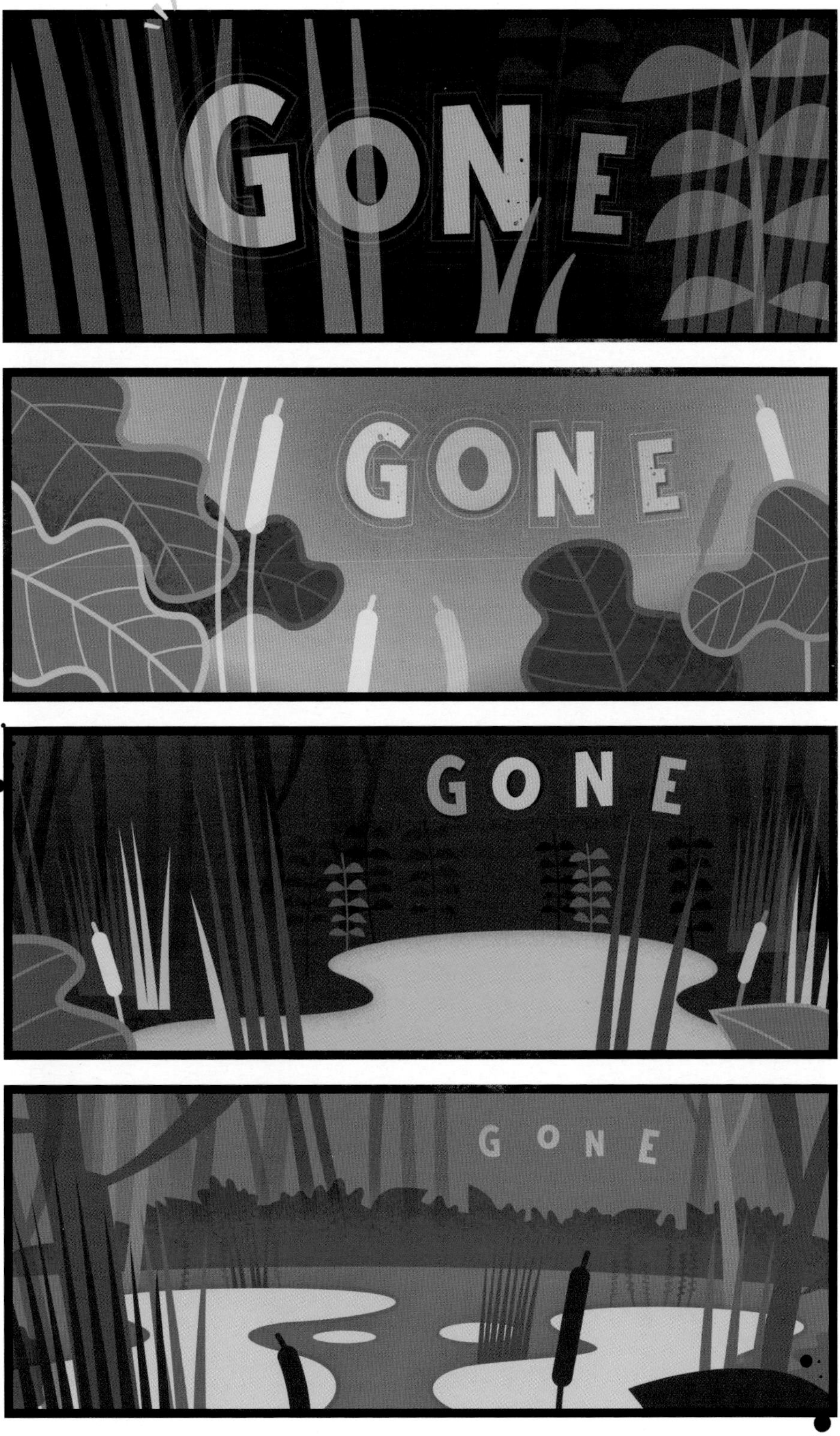
GONE
GONE
GONE
GONE

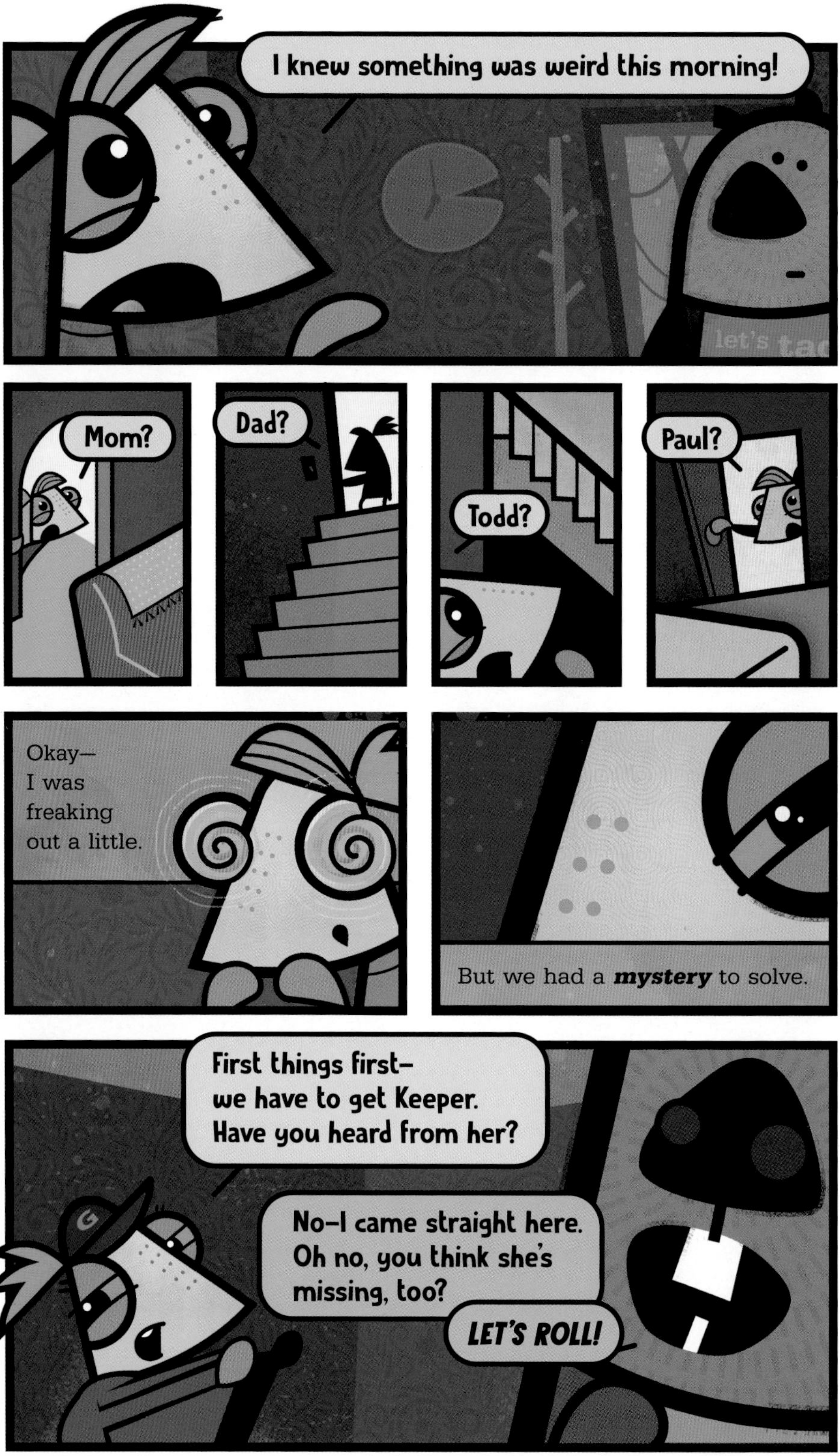

I knew something was weird this morning!
Mom?
Dad?
Todd?
Paul?
Okay—
I was
freaking
out a little.
But we had a ***mystery*** to solve.
First things first–
we have to get Keeper.
Have you heard from her?
No–I came straight here.
Oh no, you think she's
missing, too?
LET'S ROLL!

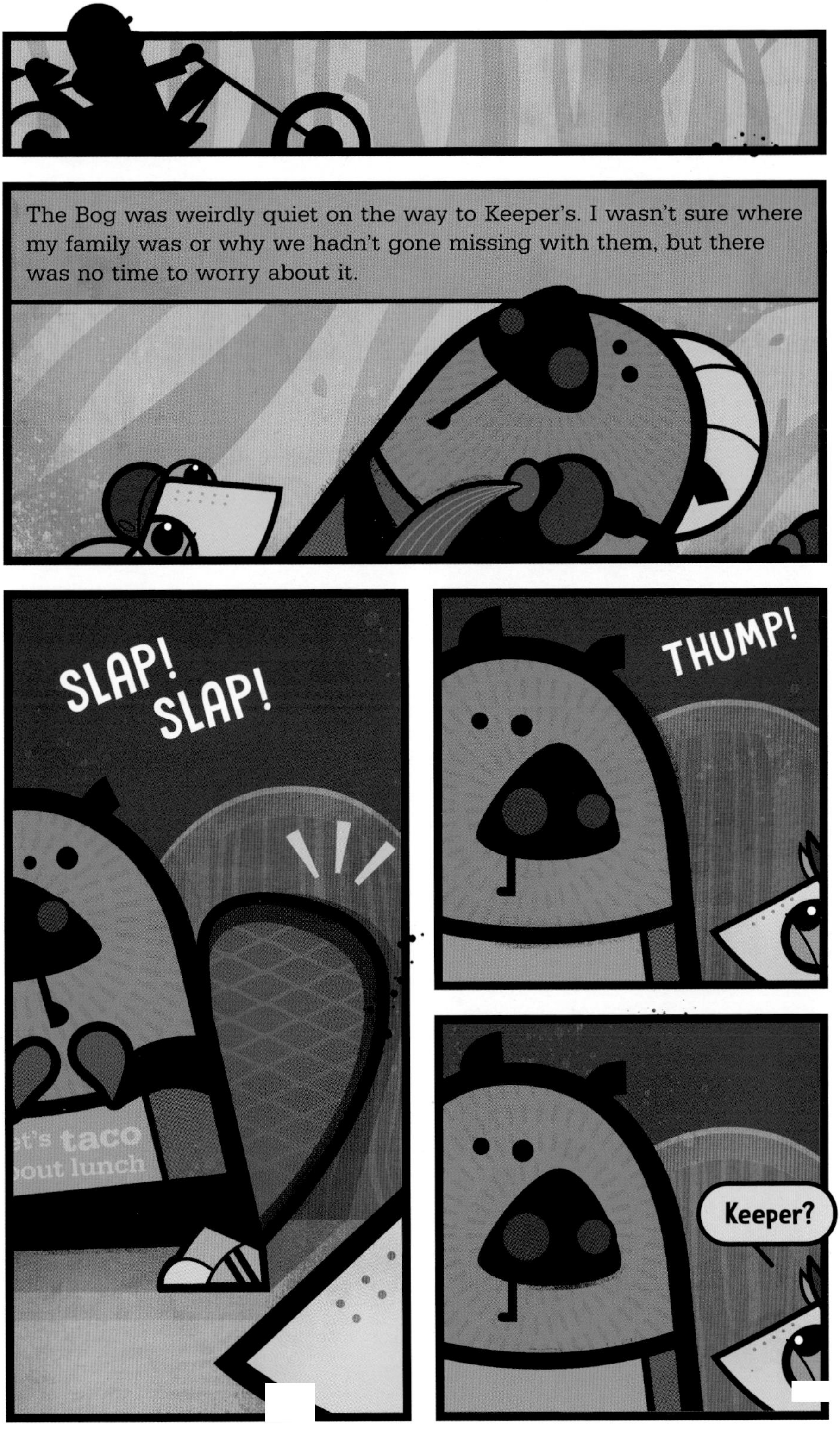
The Bog was weirdly quiet on the way to Keeper's. I wasn't sure where my family was or why we hadn't gone missing with them, but there was no time to worry about it.
SLAP! SLAP!
et's taco
out lunch
THUMP!
Keeper?

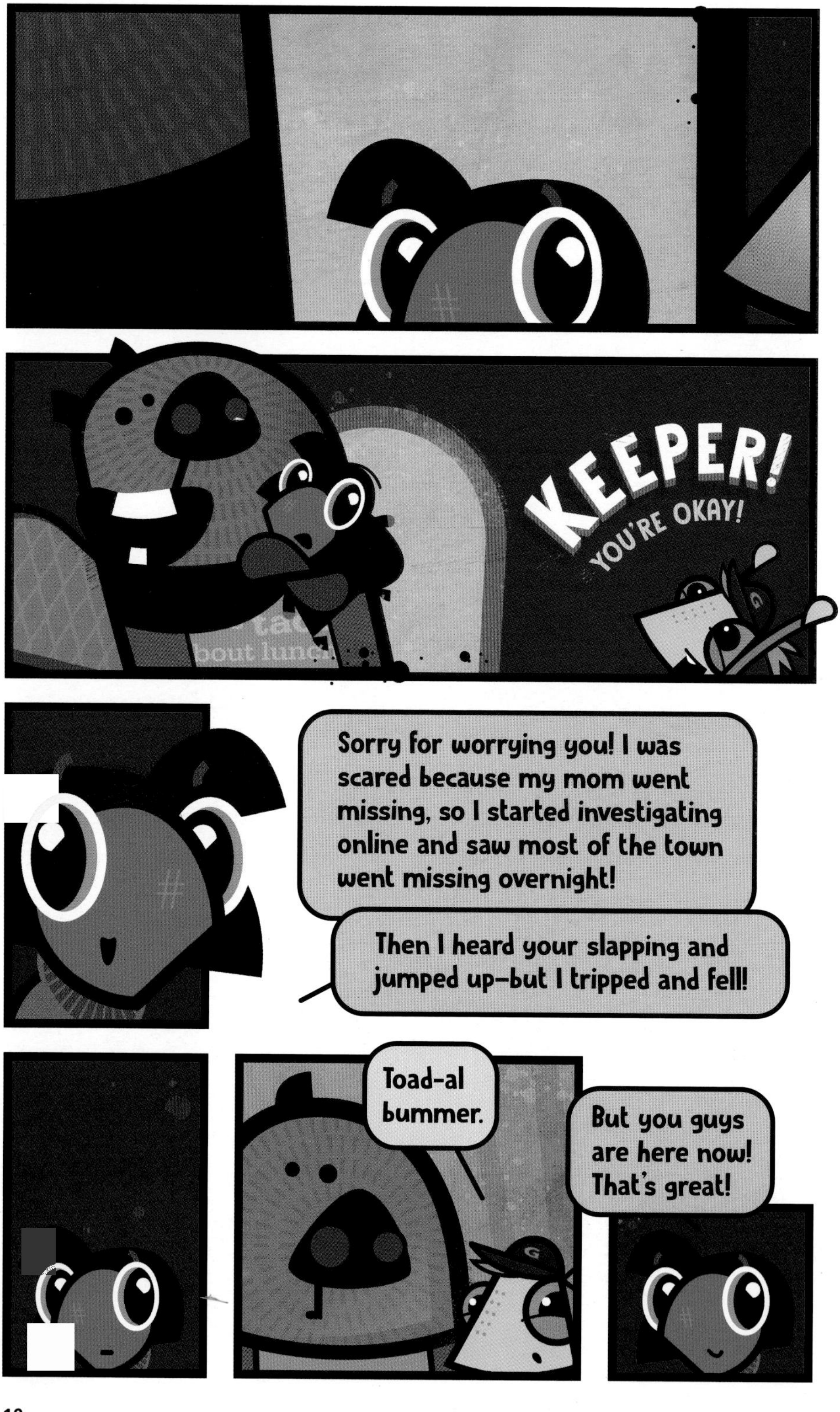
KEEPER!
YOU'RE OKAY!
Sorry for worrying you! I was scared because my mom went missing, so I started investigating online and saw most of the town went missing overnight!
Then I heard your slapping and jumped up—but I tripped and fell!
Toad-al bummer.
But you guys are here now! That's great!

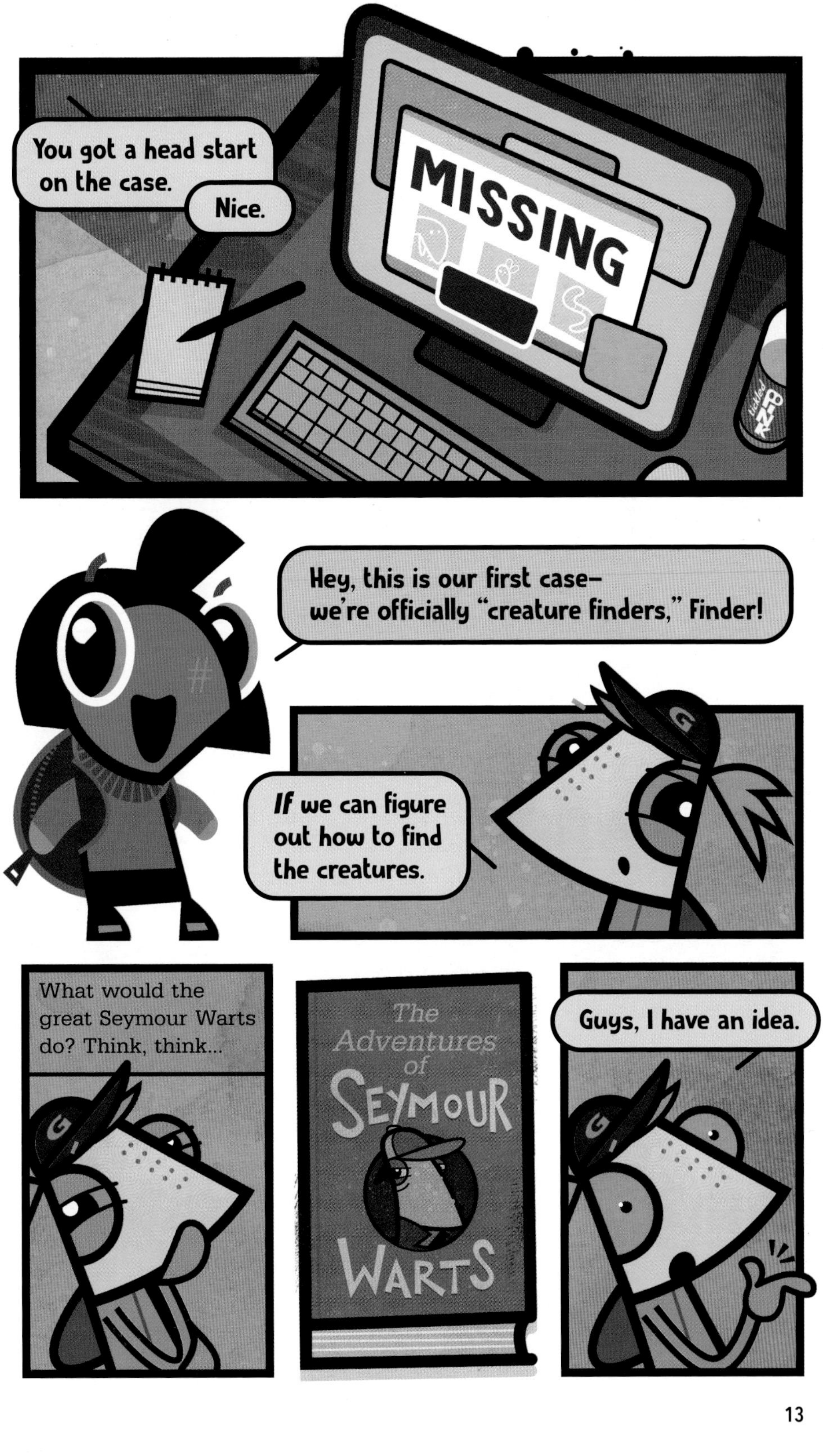
You got a head start on the case.
Nice.
MISSING
Hey, this is our first case—we're officially "creature finders," Finder!
If we can figure out how to find the creatures.
What would the great Seymour Warts do? Think, think...
The Adventures of Seymour Warts
Guys, I have an idea.

Chapter 2: Warts and Al

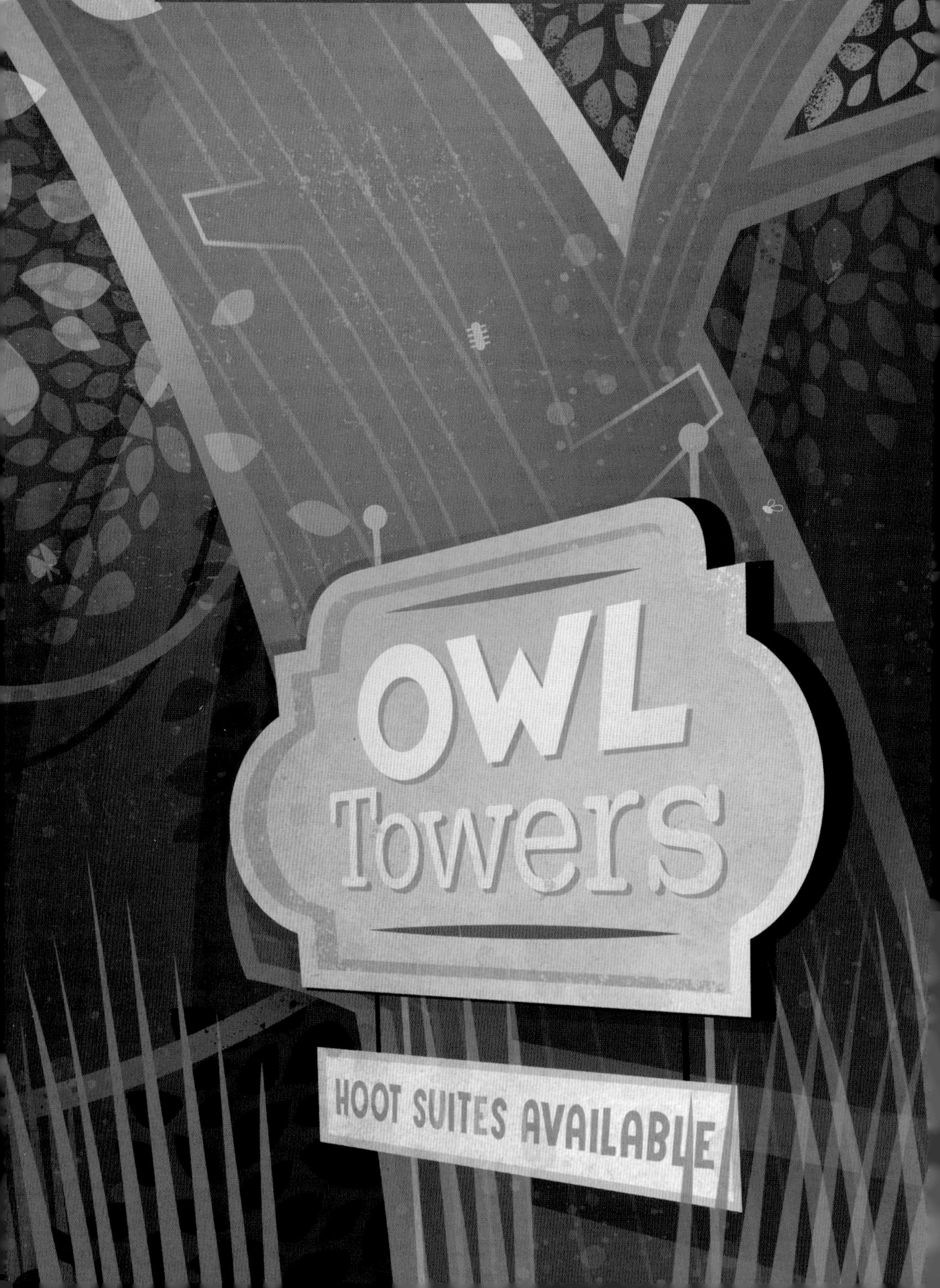
OWL
Towers
HOOT SUITES AVAILABLE

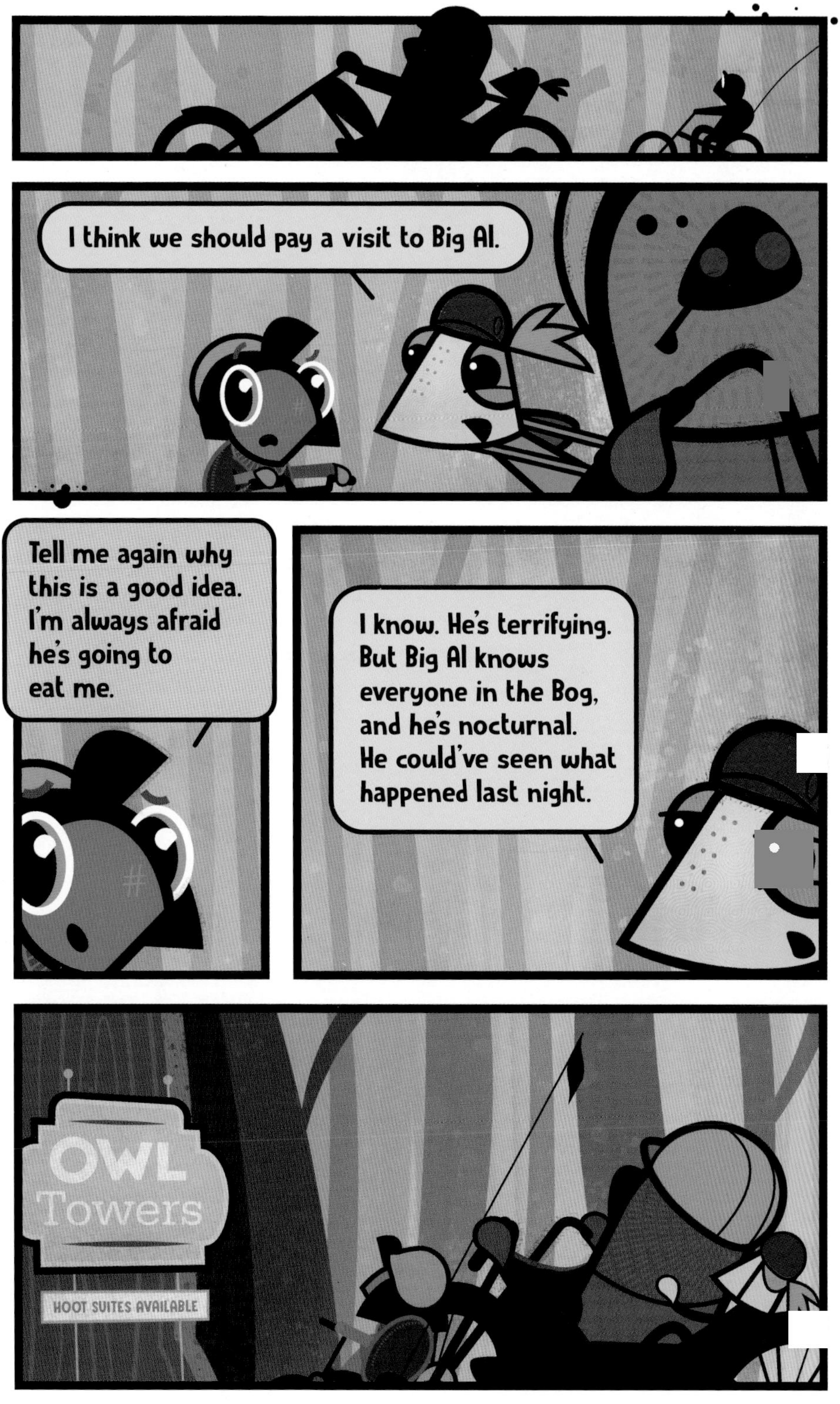
I think we should pay a visit to Big Al.
Tell me again why this is a good idea. I'm always afraid he's going to eat me.
I know. He's terrifying. But Big Al knows everyone in the Bog, and he's nocturnal. He could've seen what happened last night.
OWL Towers
HOOT SUITES AVAILABLE

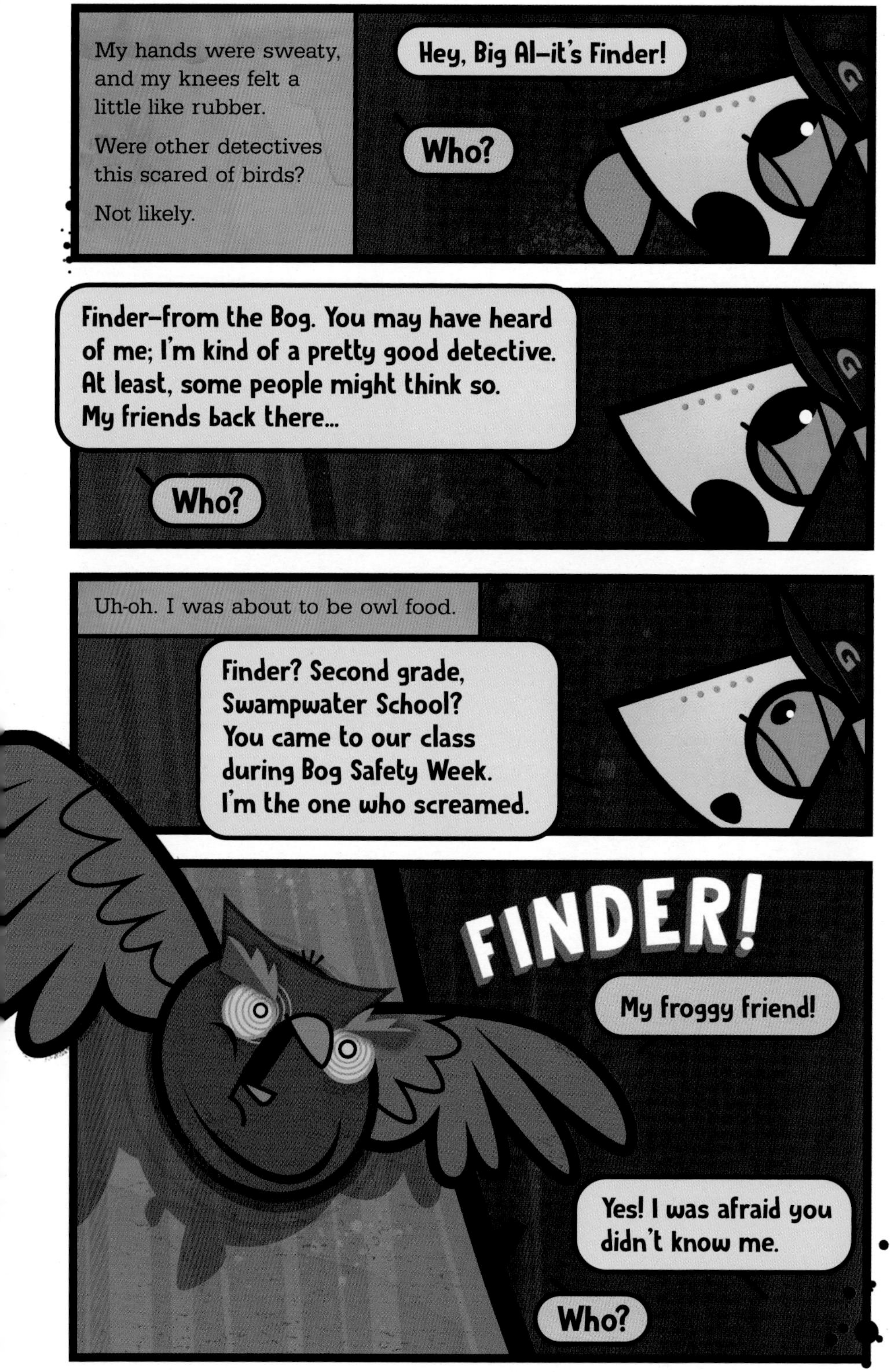
My hands were sweaty, and my knees felt a little like rubber.
Were other detectives this scared of birds?
Not likely.
Hey, Big Al—it's Finder!
Who?
Finder—from the Bog. You may have heard of me; I'm kind of a pretty good detective. At least, some people might think so. My friends back there...
Who?
Uh-oh. I was about to be owl food.
Finder? Second grade, Swampwater School? You came to our class during Bog Safety Week. I'm the one who screamed.
FINDER!
My froggy friend!
Yes! I was afraid you didn't know me.
Who?

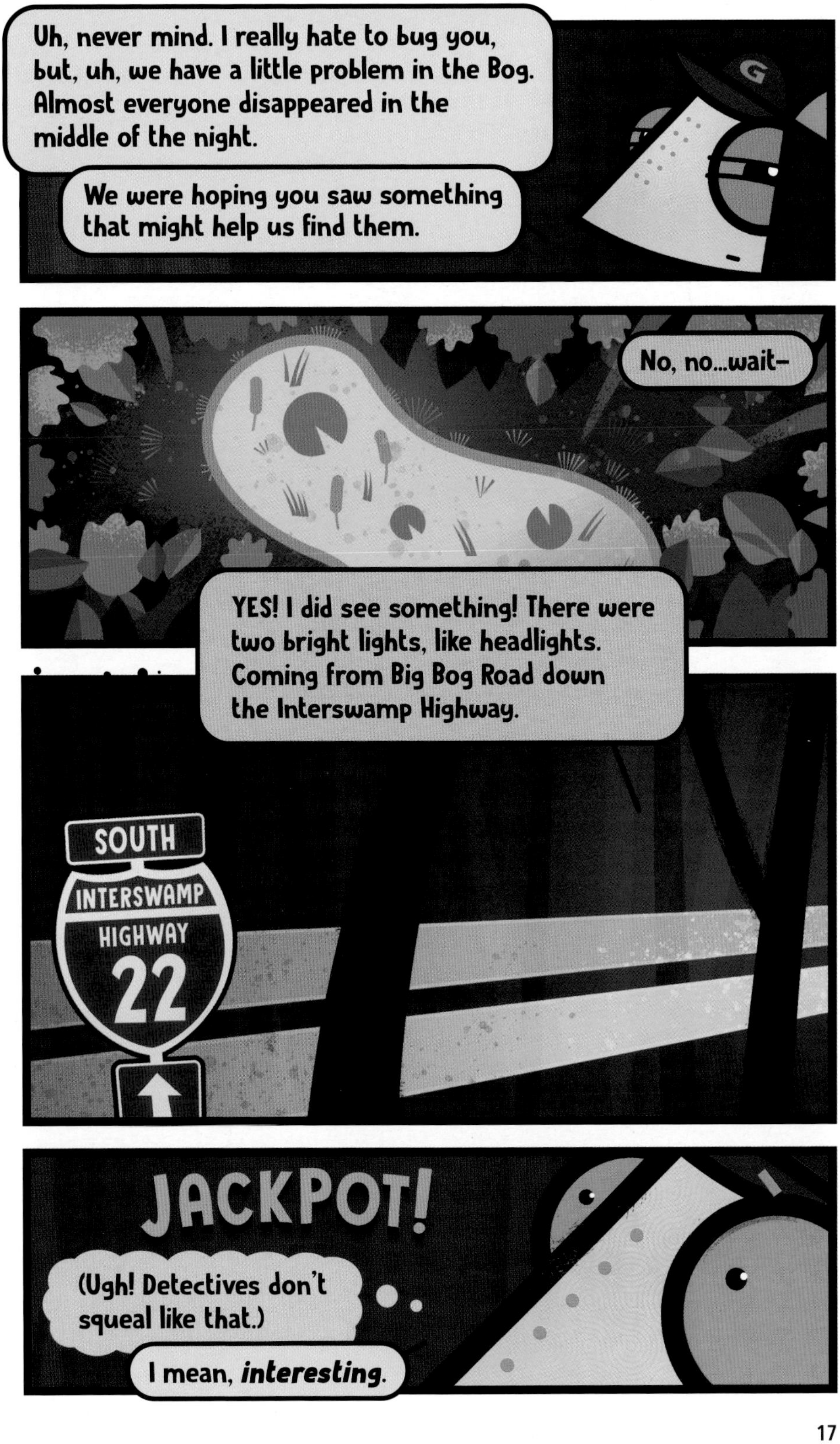
Uh, never mind. I really hate to bug you, but, uh, we have a little problem in the Bog. Almost everyone disappeared in the middle of the night.
We were hoping you saw something that might help us find them.
No, no...wait–
YES! I did see something! There were two bright lights, like headlights. Coming from Big Bog Road down the Interswamp Highway.
SOUTH
INTERSWAMP
HIGHWAY
22
JACKPOT!
(Ugh! Detectives don't squeal like that.)
I mean, *interesting*.

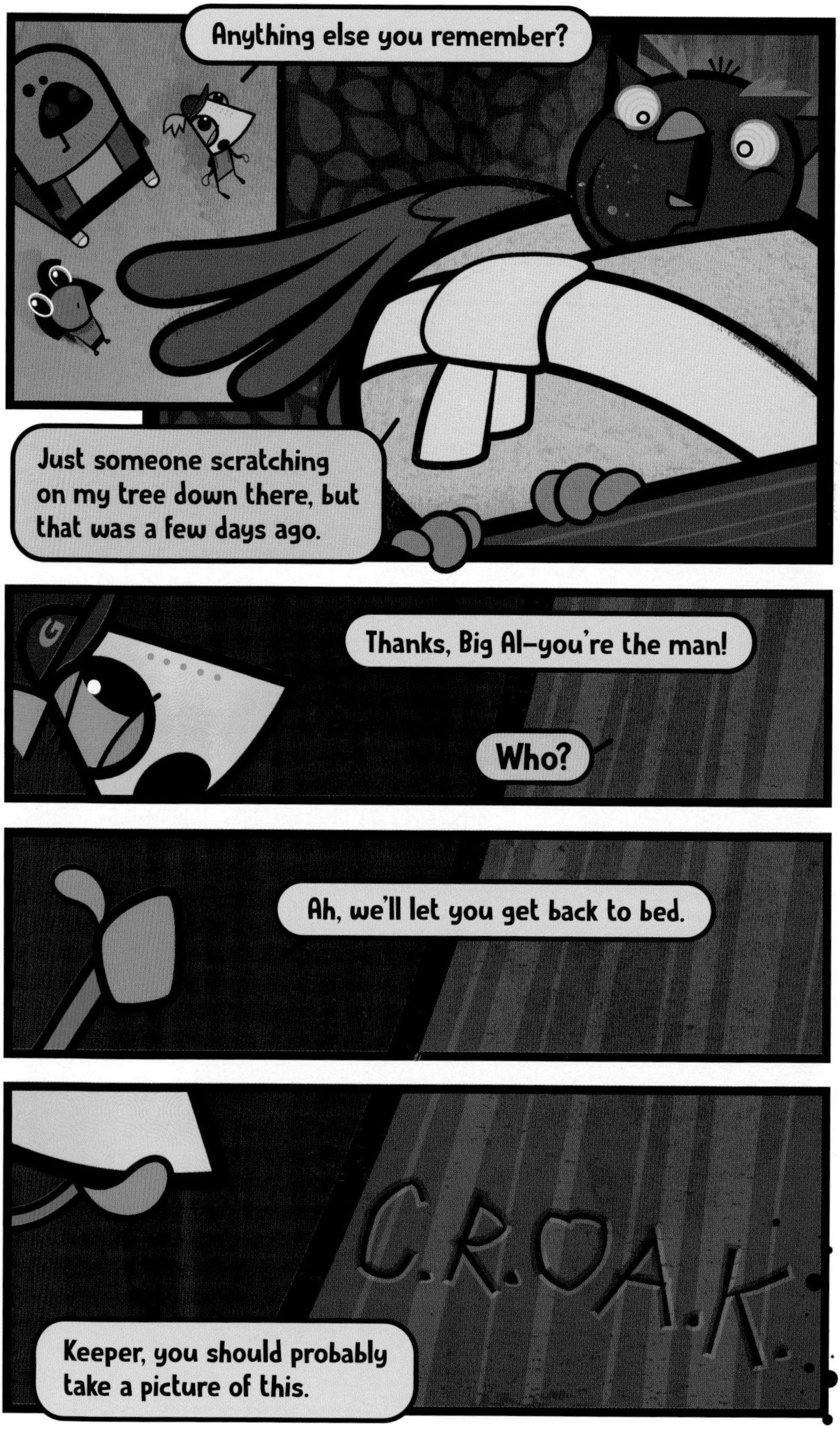
Anything else you remember?
Just someone scratching on my tree down there, but that was a few days ago.
Thanks, Big Al—you're the man!
Who?
Ah, we'll let you get back to bed.
C.R.O.A.K.
Keeper, you should probably take a picture of this.

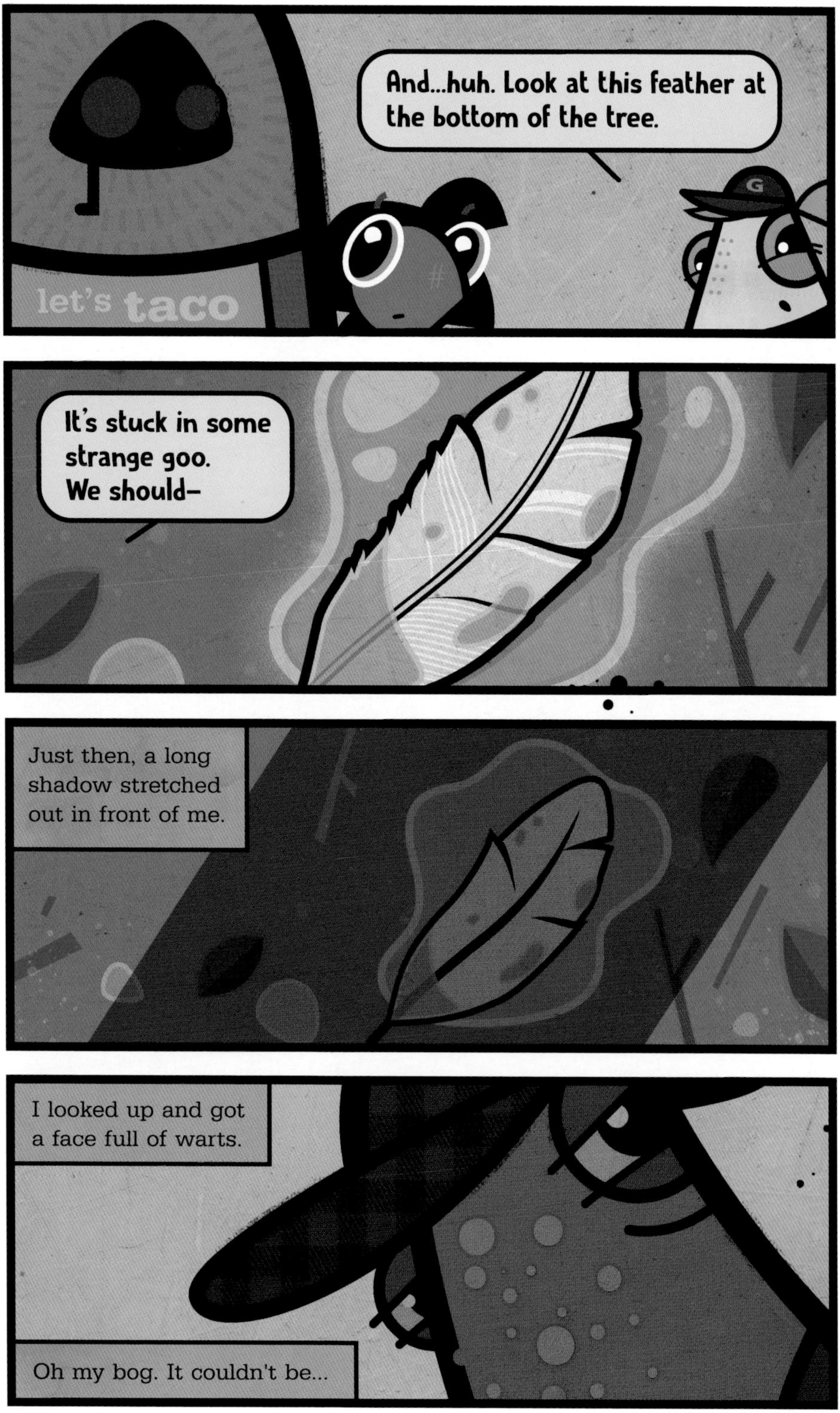
let's taco
And...huh. Look at this feather at the bottom of the tree.
It's stuck in some strange goo. We should–
Just then, a long shadow stretched out in front of me.
I looked up and got a face full of warts.
Oh my bog. It couldn't be...

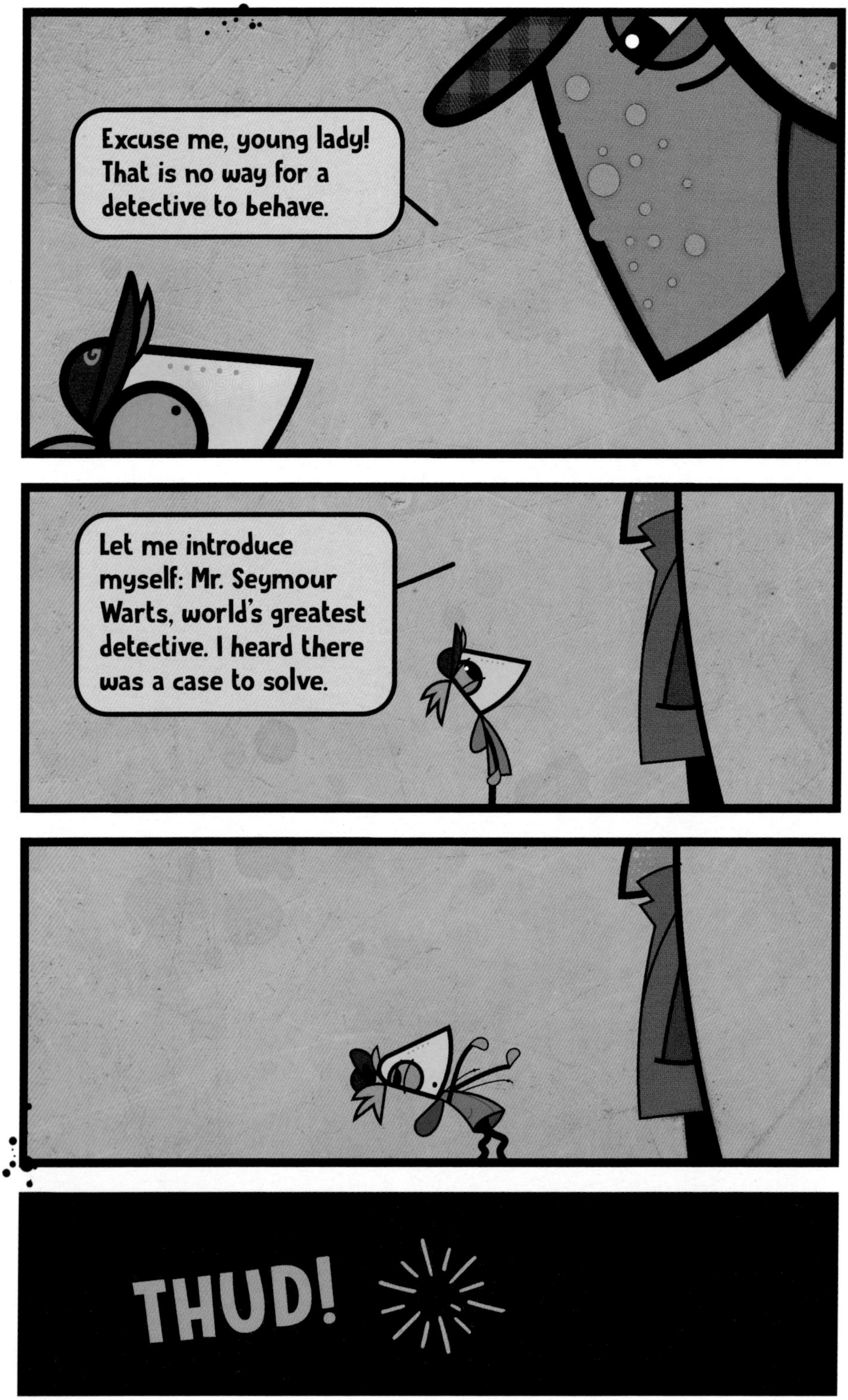
Excuse me, young lady! That is no way for a detective to behave.
Let me introduce myself: Mr. Seymour Warts, world's greatest detective. I heard there was a case to solve.
THUD!

Chapter 3: Agents of C.R.O.A.K.

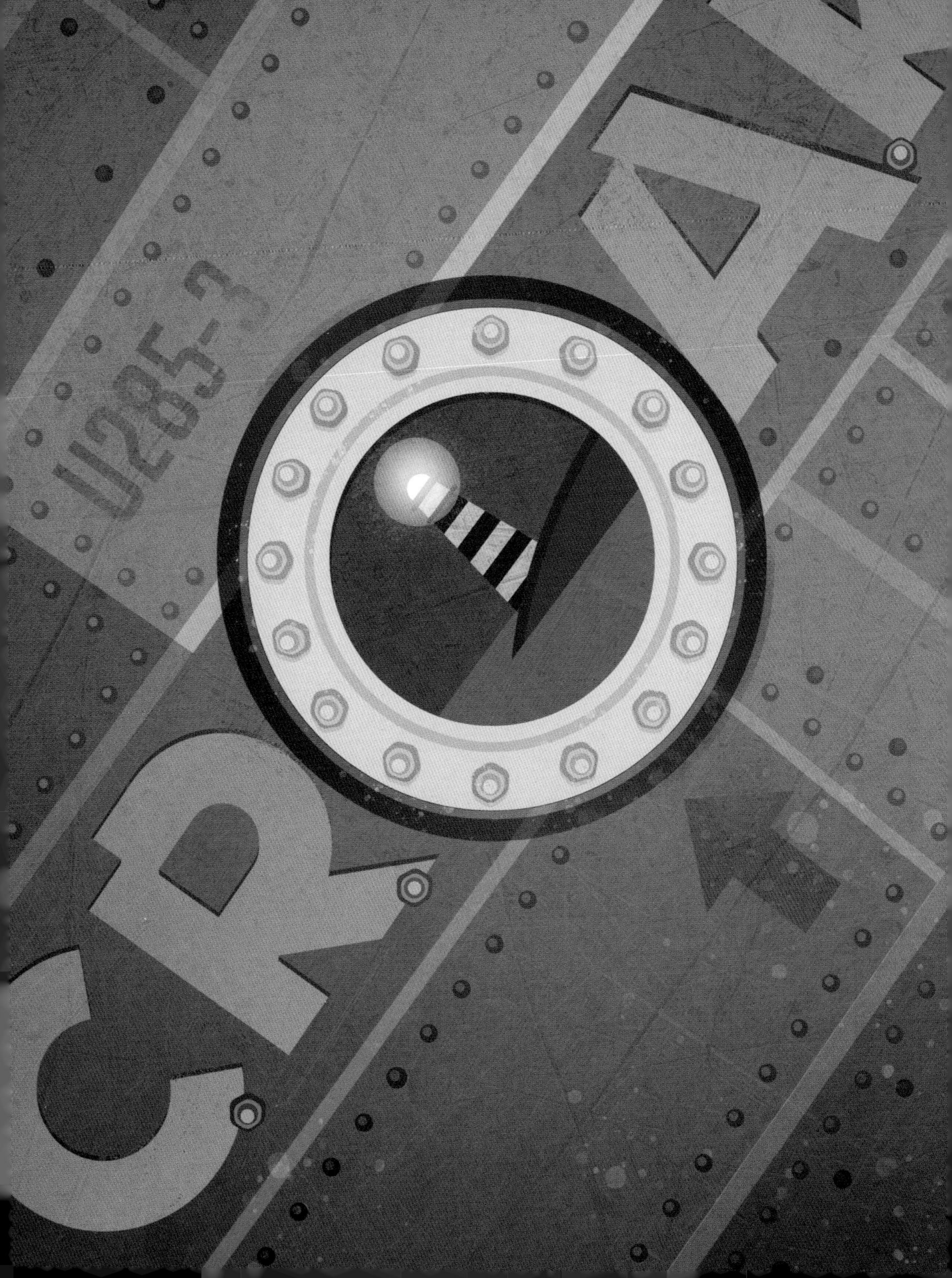
U285-3

When I came to, my head was hurting, and I had a vague memory of meeting my biggest hero before everything went blank. But that had to have been a dream, right?

What happened?

You fainted. Mr. Warts read the letters on the tree and ran off to investigate. He felt bad to leave so soon, though, so he left his card for us.

Chopper had to drag you back on his tail.

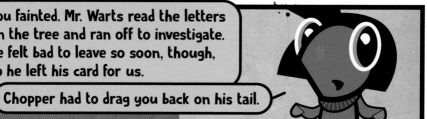

We are not to speak of this.

Deal.

let's taco

22

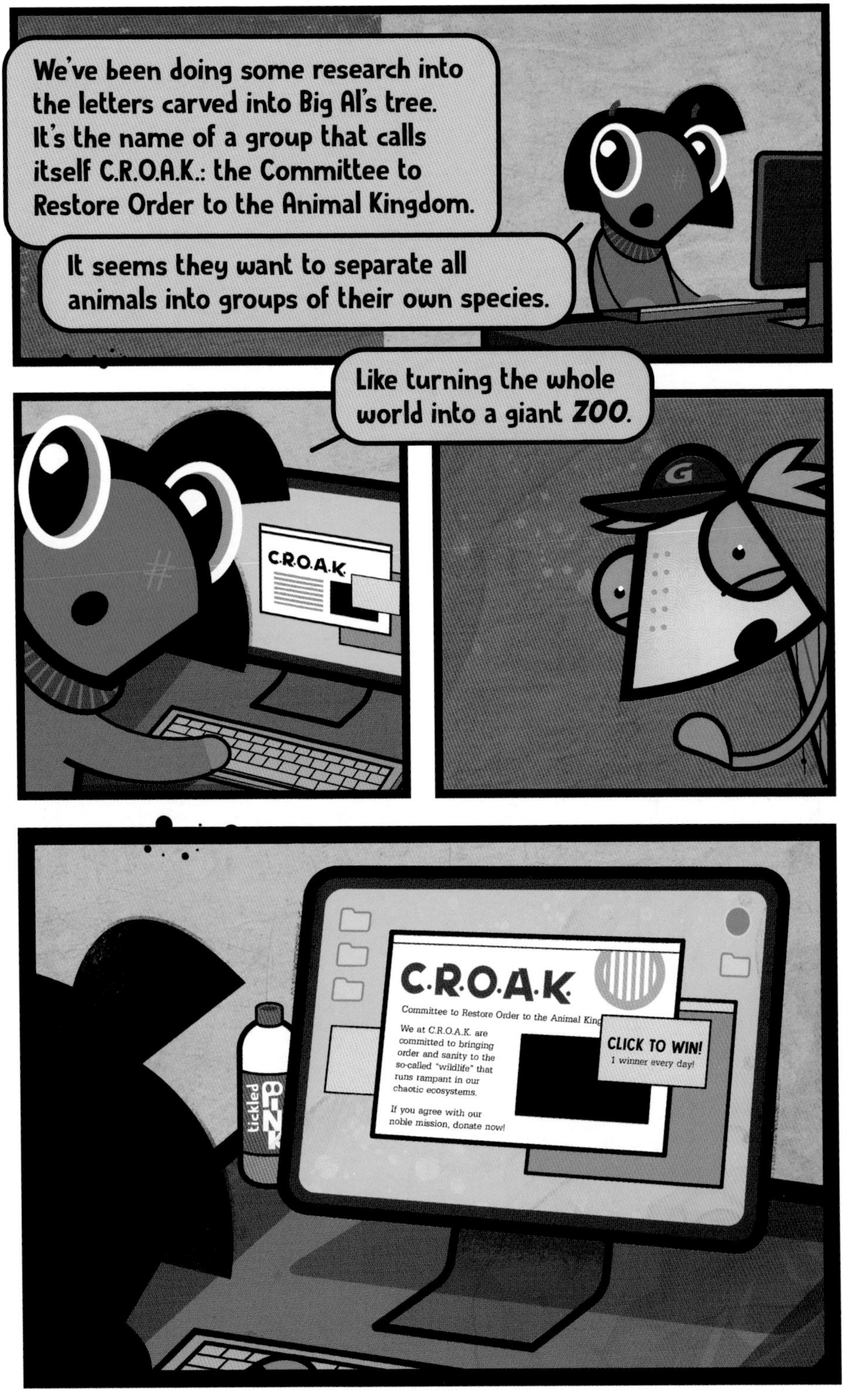
We've been doing some research into the letters carved into Big Al's tree. It's the name of a group that calls itself C.R.O.A.K.: the Committee to Restore Order to the Animal Kingdom.
It seems they want to separate all animals into groups of their own species.
Like turning the whole world into a giant ZOO.
C.R.O.A.K.
C.R.O.A.K
Committee to Restore Order to the Animal King
We at C.R.O.A.K. are committed to bringing order and sanity to the so-called "wildlife" that runs rampant in our chaotic ecosystems.
If you agree with our noble mission, donate now!
CLICK TO WIN!
1 winner every day!
tickled PINK

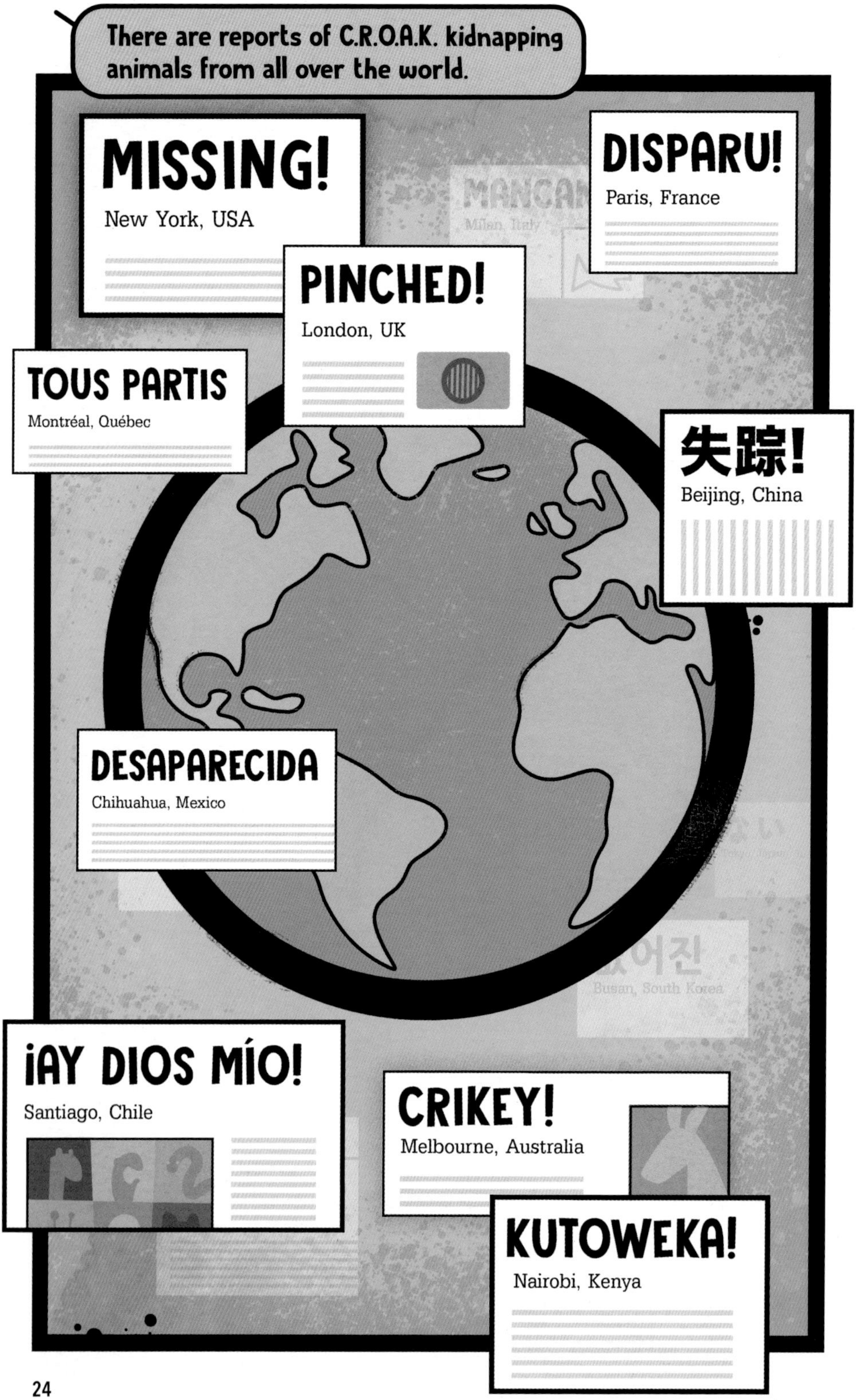
There are reports of C.R.O.A.K. kidnapping animals from all over the world.
MISSING!
New York, USA
DISPARU!
Paris, France
Milan, Italy
PINCHED!
London, UK
TOUS PARTIS
Montréal, Québec
失踪!
Beijing, China
DESAPARECIDA
Chihuahua, Mexico
Busan, South Korea
¡AY DIOS MÍO!
Santiago, Chile
CRIKEY!
Melbourne, Australia
KUTOWEKA!
Nairobi, Kenya

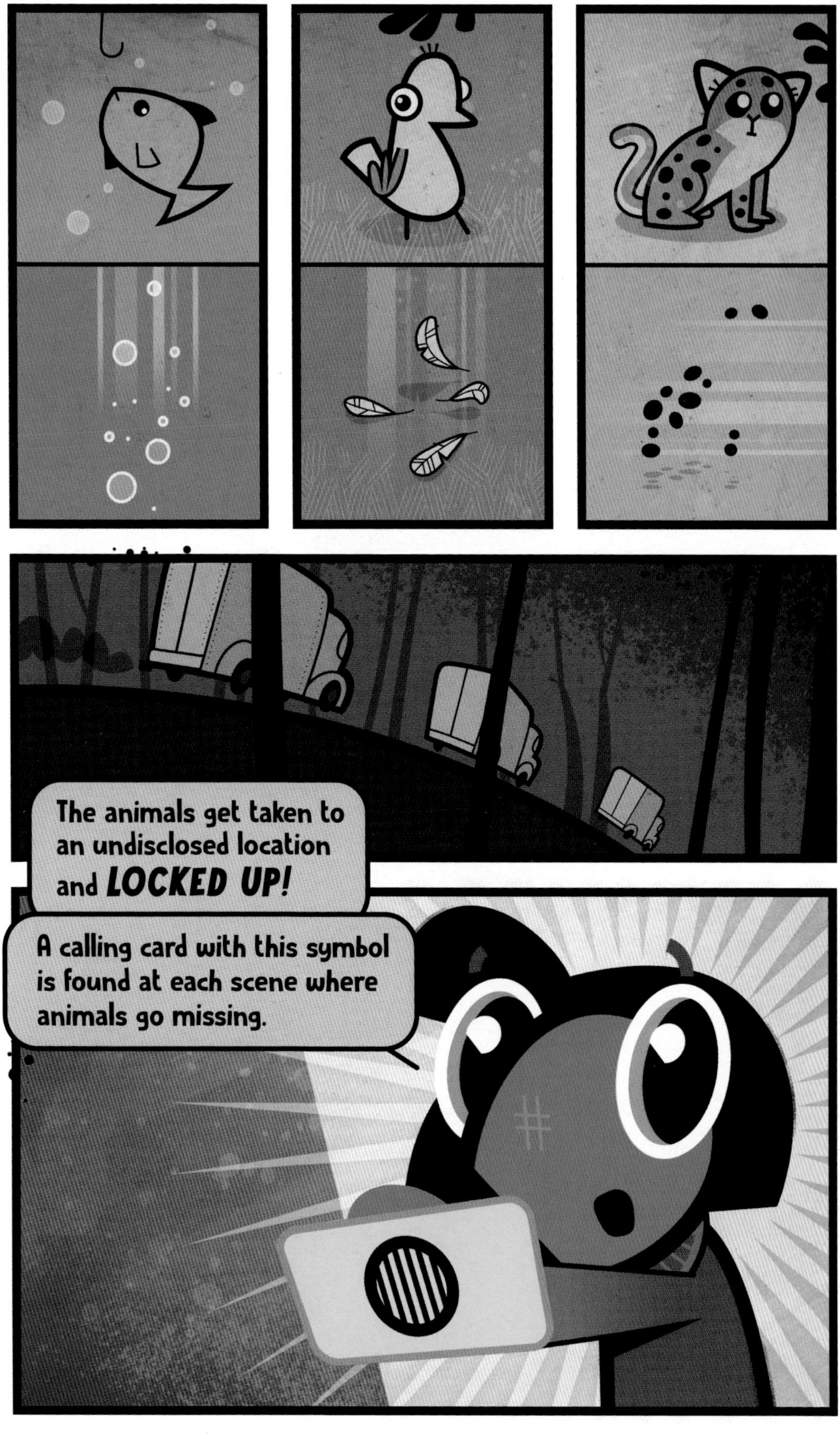
The animals get taken to an undisclosed location and LOCKED UP!
A calling card with this symbol is found at each scene where animals go missing.

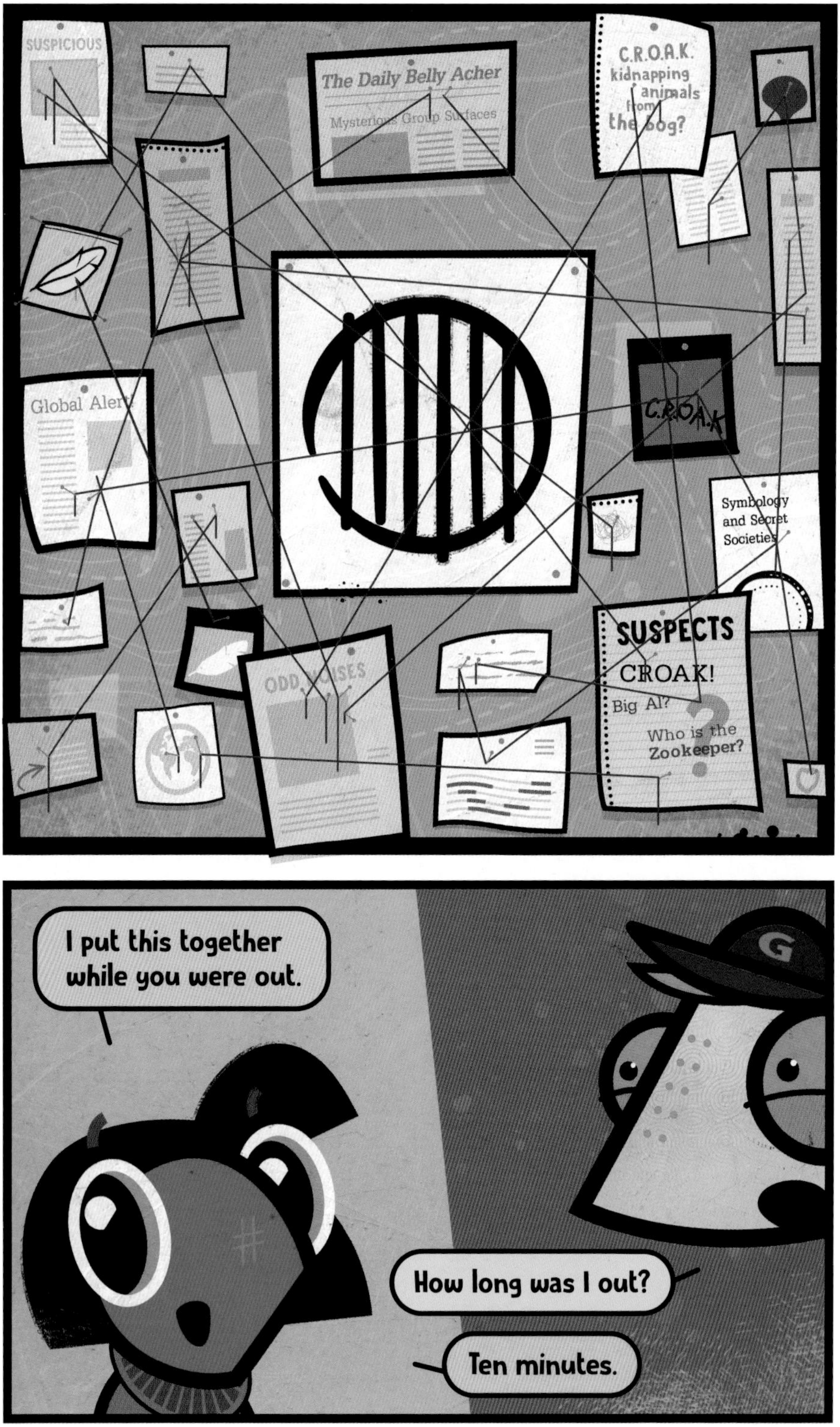
SUSPICIOUS
The Daily Belly Acher
Mysterious Group Surfaces
C.R.O.A.K.
kidnapping animals from the bog?
Global Alert
C.R.O.A.K
Symbology and Secret Societies
SUSPECTS
CROAK!
Big Al?
Who is the Zookeeper?
ODD NOISES
I put this together while you were out.
How long was I out?
Ten minutes.

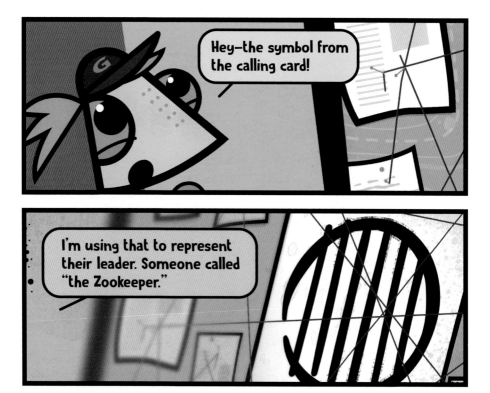

Hey—the symbol from the calling card!

I'm using that to represent their leader. Someone called "the Zookeeper."

This "Zookeeper" seemed like the natural culprit, but it felt like we were missing something. How had they kidnapped everyone in the bog in one night?

SUSPECTS

CROAK!

Big Al?

?

...ho is the ...er?

This case was seeming trickier by the minute. I couldn't help but wonder if Seymour Warts's investigation was going any better...

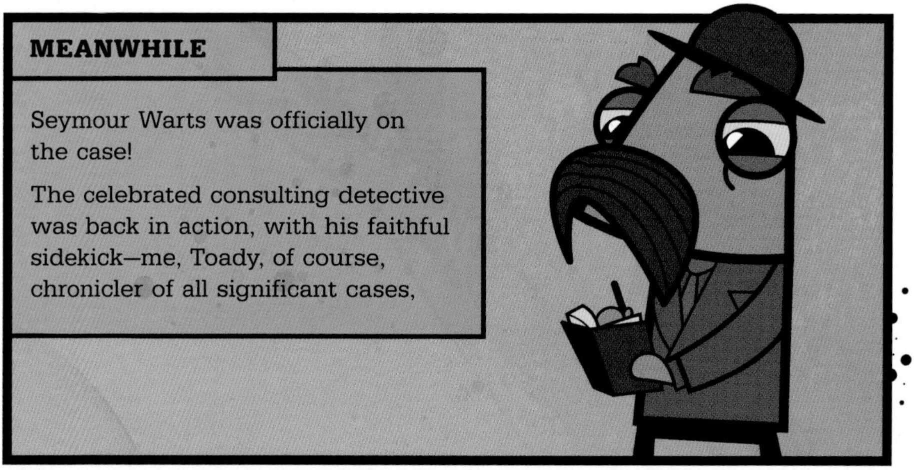
MEANWHILE
Seymour Warts was officially on the case!
The celebrated consulting detective was back in action, with his faithful sidekick—me, Toady, of course, chronicler of all significant cases,

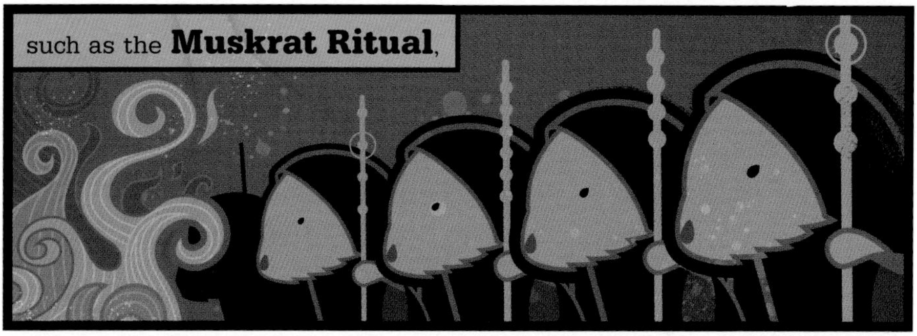
such as the **Muskrat Ritual**,

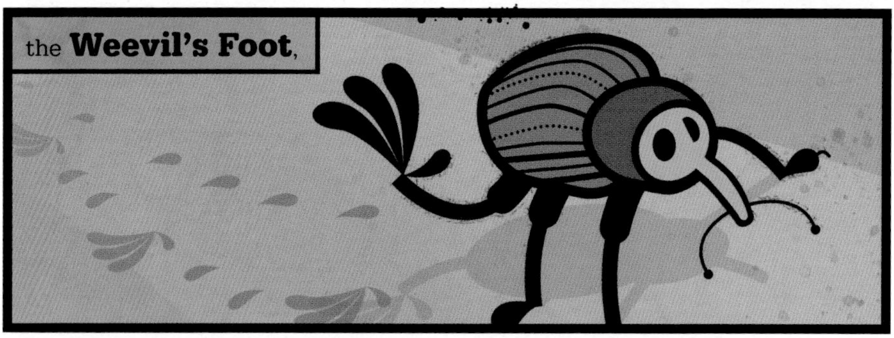
the **Weevil's Foot**,

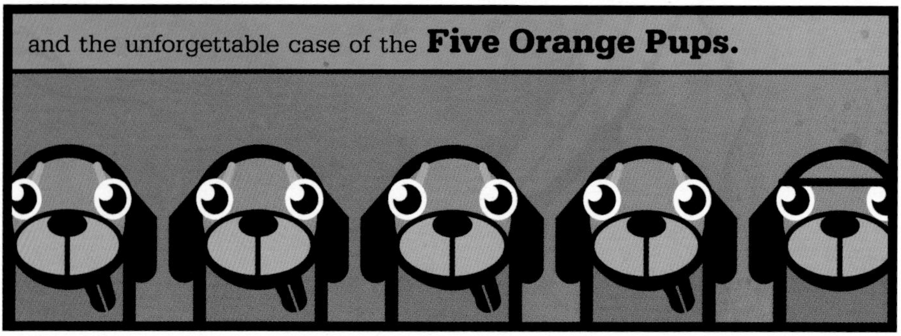
and the unforgettable case of the **Five Orange Pups.**

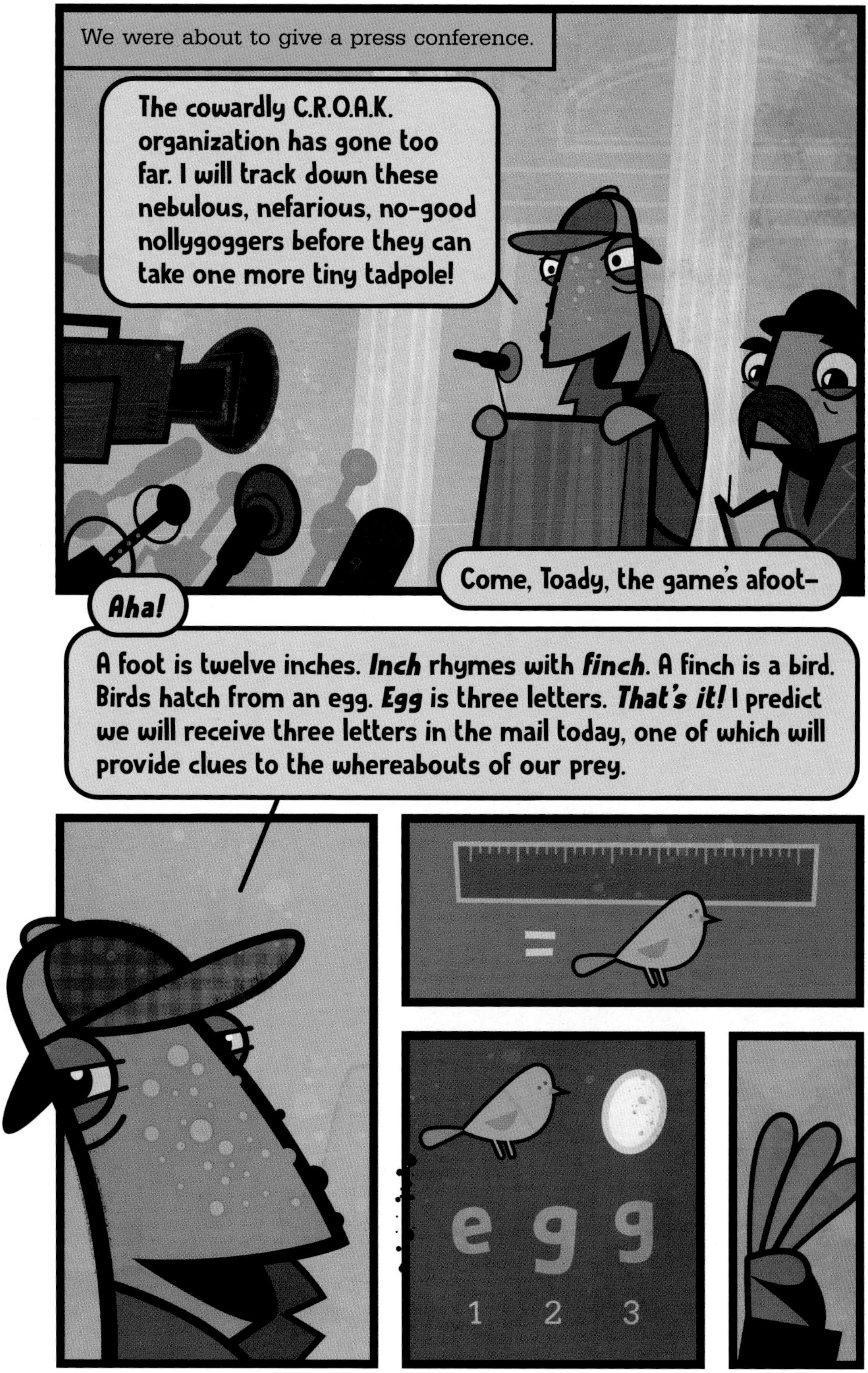
We were about to give a press conference.
The cowardly C.R.O.A.K. organization has gone too far. I will track down these nebulous, nefarious, no-good nollygoggers before they can take one more tiny tadpole!
Come, Toady, the game's afoot—
Aha!
A foot is twelve inches. *Inch* rhymes with *finch*. A finch is a bird. Birds hatch from an egg. *Egg* is three letters. *That's it!* I predict we will receive three letters in the mail today, one of which will provide clues to the whereabouts of our prey.
=
egg
1 2 3

Chapter 4: Goose-Liver Goo

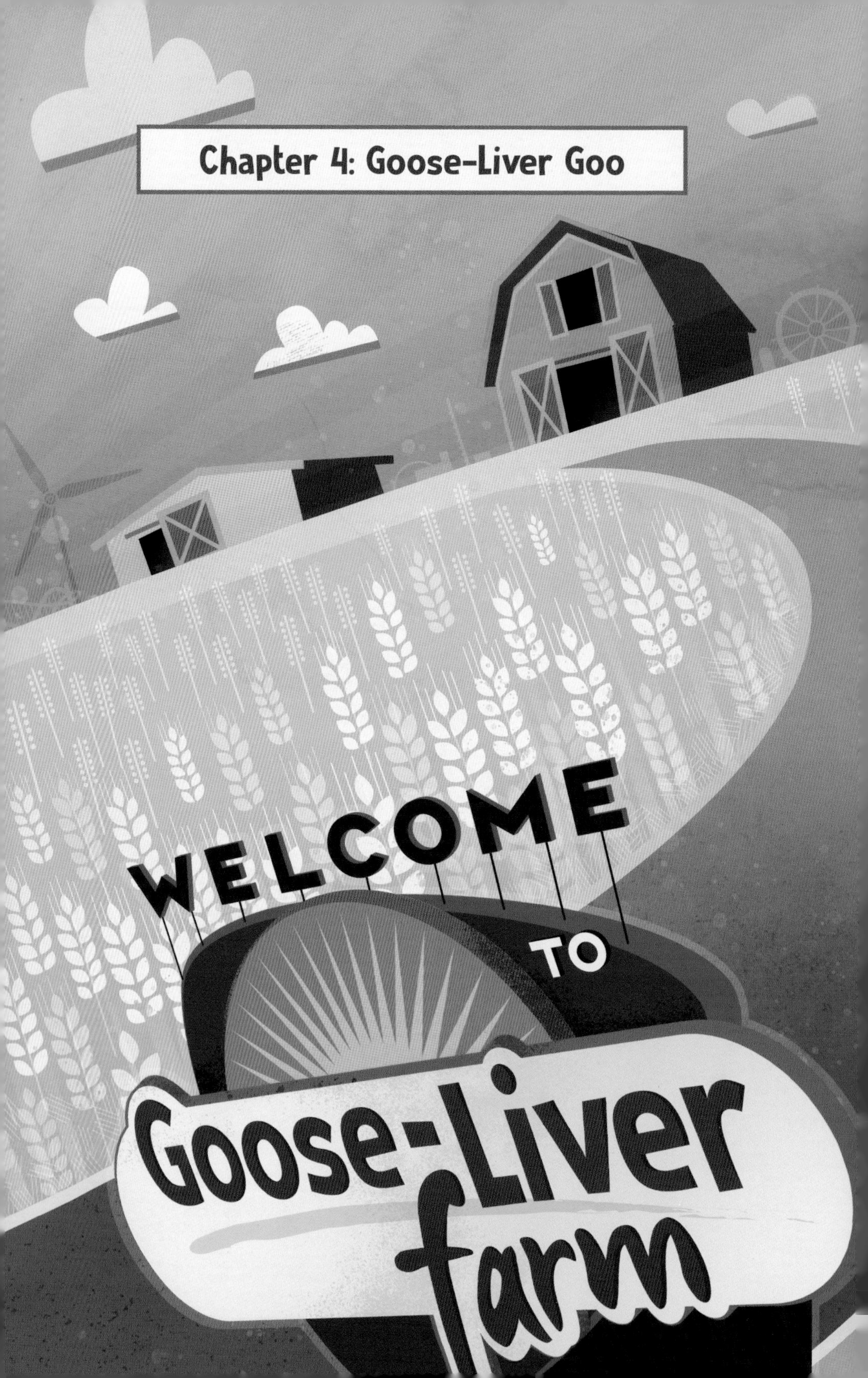
WELCOME
TO
Goose-Liver
farm

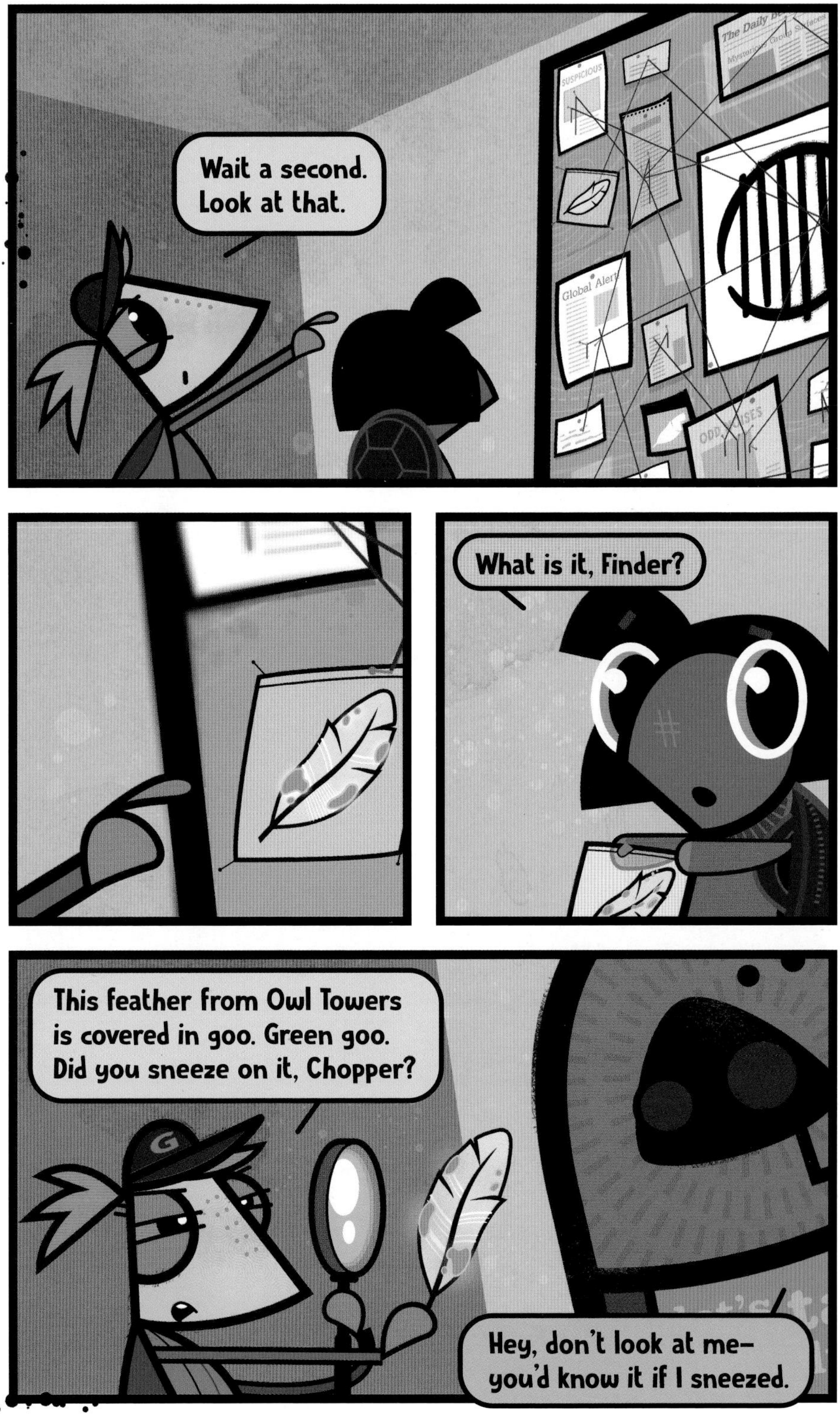
Wait a second. Look at that.
SUSPICIOUS
What is it, Finder?
This feather from Owl Towers is covered in goo. Green goo. Did you sneeze on it, Chopper?
Hey, don't look at me— you'd know it if I sneezed.

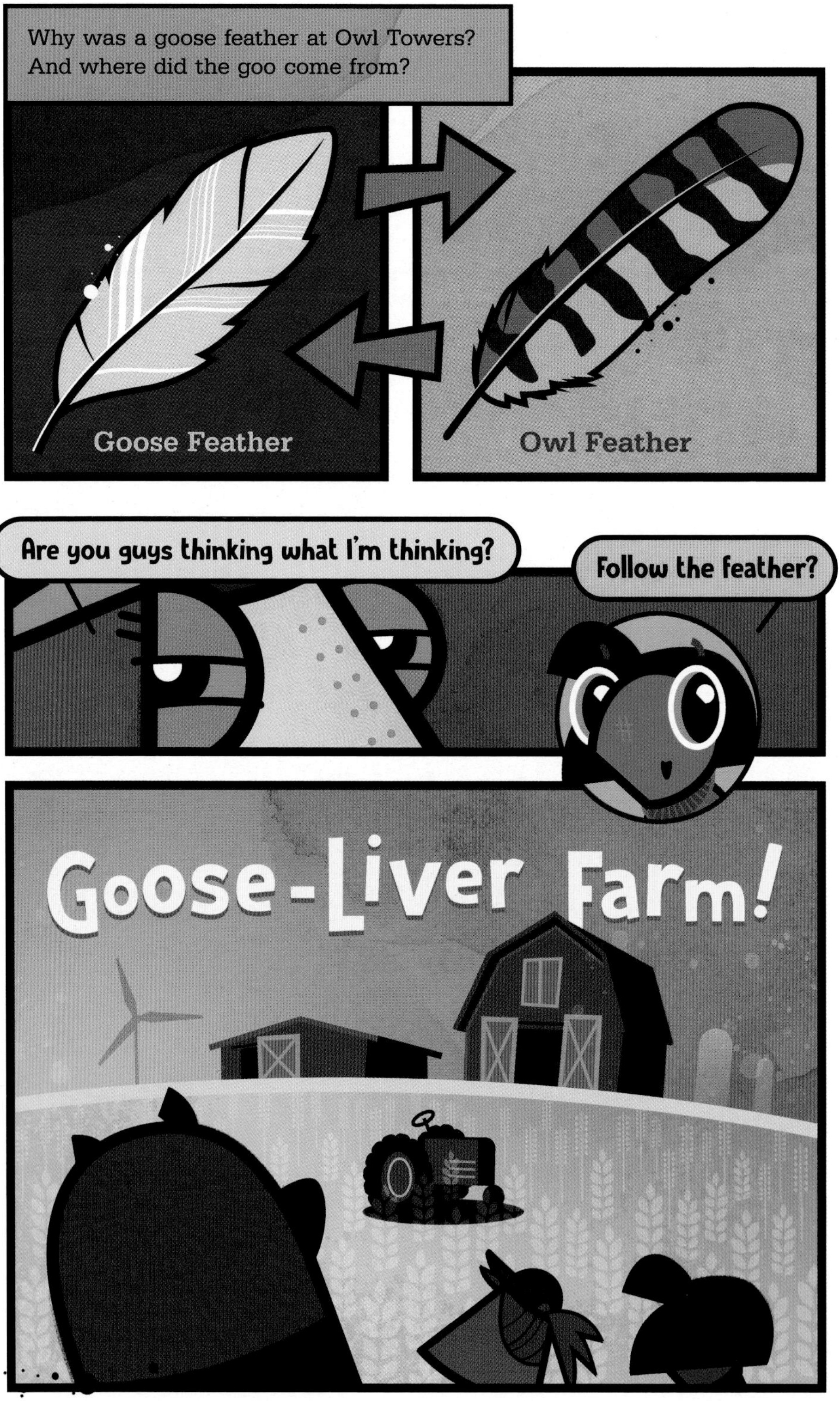
Why was a goose feather at Owl Towers? And where did the goo come from?
Goose Feather
Owl Feather
Are you guys thinking what I'm thinking?
Follow the feather?
Goose-Liver Farm!

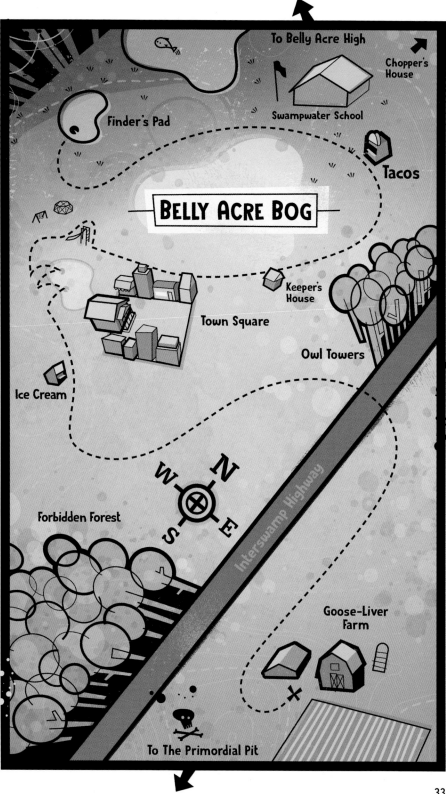

To Belly Acre High

Chopper's House

Swampwater School

Finder's Pad

Tacos

BELLY ACRE BOG

Keeper's House

Town Square

Owl Towers

Ice Cream

Forbidden Forest

N W E S

Interswamp Highway

Goose-Liver Farm

To The Primordial Pit

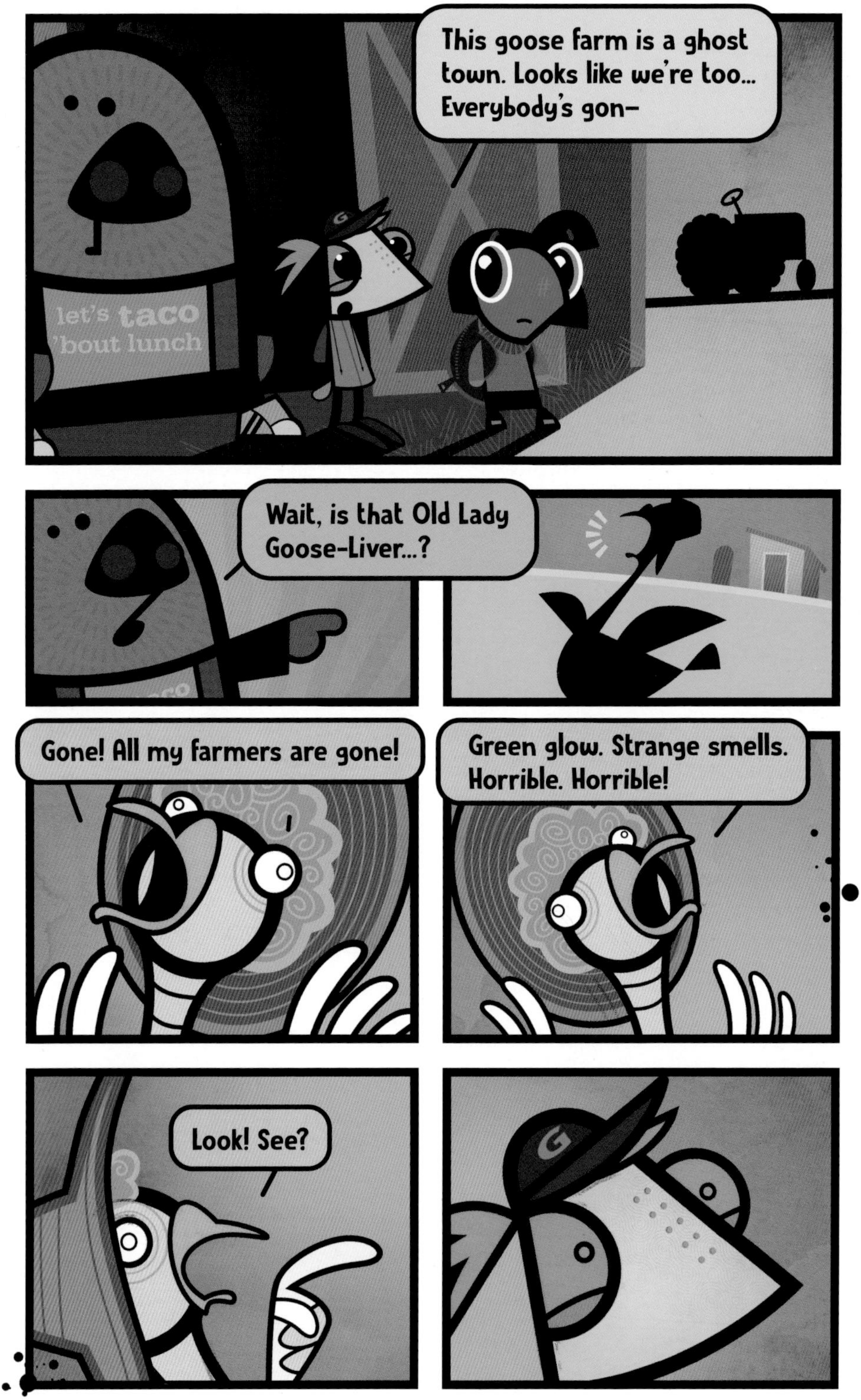
let's taco 'bout lunch
This goose farm is a ghost town. Looks like we're too... Everybody's gon–
Wait, is that Old Lady Goose-Liver...?
Gone! All my farmers are gone!
Green glow. Strange smells. Horrible. Horrible!
Look! See?

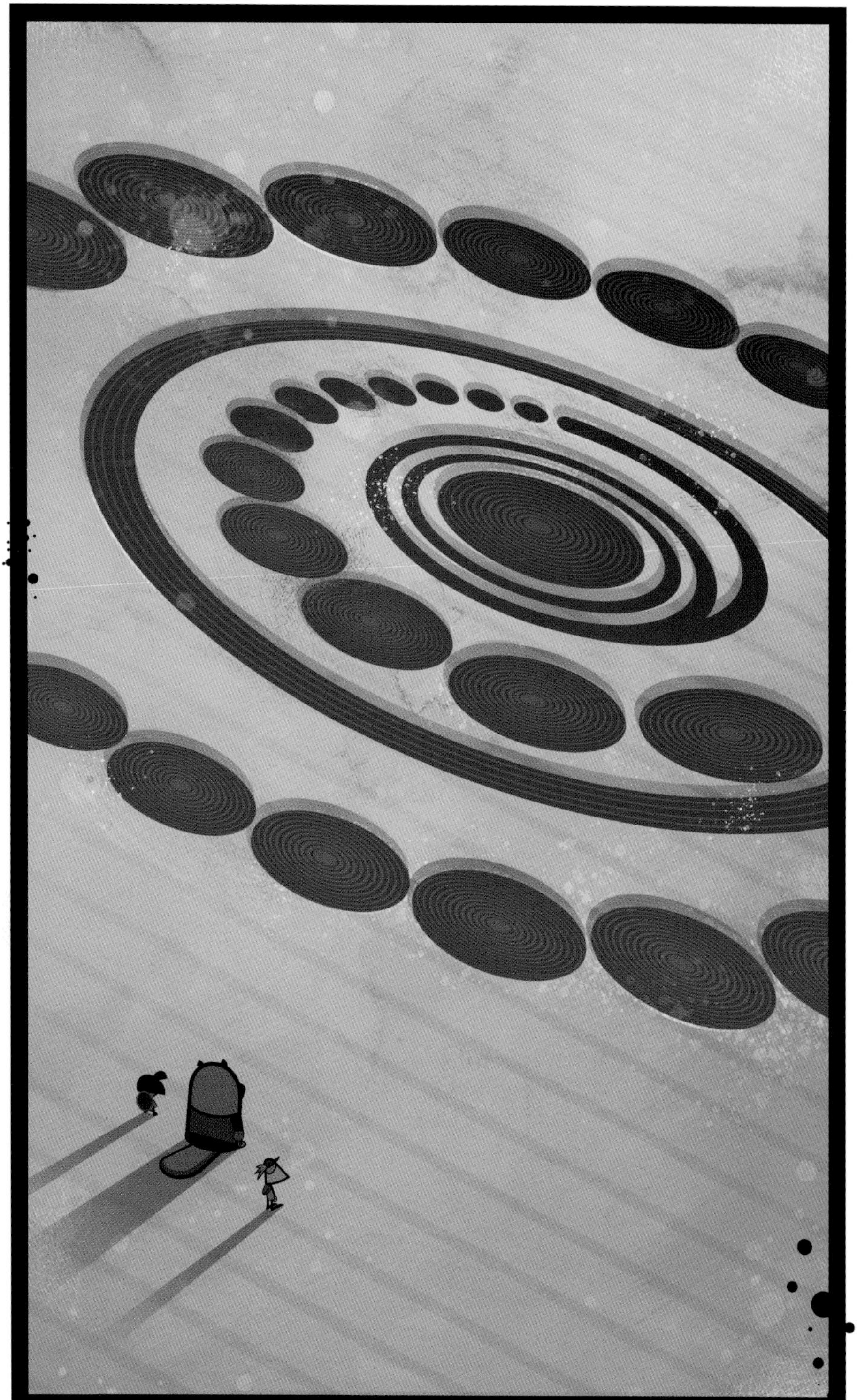

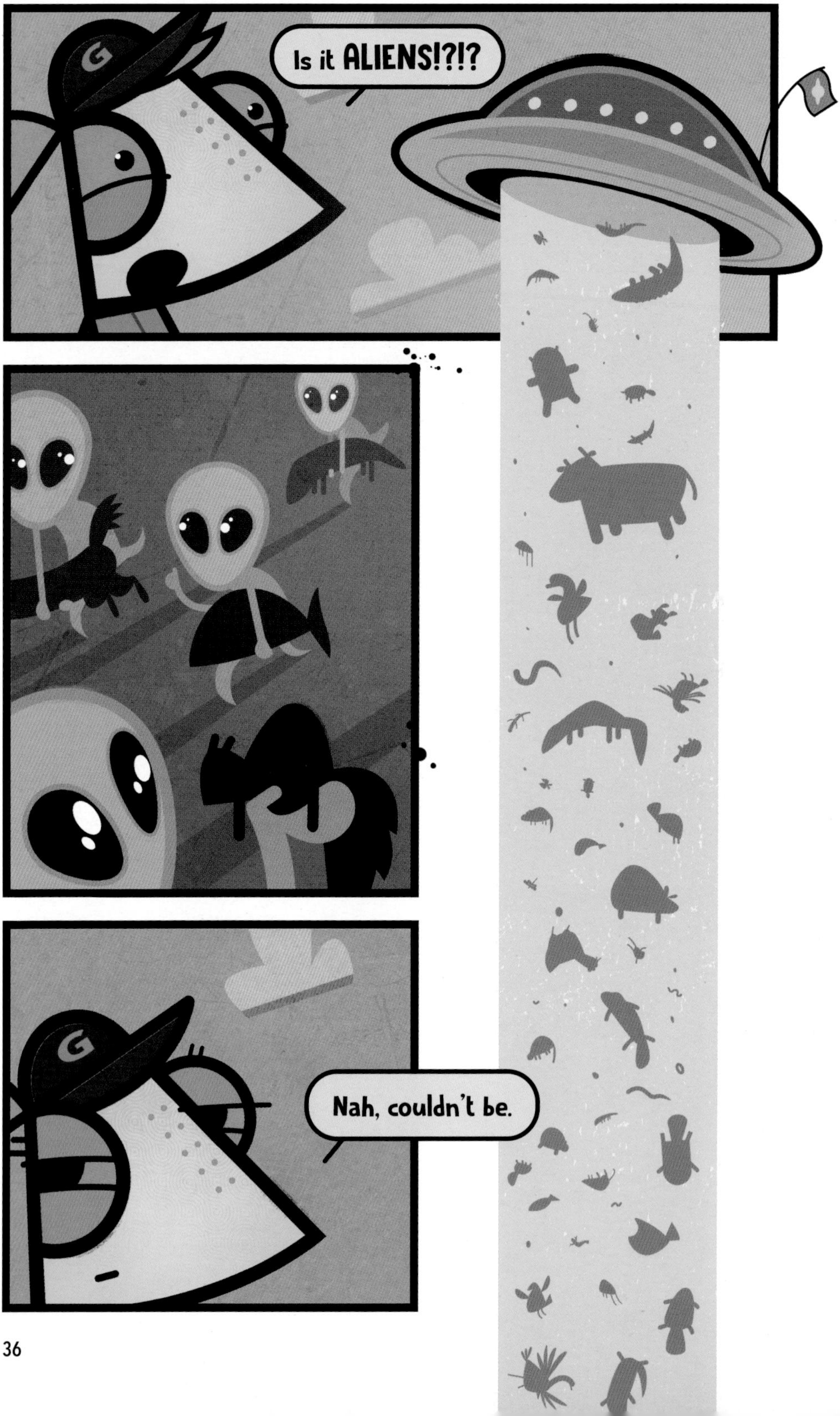
Is it ALIENS!?!?
Nah, couldn't be.

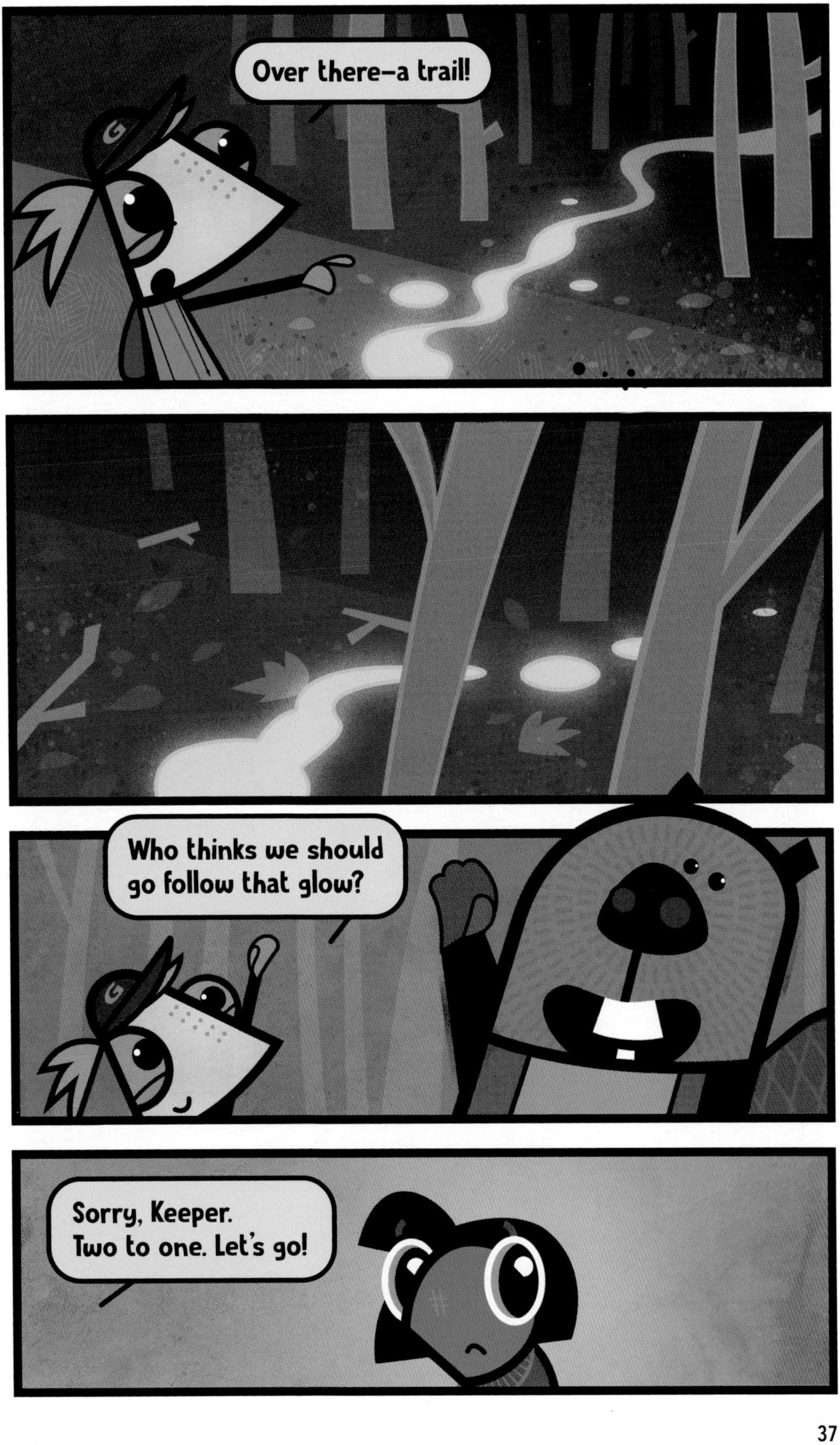
Over there—a trail!
Who thinks we should go follow that glow?
Sorry, Keeper. Two to one. Let's go!

Chapter 5: Creature Camp

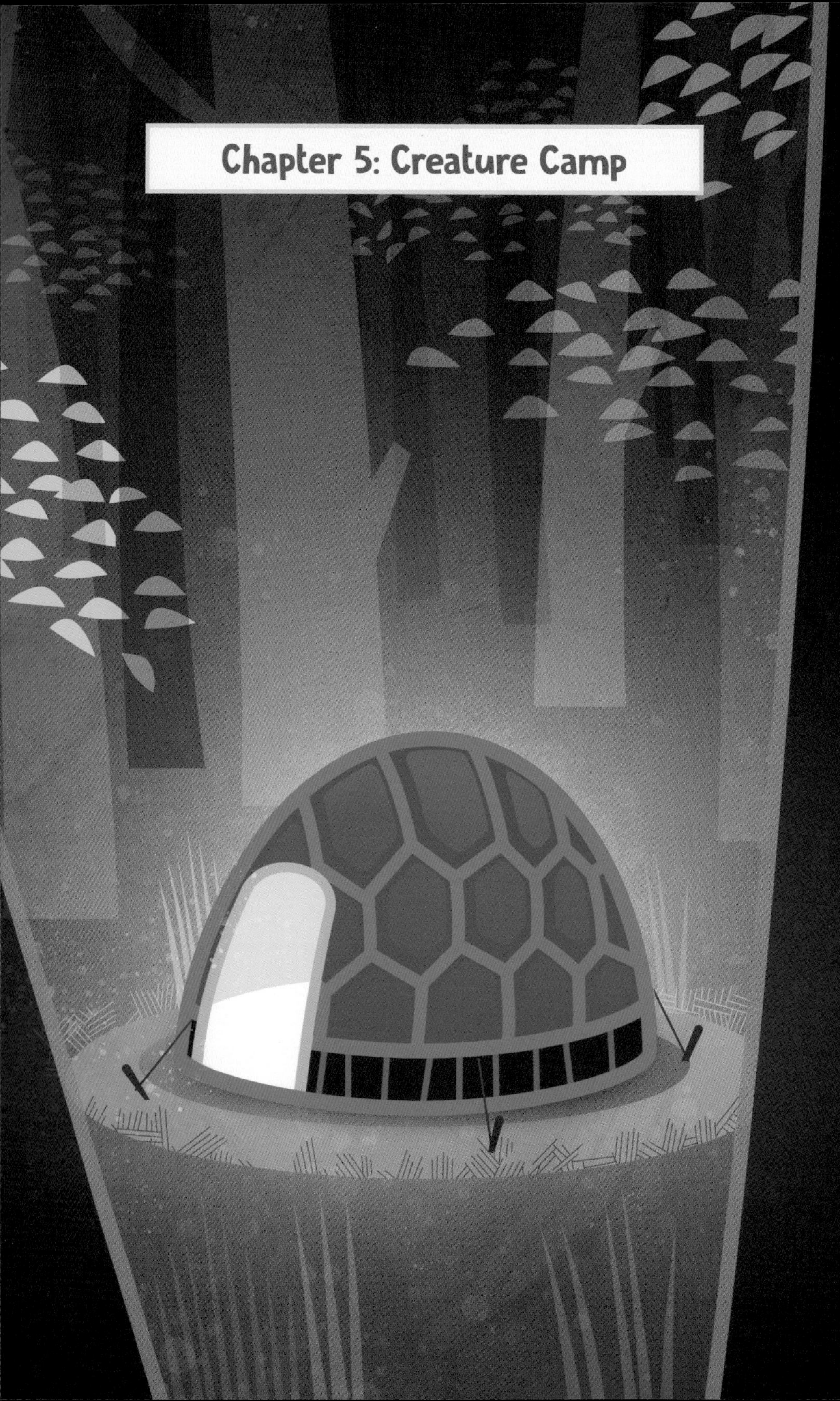

I'll bring up the rear.

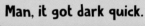

Man, it got dark quick.

What do you think, guys?

We're not going to find any clues like this. Maybe we should set up camp and search more in the morning.

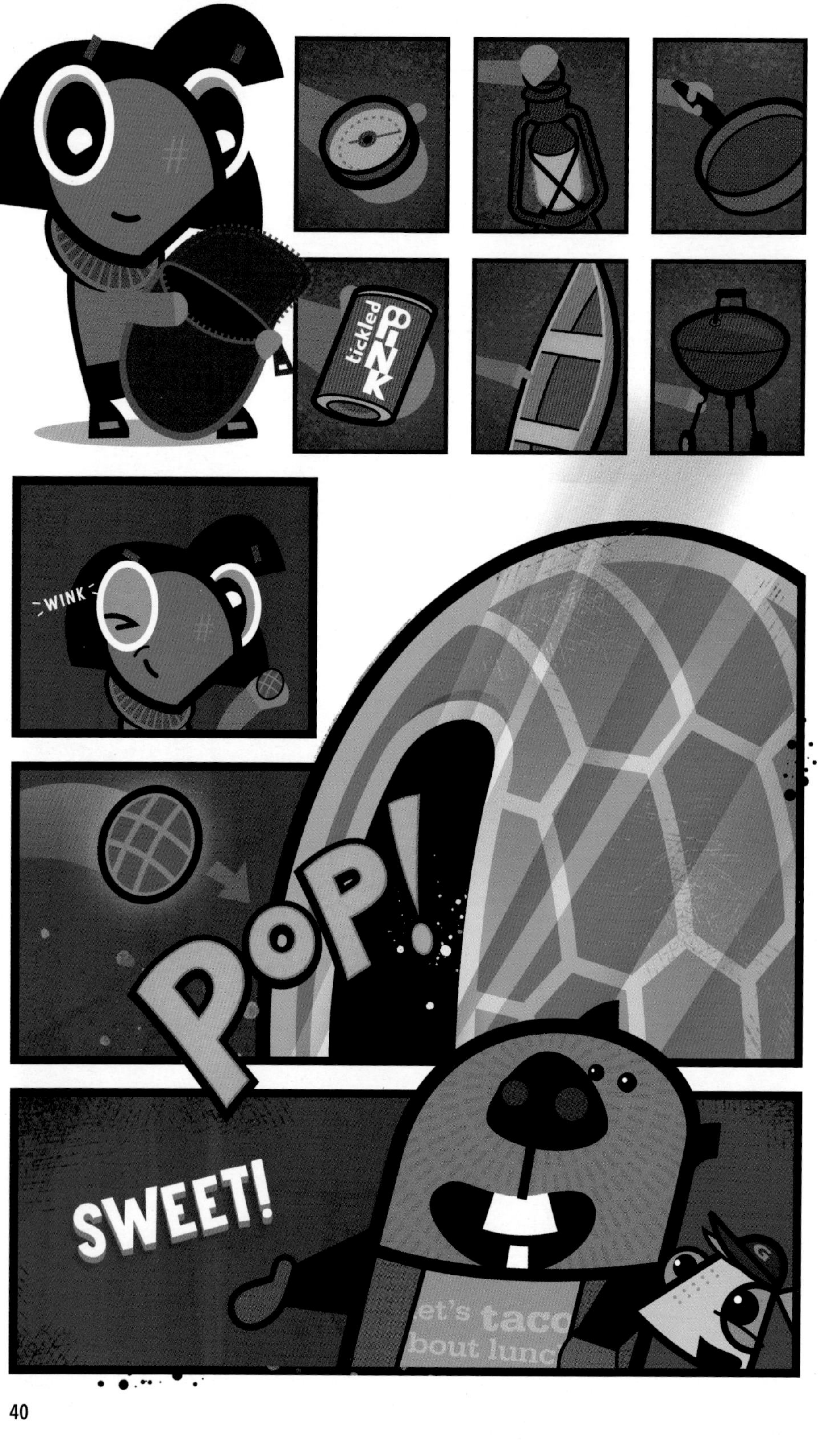
tickled
PINK
WINK
POP!
SWEET!

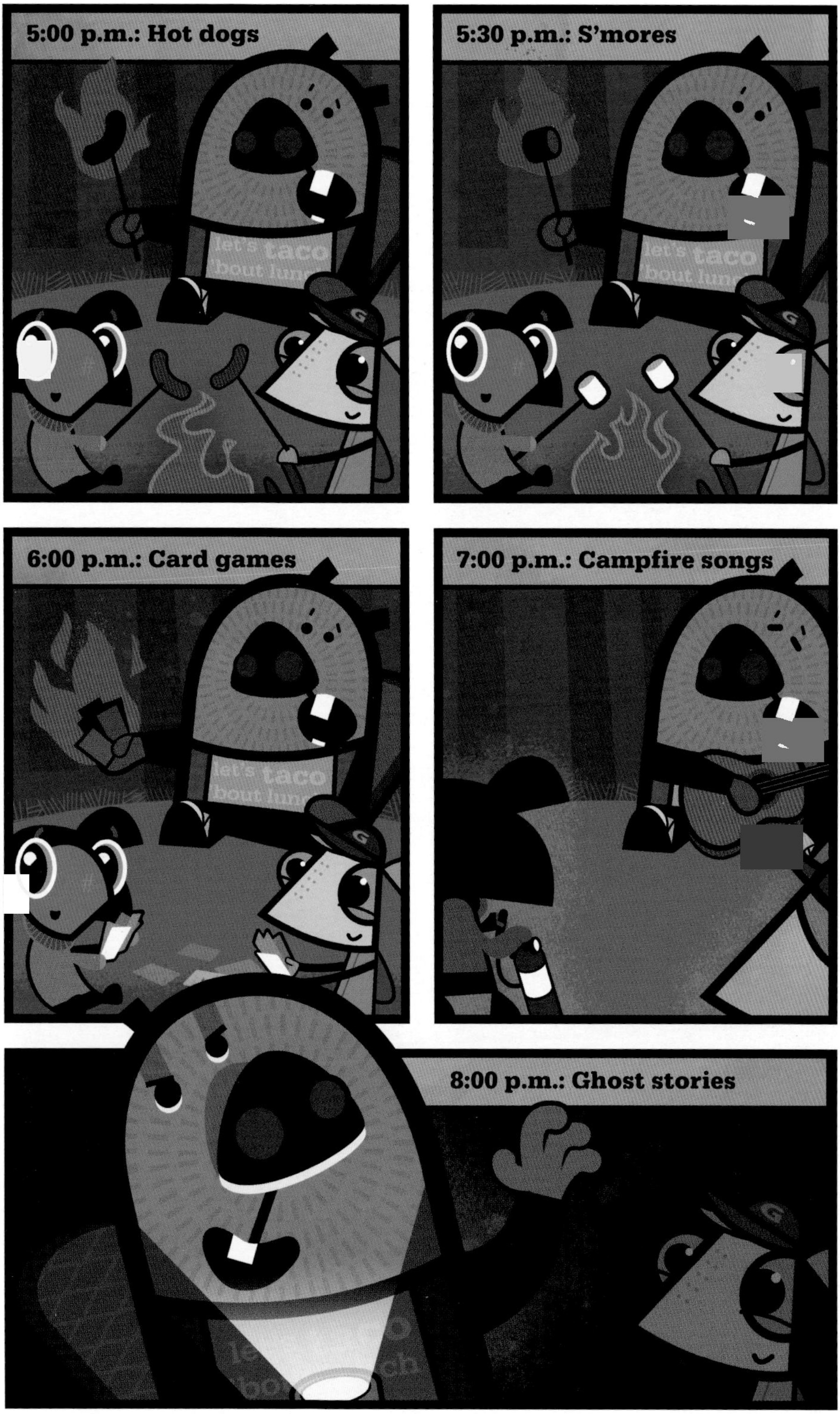
5:00 p.m.: Hot dogs
5:30 p.m.: S'mores
6:00 p.m.: Card games
7:00 p.m.: Campfire songs
8:00 p.m.: Ghost stories

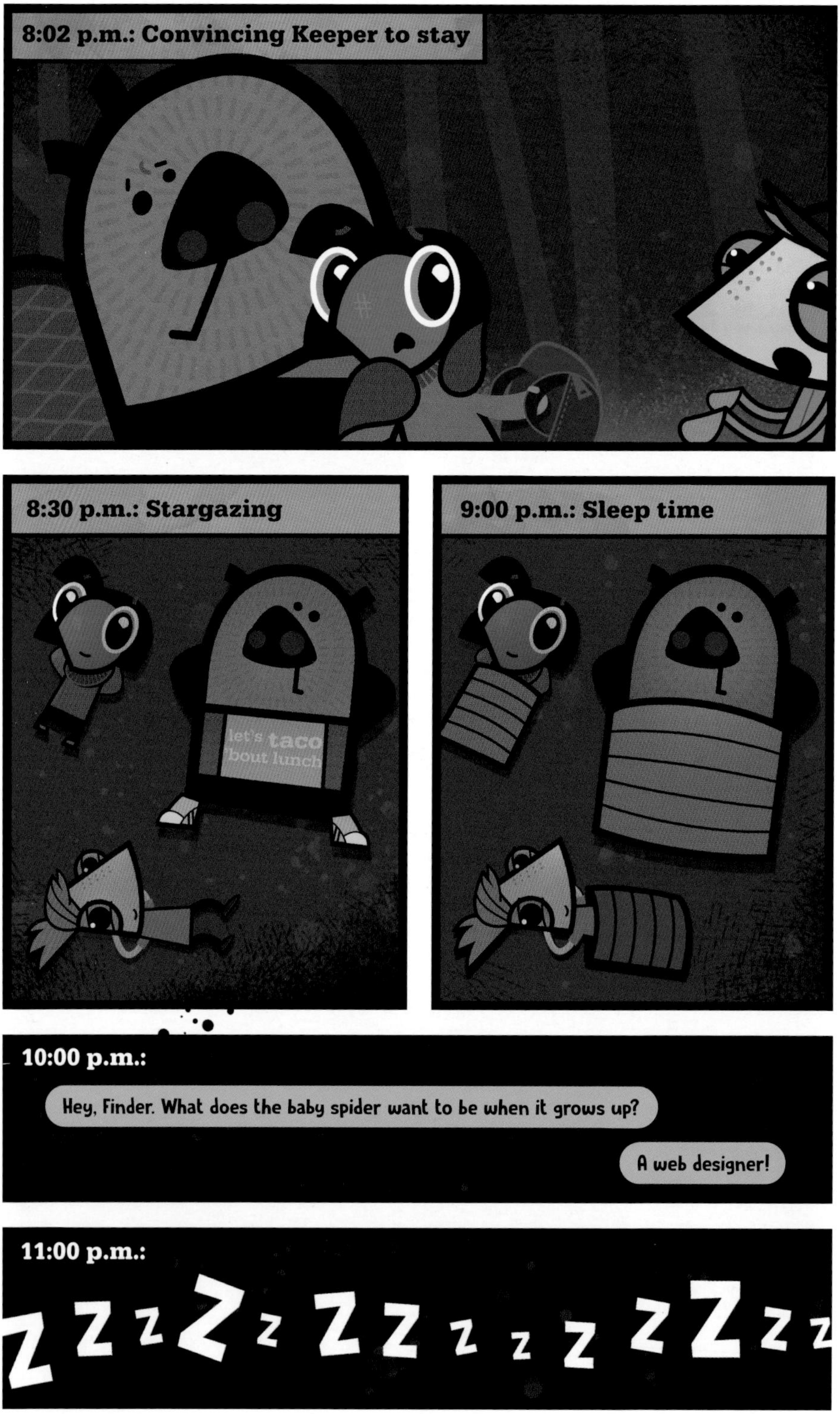
8:02 p.m.: Convincing Keeper to stay
8:30 p.m.: Stargazing
let's taco 'bout lunch
9:00 p.m.: Sleep time
10:00 p.m.:
Hey, Finder. What does the baby spider want to be when it grows up?
A web designer!
11:00 p.m.:
Z Z z Z z Z Z z z Z Z Z z z

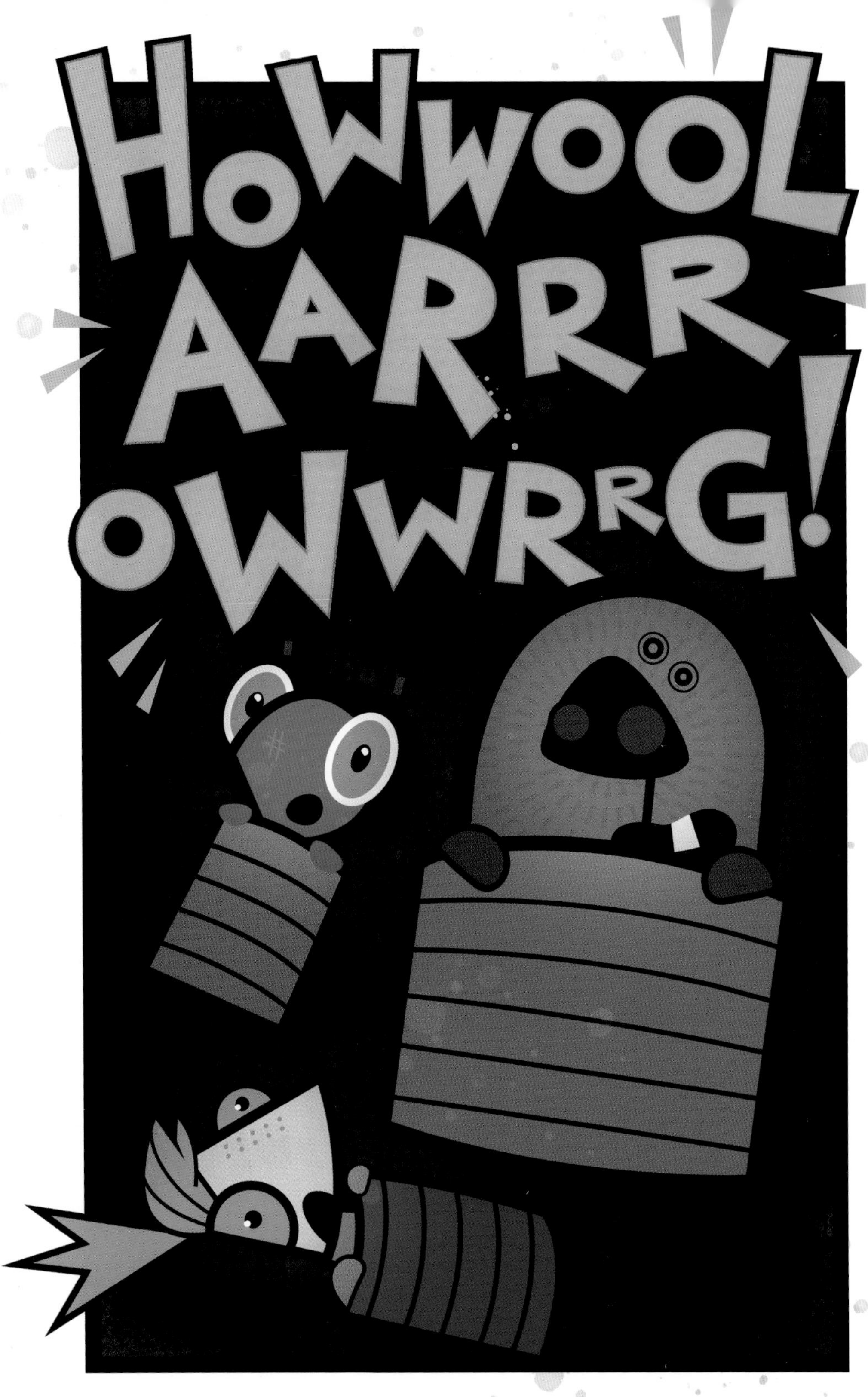
HOWWOOL
AARRR
OWWRRG!

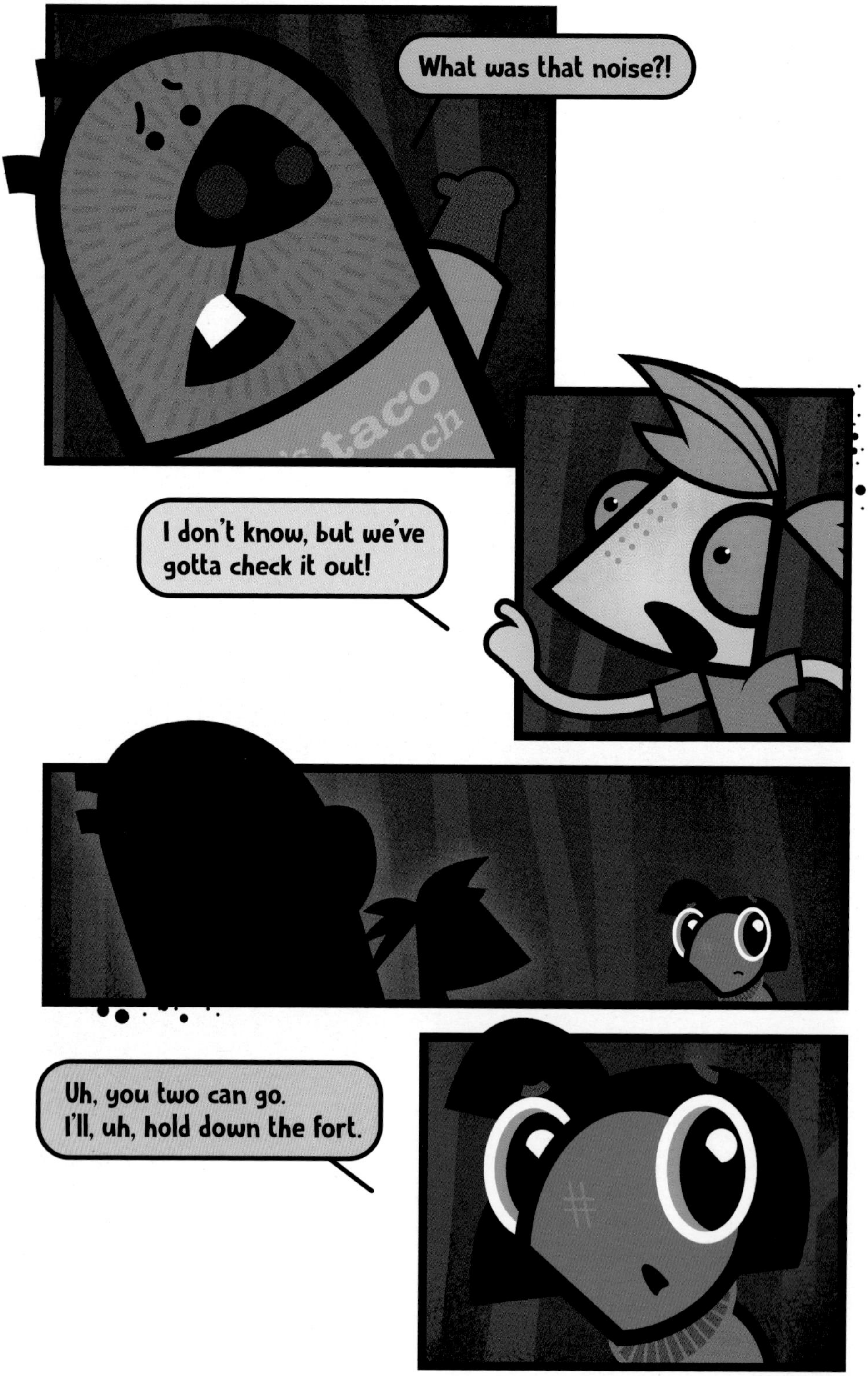
What was that noise?!
I don't know, but we've gotta check it out!
Uh, you two can go. I'll, uh, hold down the fort.

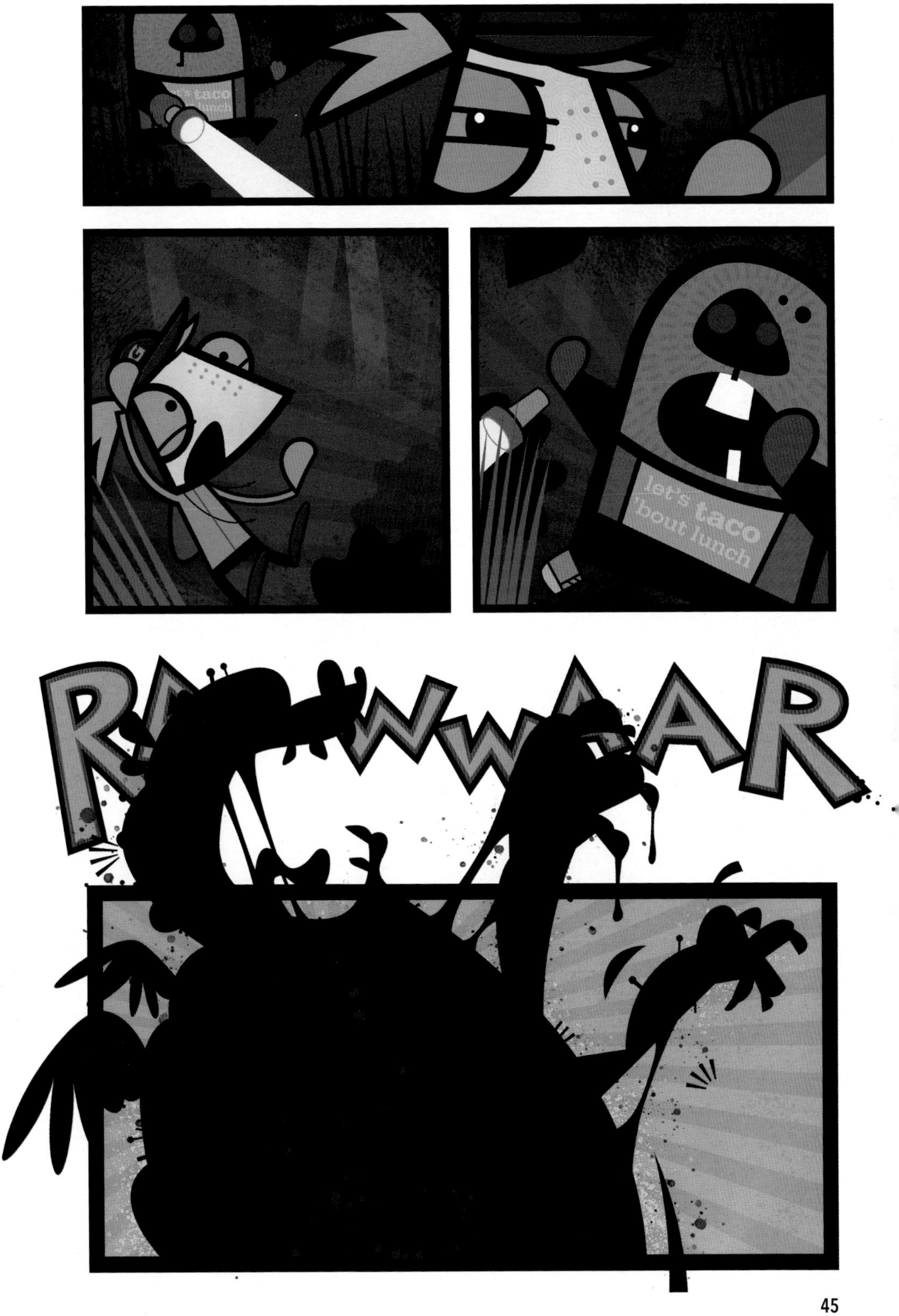
let's taco 'bout lunch
let's taco 'bout lunch
RAWWAAR

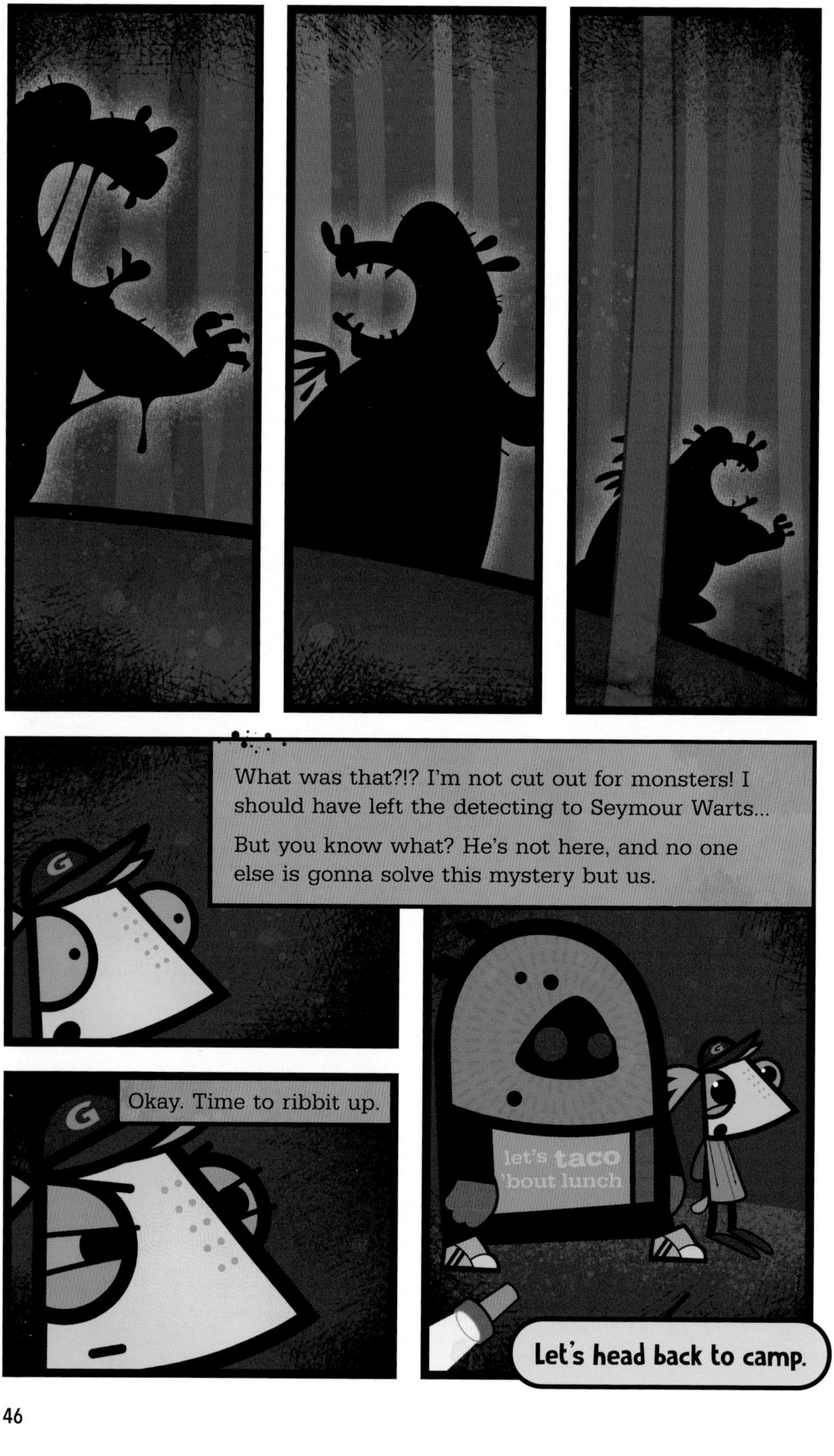
What was that?!? I'm not cut out for monsters! I should have left the detecting to Seymour Warts...
But you know what? He's not here, and no one else is gonna solve this mystery but us.
Okay. Time to ribbit up.
let's taco 'bout lunch
Let's head back to camp.

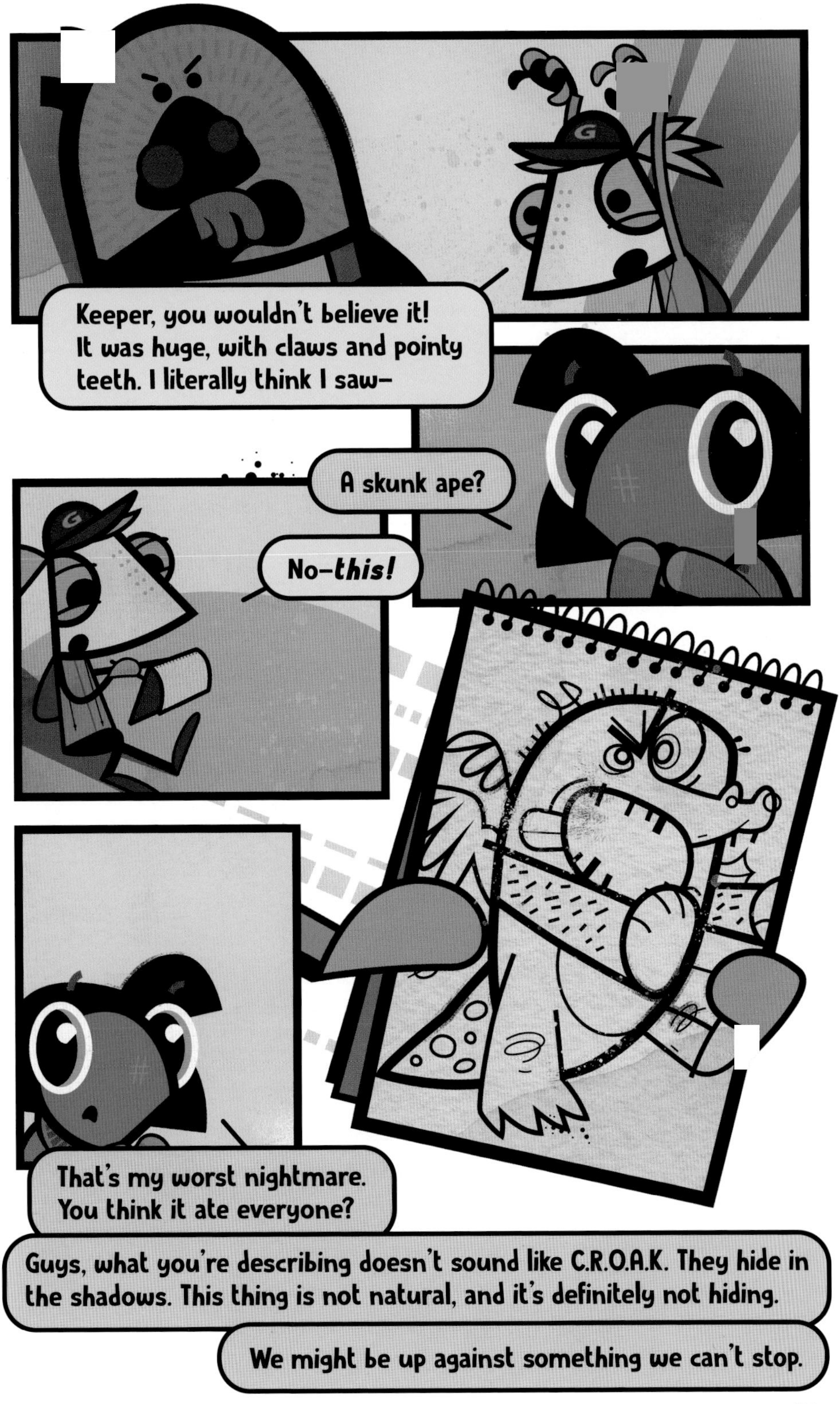
Keeper, you wouldn't believe it!
It was huge, with claws and pointy teeth. I literally think I saw–
A skunk ape?
No–*this!*
That's my worst nightmare.
You think it ate everyone?
Guys, what you're describing doesn't sound like C.R.O.A.K. They hide in the shadows. This thing is not natural, and it's definitely not hiding.
We might be up against something we can't stop.

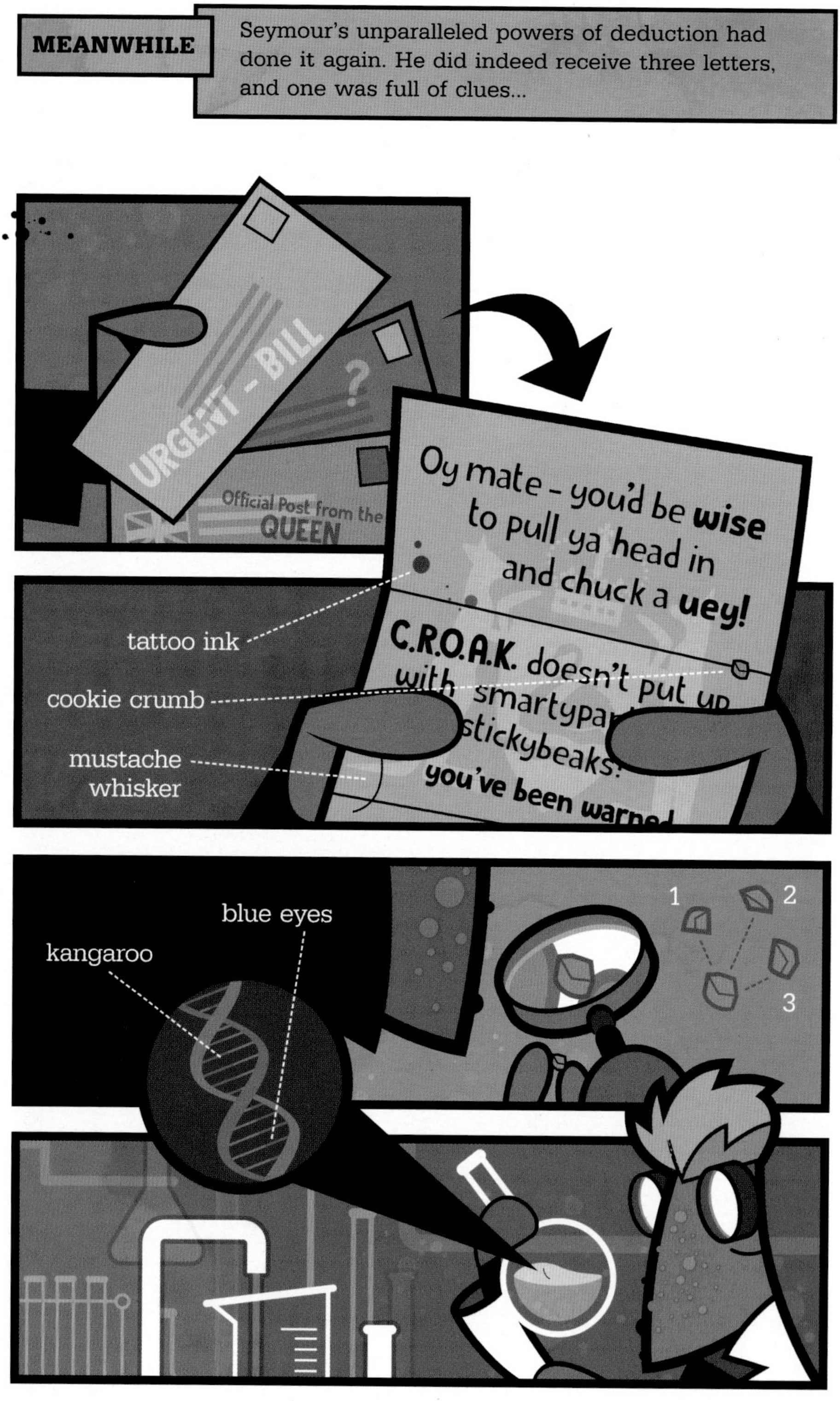
MEANWHILE
Seymour's unparalleled powers of deduction had done it again. He did indeed receive three letters, and one was full of clues...
URGENT - BILL
?
Official Post from the QUEEN
Oy mate – you'd be **wise** to pull ya head in and chuck a **uey!**
C.R.O.A.K. doesn't put up
with smartypa
stickybeaks!
you've been warne
tattoo ink
cookie crumb
mustache whisker
1
2
3
blue eyes
kangaroo

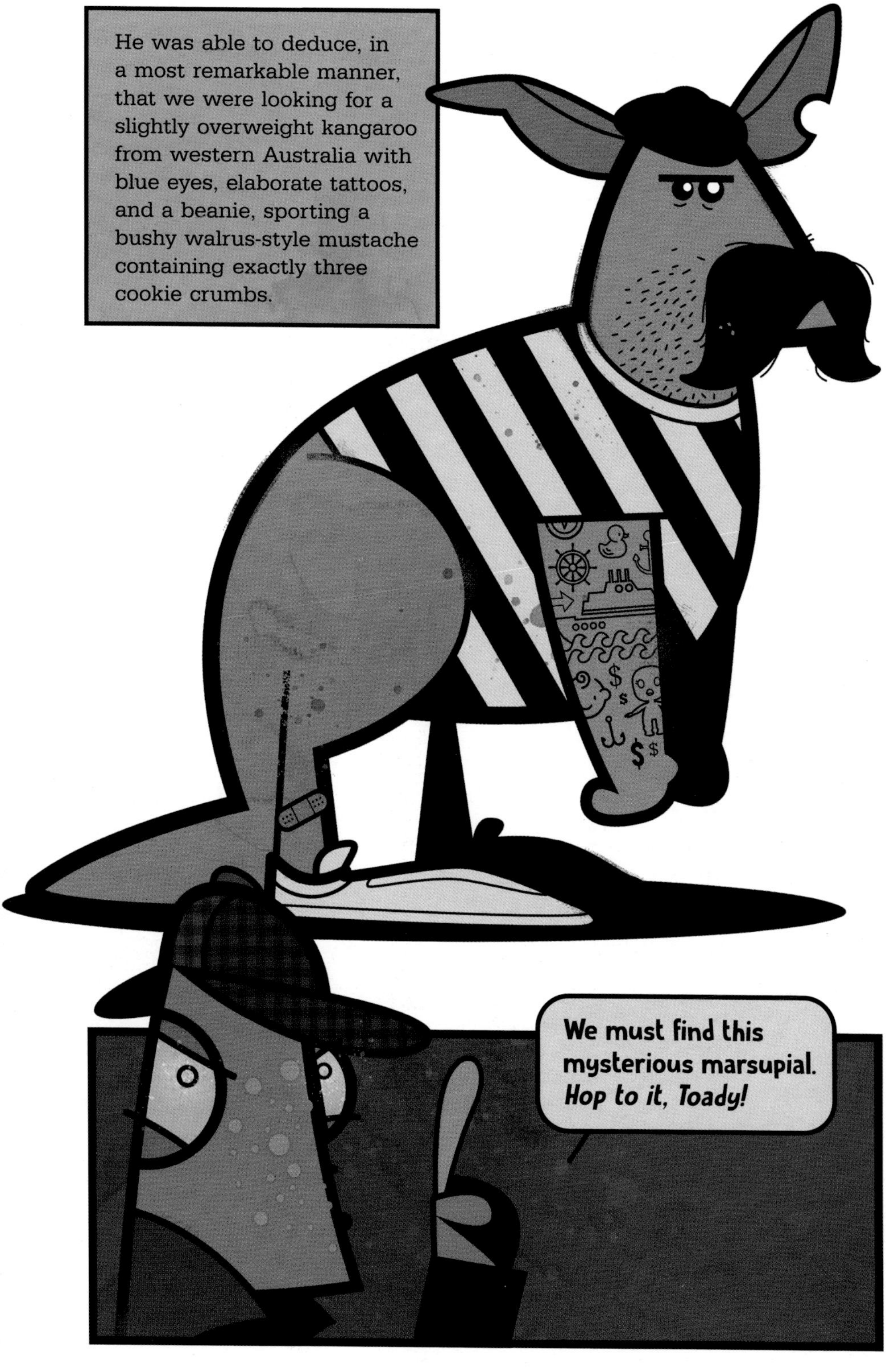
He was able to deduce, in a most remarkable manner, that we were looking for a slightly overweight kangaroo from western Australia with blue eyes, elaborate tattoos, and a beanie, sporting a bushy walrus-style mustache containing exactly three cookie crumbs.
We must find this mysterious marsupial. *Hop to it, Toady!*

Chapter 6: Later, Gator!

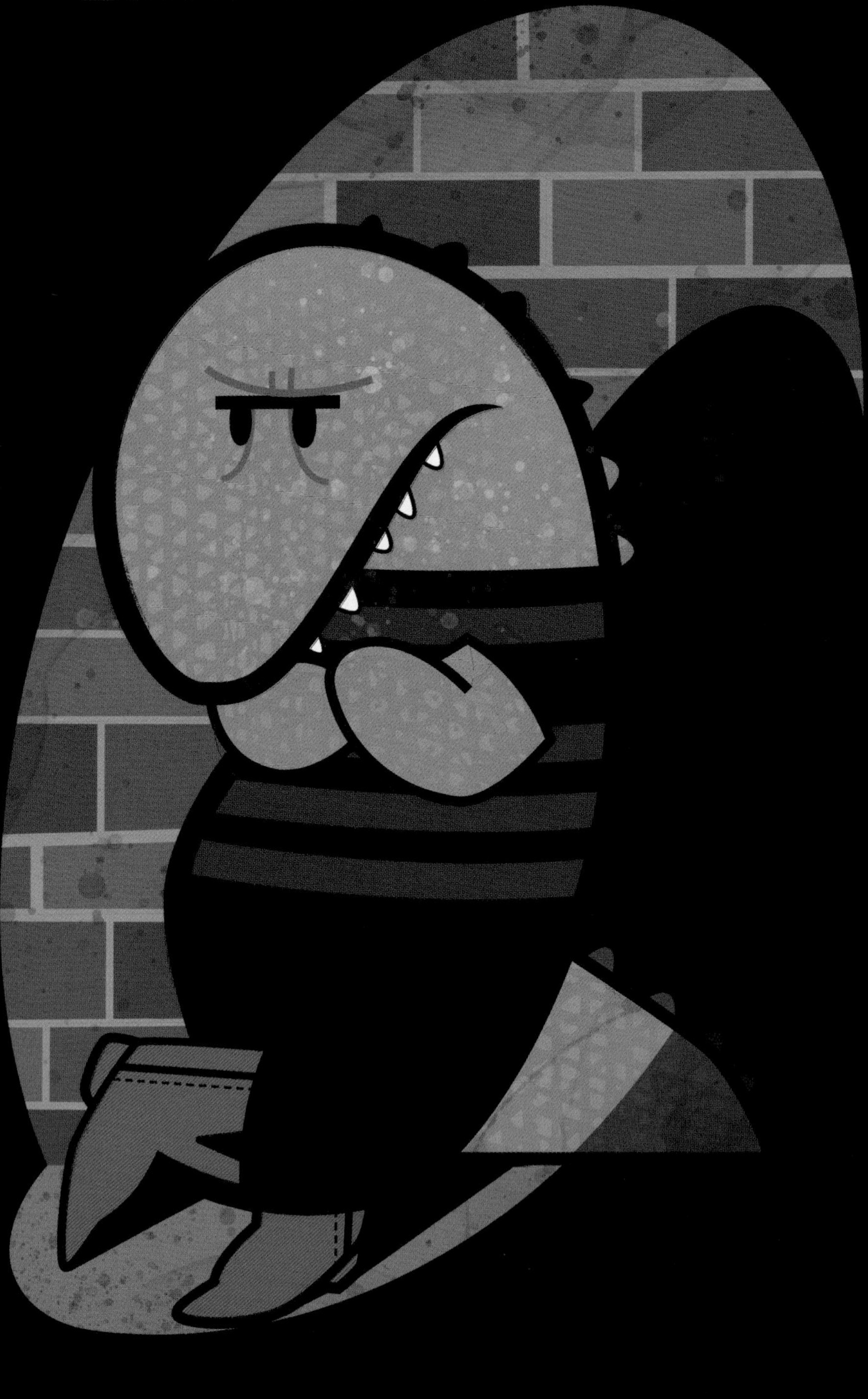

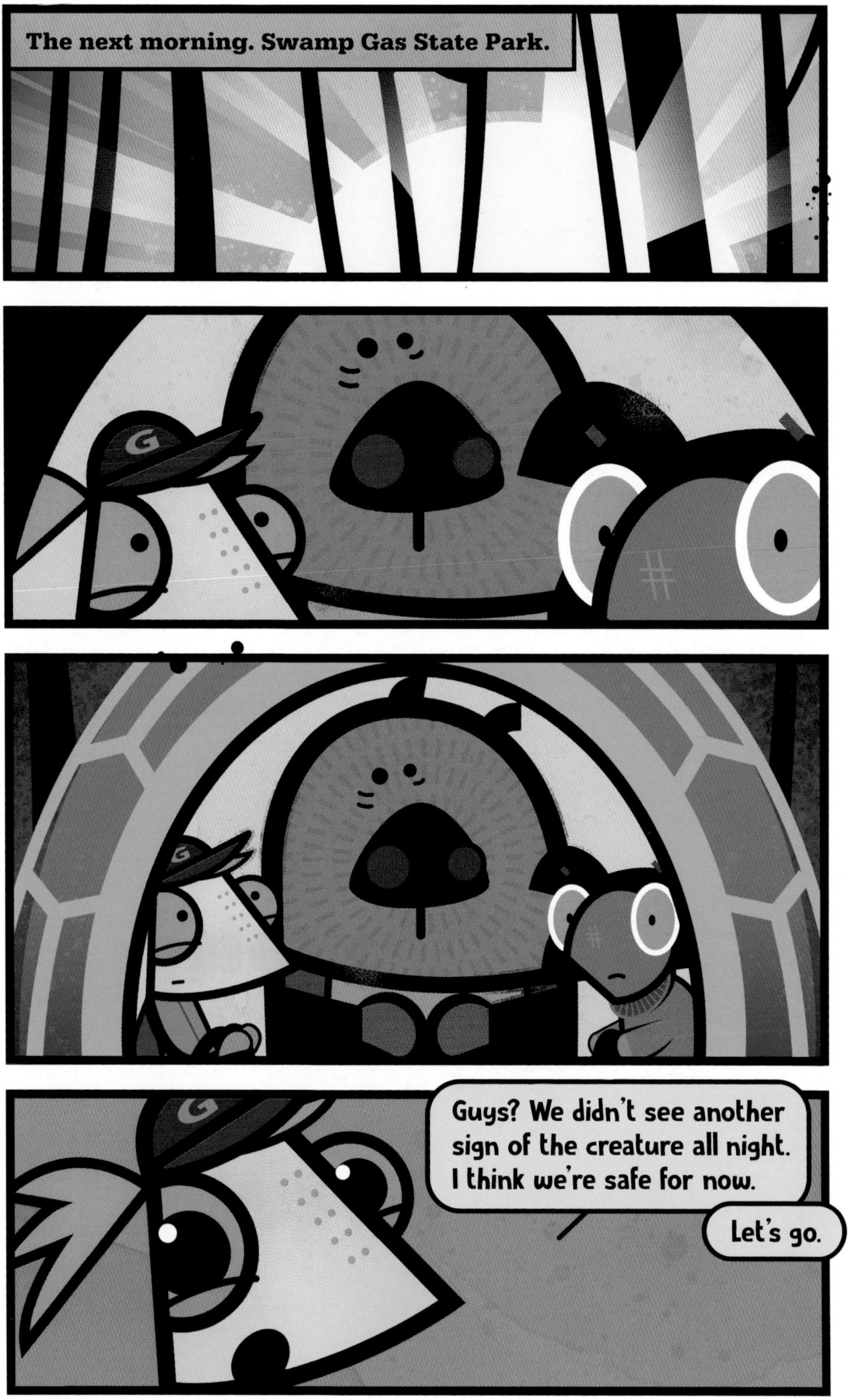
The next morning. Swamp Gas State Park.
Guys? We didn't see another sign of the creature all night. I think we're safe for now.
Let's go.

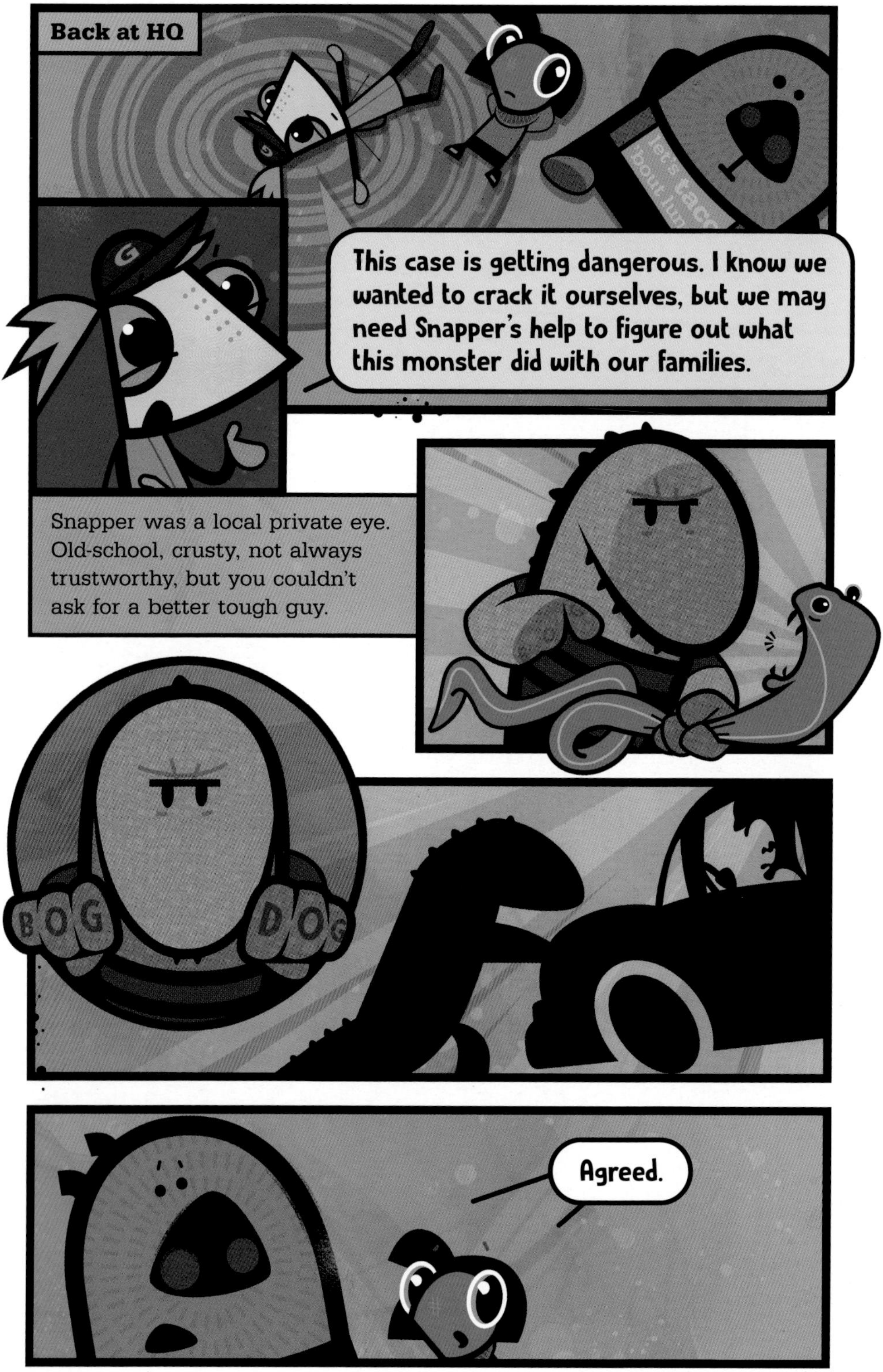
Back at HQ
This case is getting dangerous. I know we wanted to crack it ourselves, but we may need Snapper's help to figure out what this monster did with our families.
Snapper was a local private eye. Old-school, crusty, not always trustworthy, but you couldn't ask for a better tough guy.
BOG DOG
Agreed.

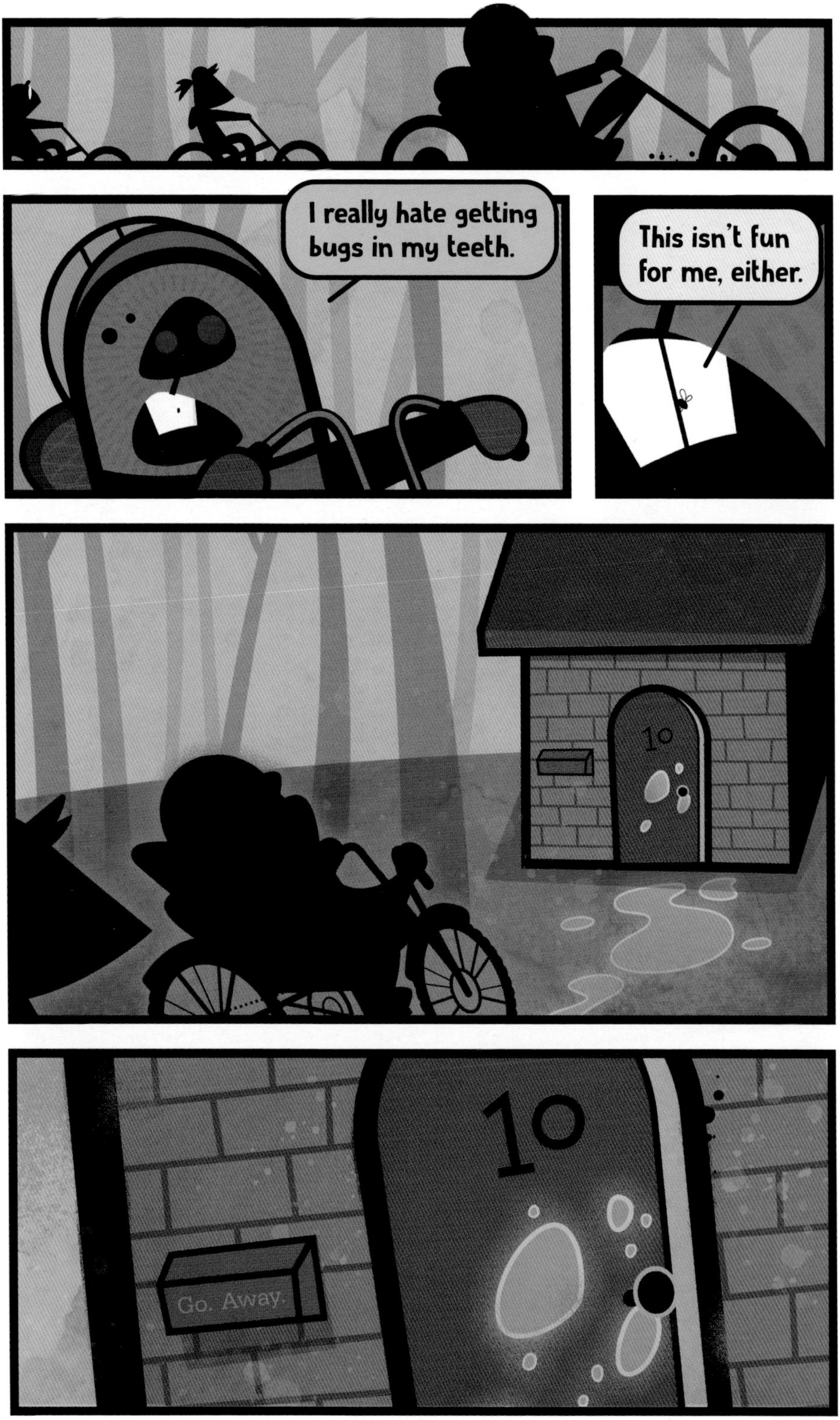
I really hate getting bugs in my teeth.
This isn't fun for me, either.
10
Go. Away.
10

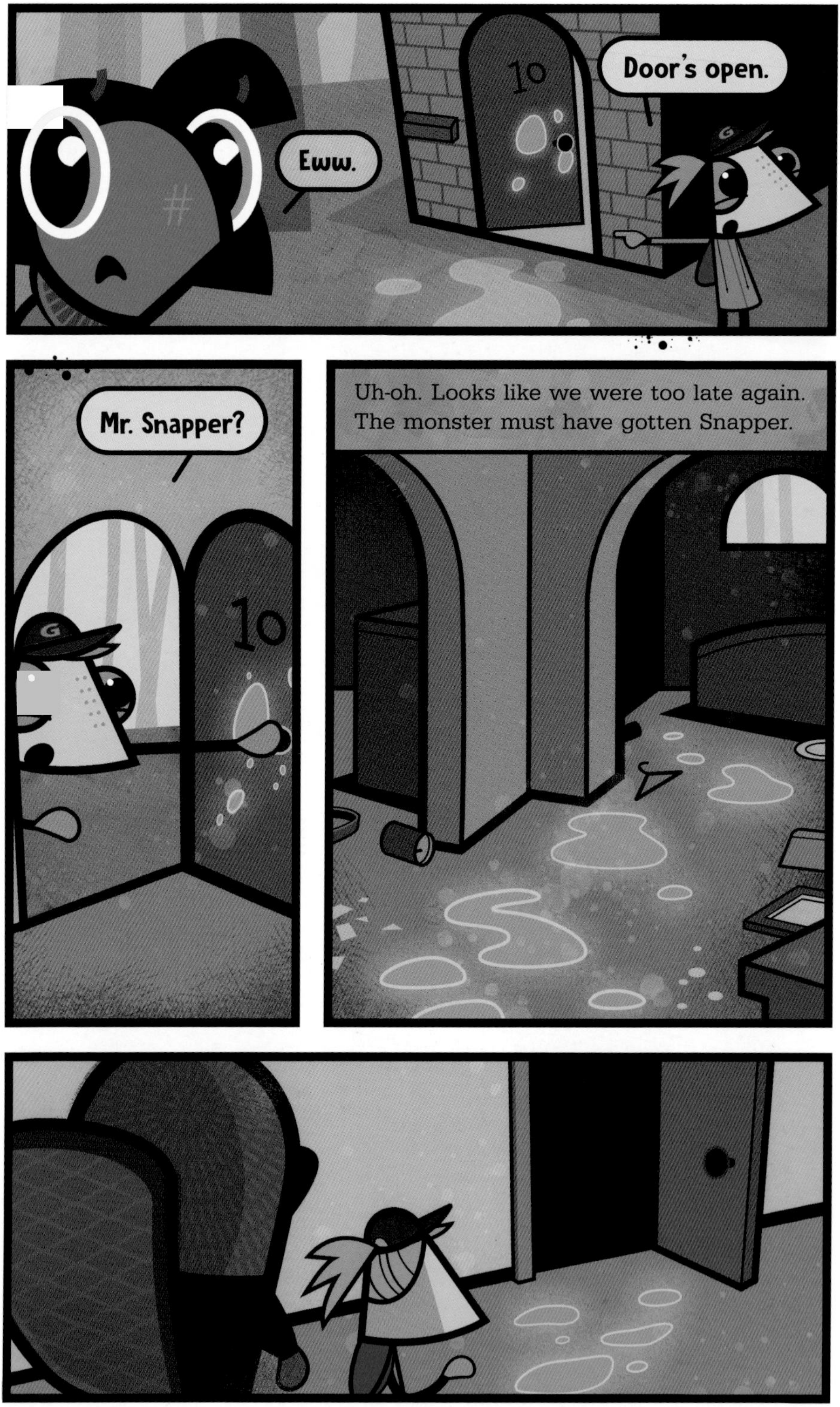
Door's open.
Eww.
Mr. Snapper?
Uh-oh. Looks like we were too late again.
The monster must have gotten Snapper.

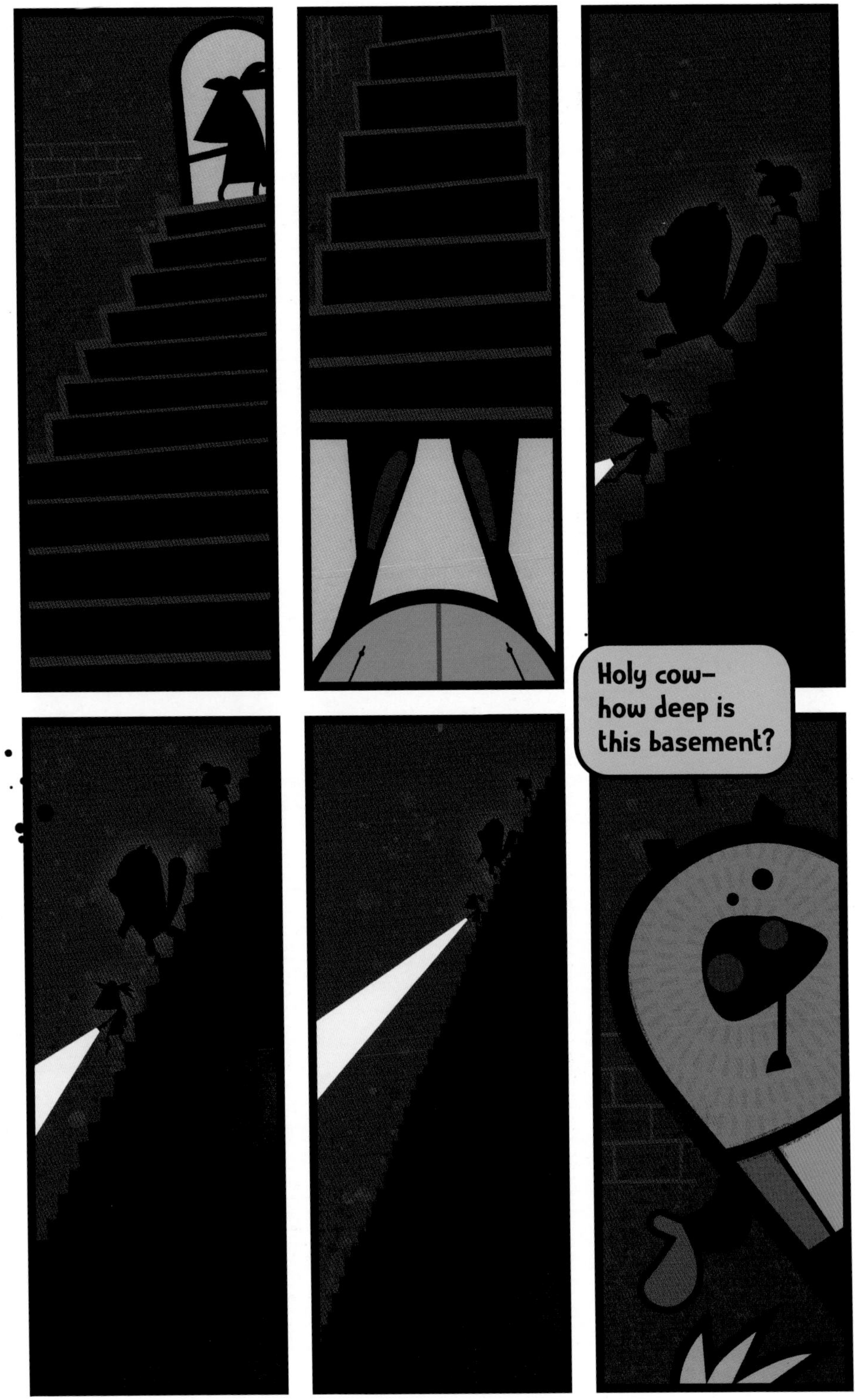
Holy cow—how deep is this basement?

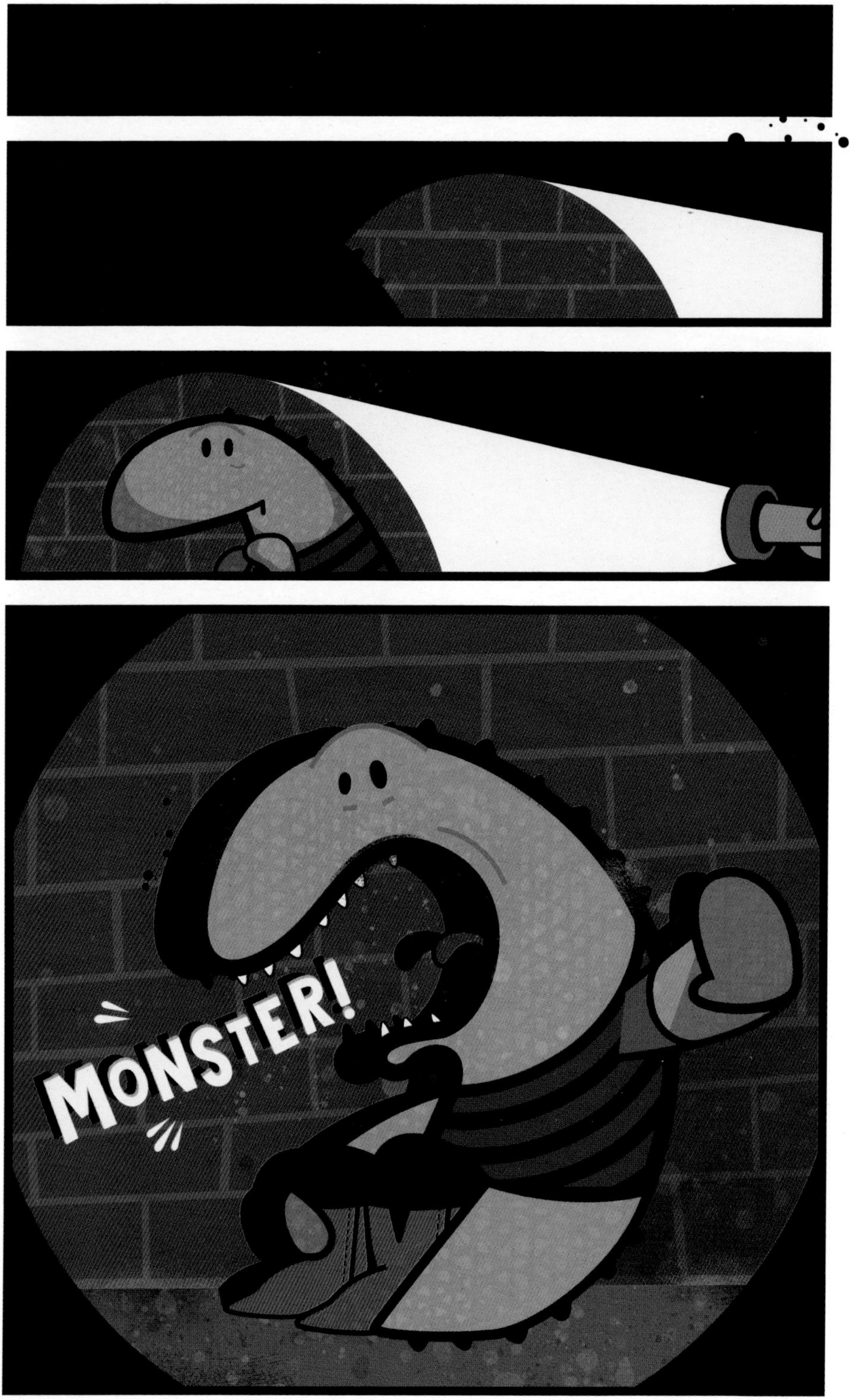
MONSTER!

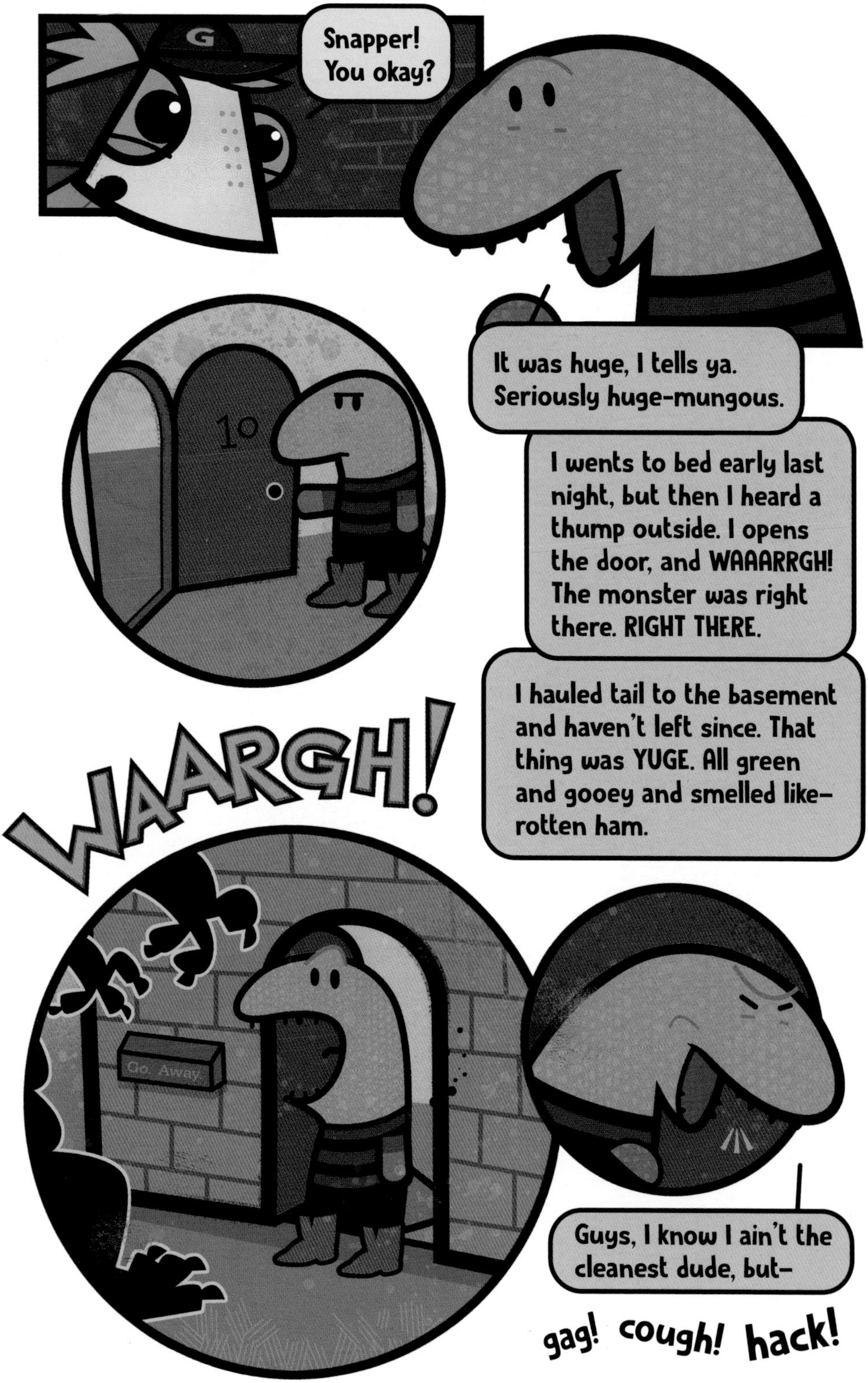
Snapper!
You okay?
It was huge, I tells ya. Seriously huge-mungous.
I wents to bed early last night, but then I heard a thump outside. I opens the door, and WAAARRGH! The monster was right there. RIGHT THERE.
I hauled tail to the basement and haven't left since. That thing was YUGE. All green and gooey and smelled like—rotten ham.
WAARGH!
Go Away
Guys, I know I ain't the cleanest dude, but—
gag! cough! hack!

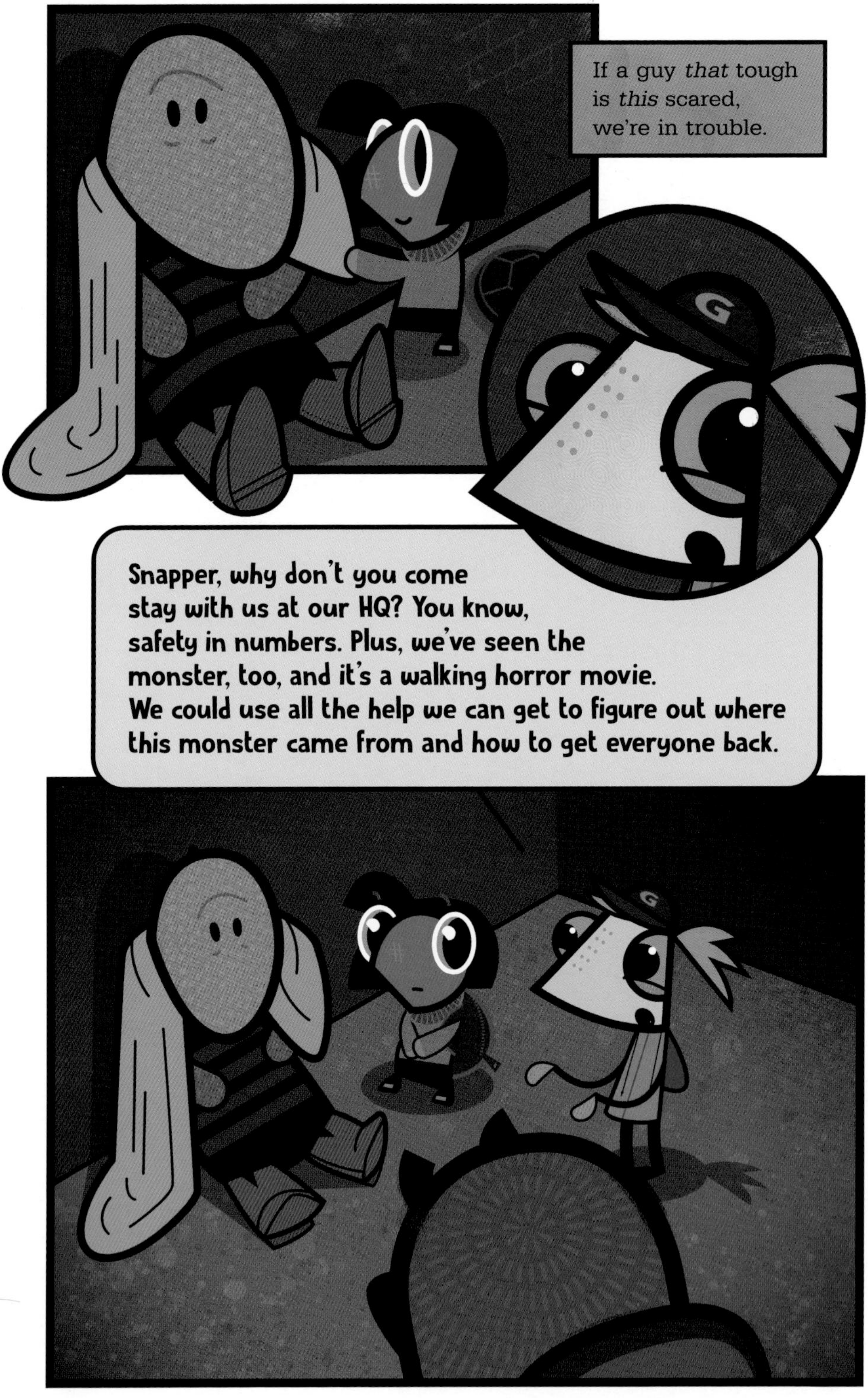
If a guy *that* tough is *this* scared, we're in trouble.
Snapper, why don't you come stay with us at our HQ? You know, safety in numbers. Plus, we've seen the monster, too, and it's a walking horror movie. We could use all the help we can get to figure out where this monster came from and how to get everyone back.

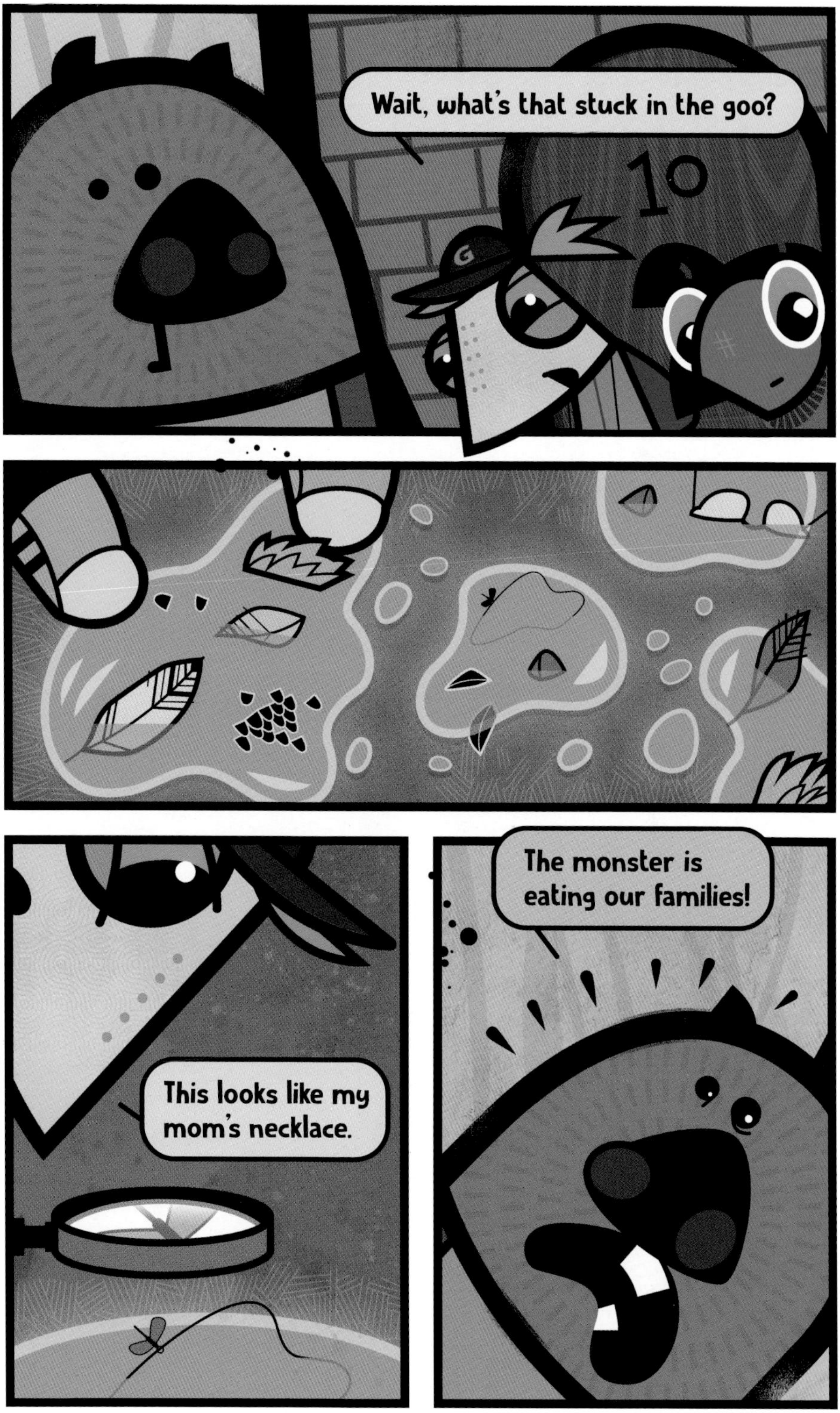
Wait, what's that stuck in the goo?
10
This looks like my mom's necklace.
The monster is eating our families!

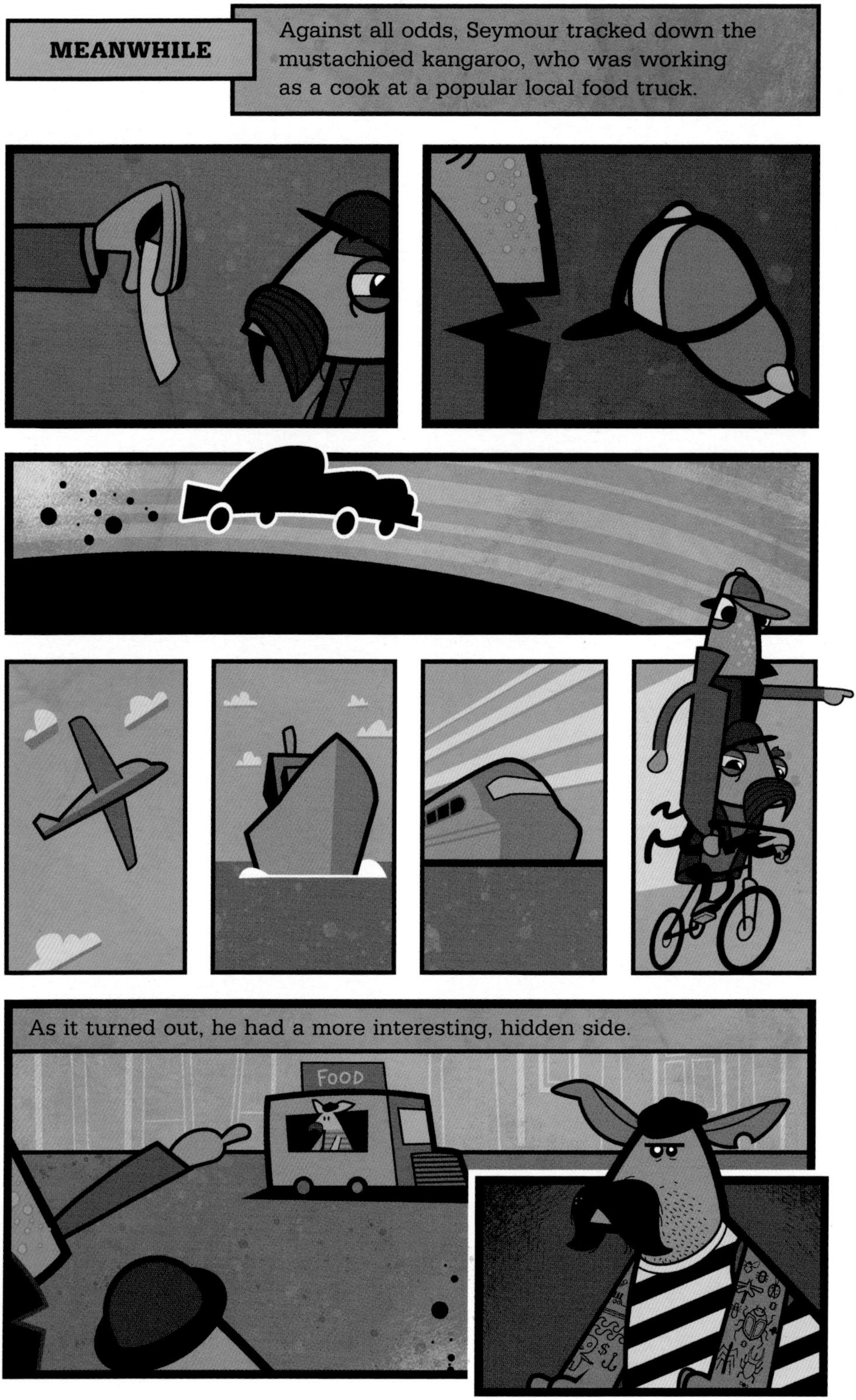
MEANWHILE
Against all odds, Seymour tracked down the mustachioed kangaroo, who was working as a cook at a popular local food truck.
As it turned out, he had a more interesting, hidden side.
FOOD

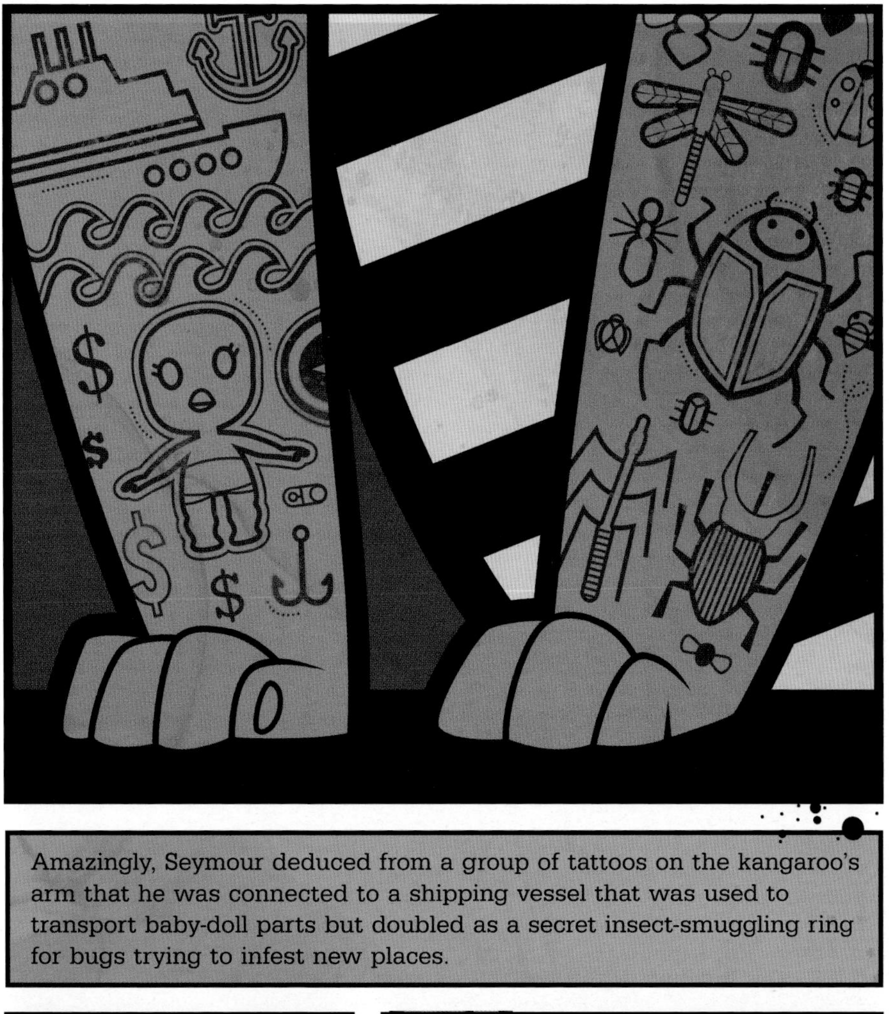

Amazingly, Seymour deduced from a group of tattoos on the kangaroo's arm that he was connected to a shipping vessel that was used to transport baby-doll parts but doubled as a secret insect-smuggling ring for bugs trying to infest new places.

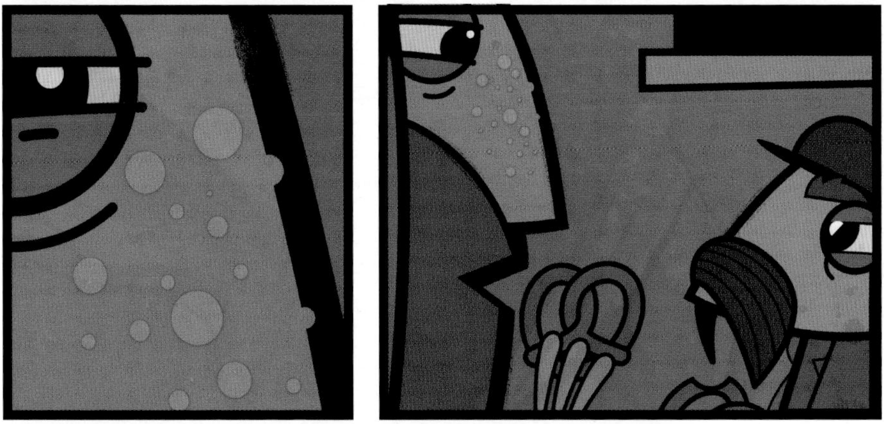

And, just like that, we were off on a ship hunt!

Chapter 7: The Trap Is Set

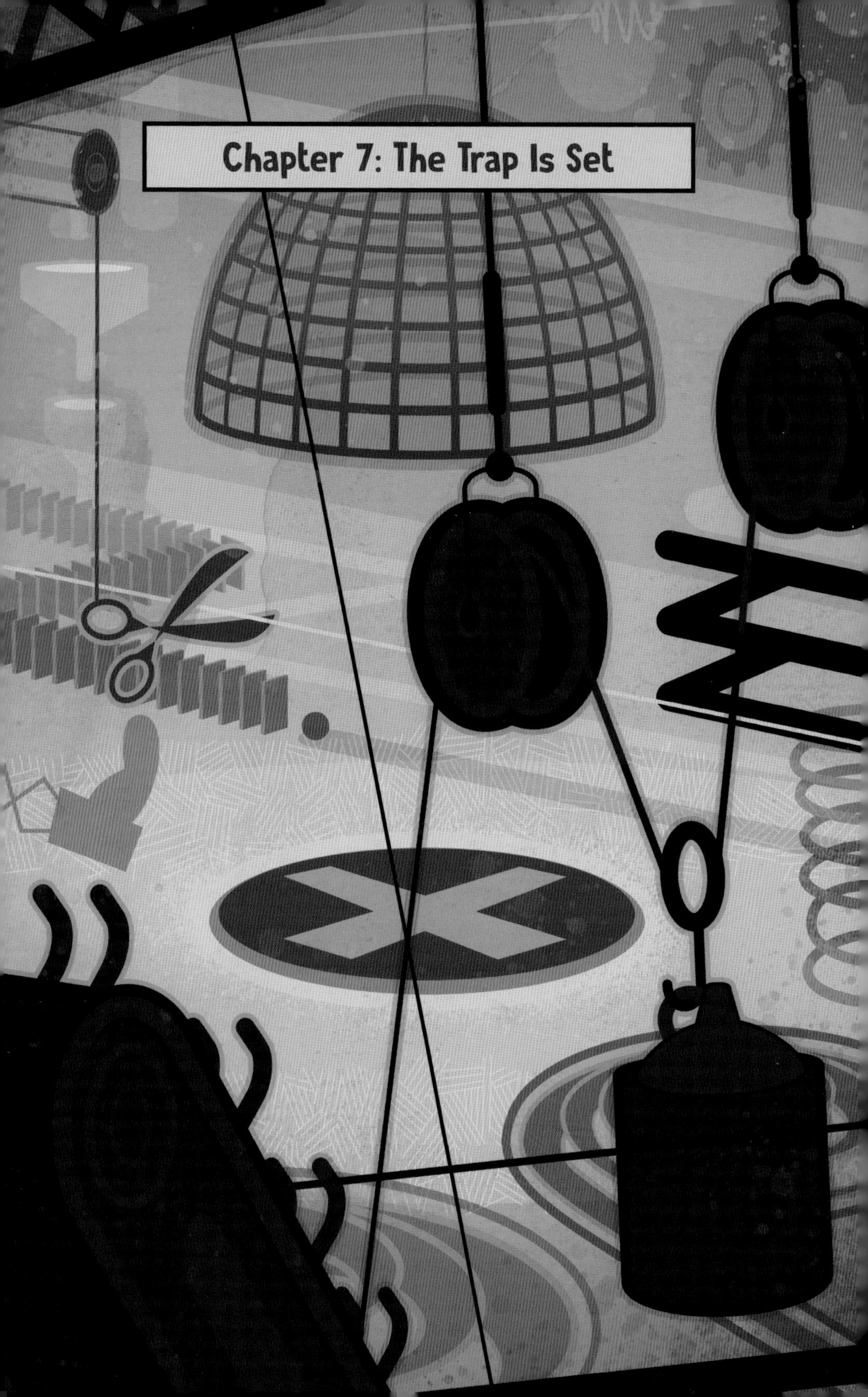

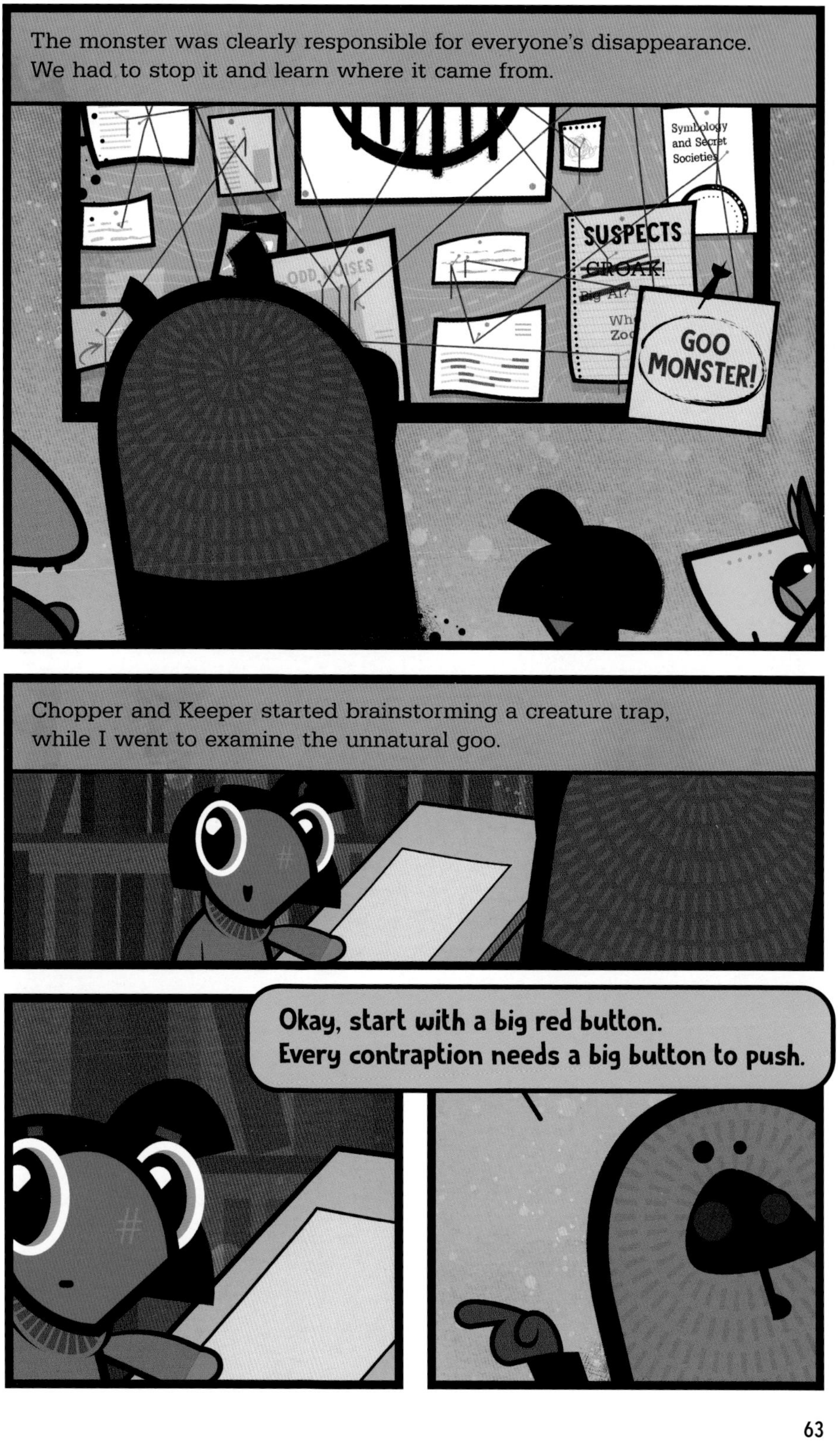

The monster was clearly responsible for everyone's disappearance. We had to stop it and learn where it came from.
Symbology and Secret Societies
SUSPECTS
GROAK!
Big Al?
GOO MONSTER!
Chopper and Keeper started brainstorming a creature trap, while I went to examine the unnatural goo.
Okay, start with a big red button.
Every contraption needs a big button to push.

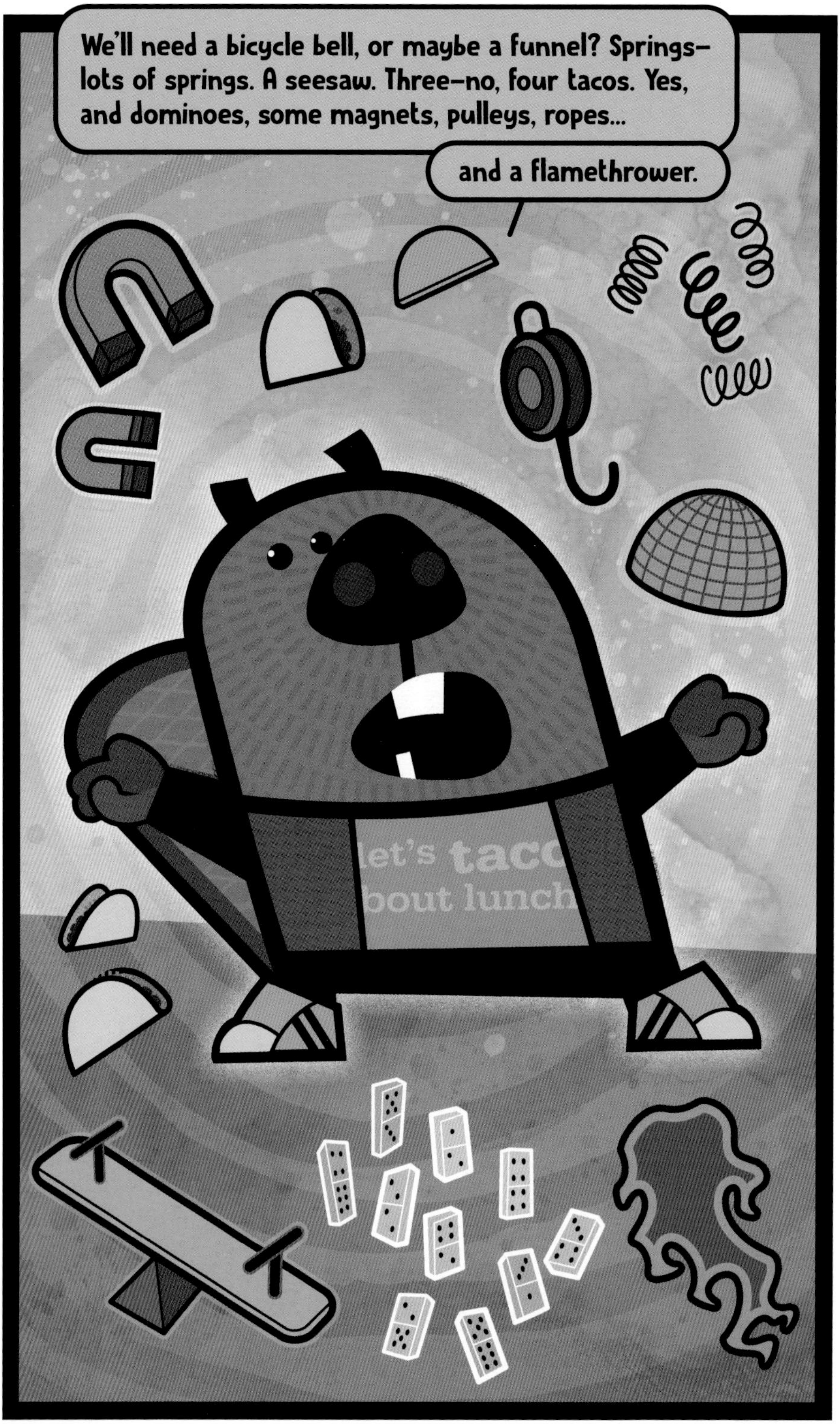
We'll need a bicycle bell, or maybe a funnel? Springs–lots of springs. A seesaw. Three–no, four tacos. Yes, and dominoes, some magnets, pulleys, ropes...
and a flamethrower.
let's taco bout lunch

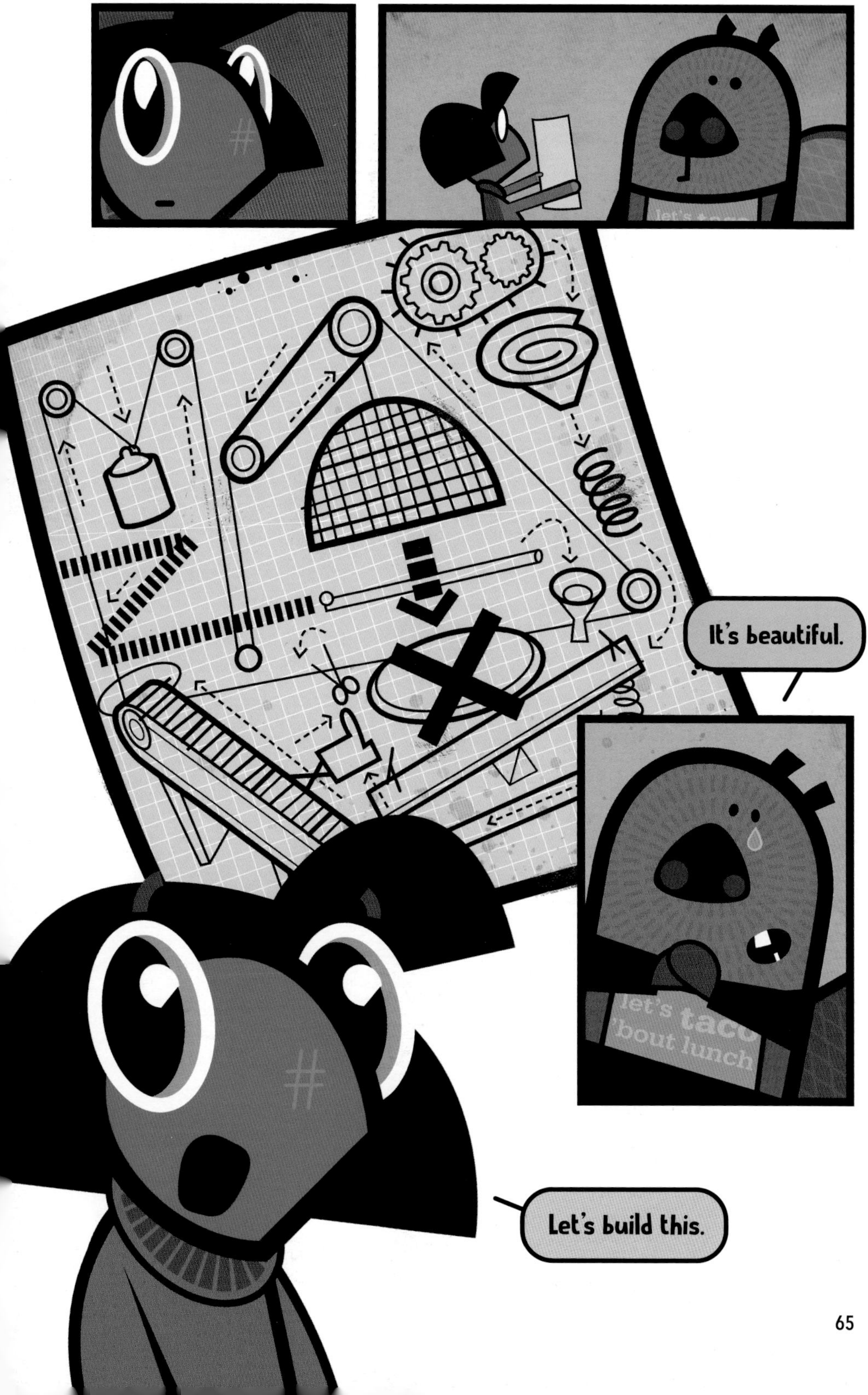
let's taco
'bout lunch
It's beautiful.
Let's build this.

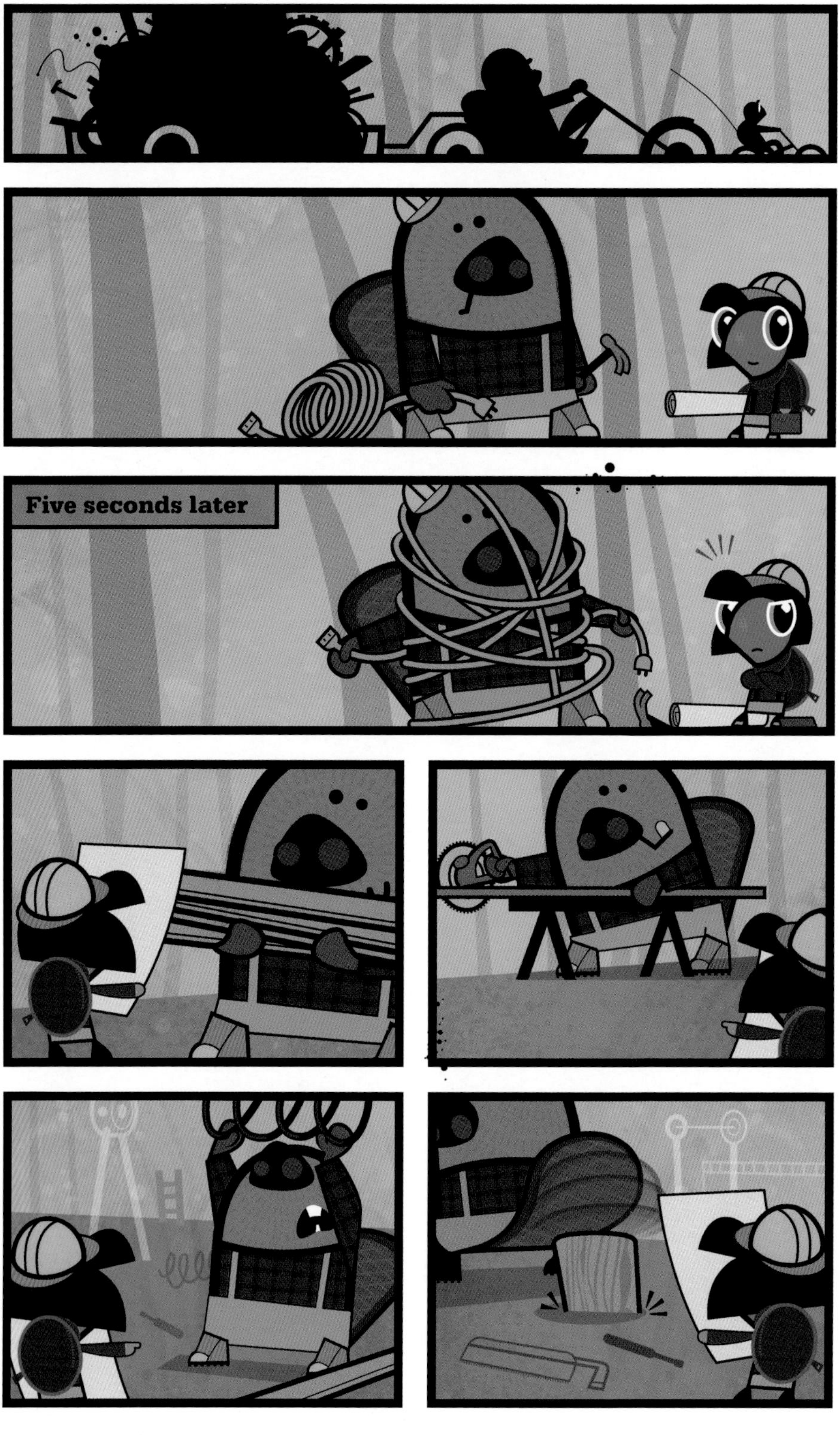
Five seconds later

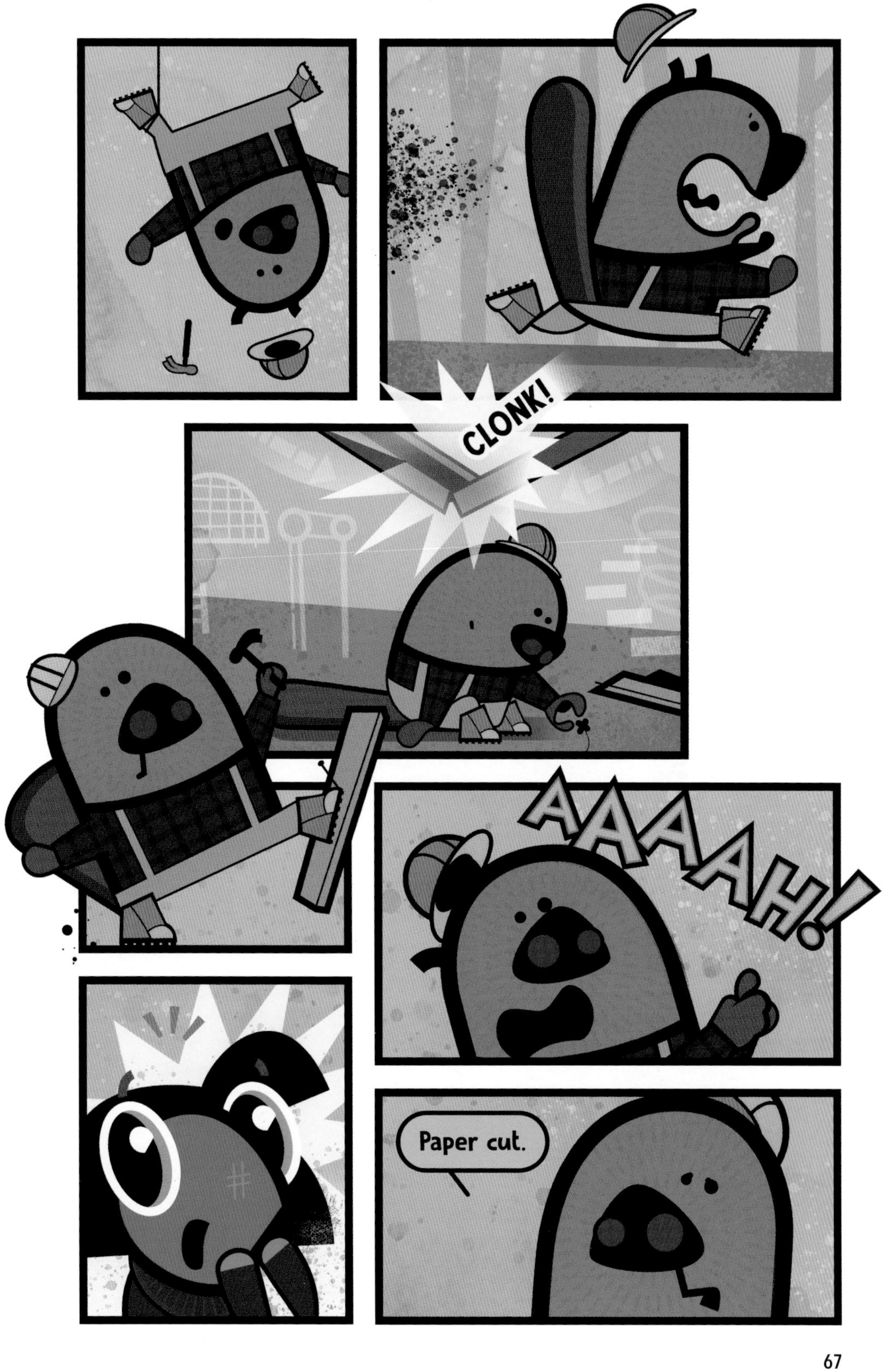
CLONK!
AAAAAH!
Paper cut.

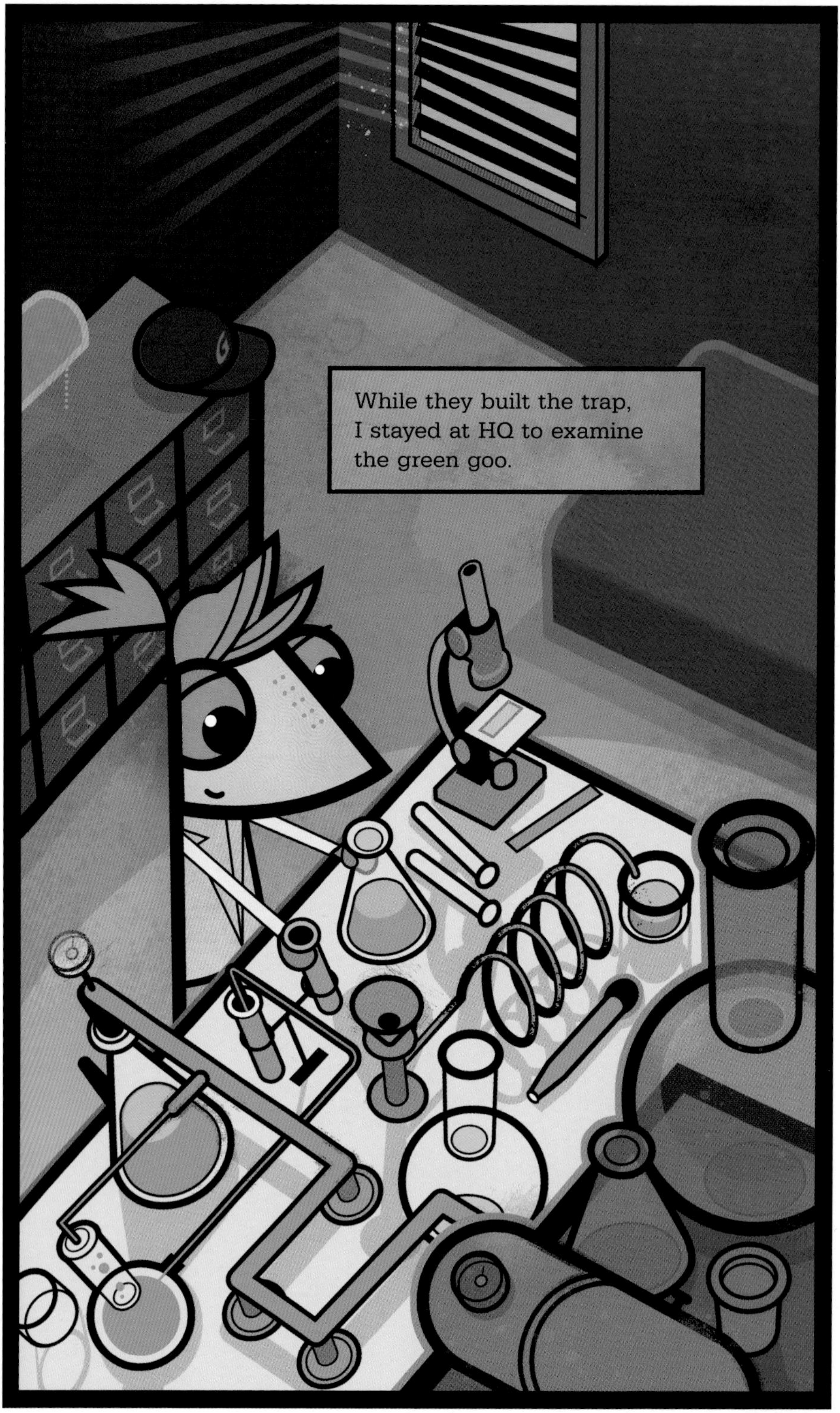
While they built the trap, I stayed at HQ to examine the green goo.

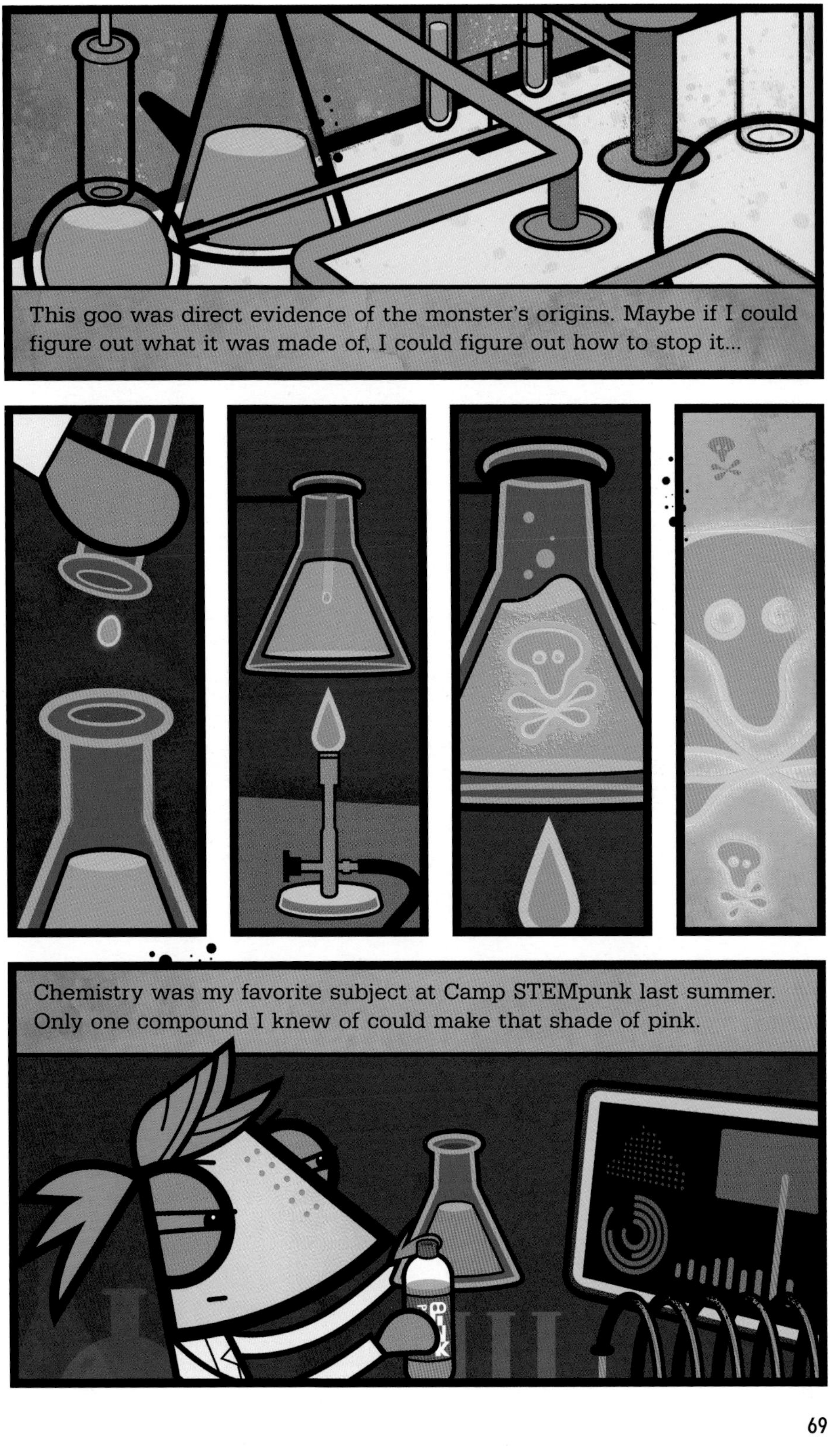
This goo was direct evidence of the monster's origins. Maybe if I could figure out what it was made of, I could figure out how to stop it...
Chemistry was my favorite subject at Camp STEMpunk last summer. Only one compound I knew of could make that shade of pink.

Chapter 8: A Matter of Factory

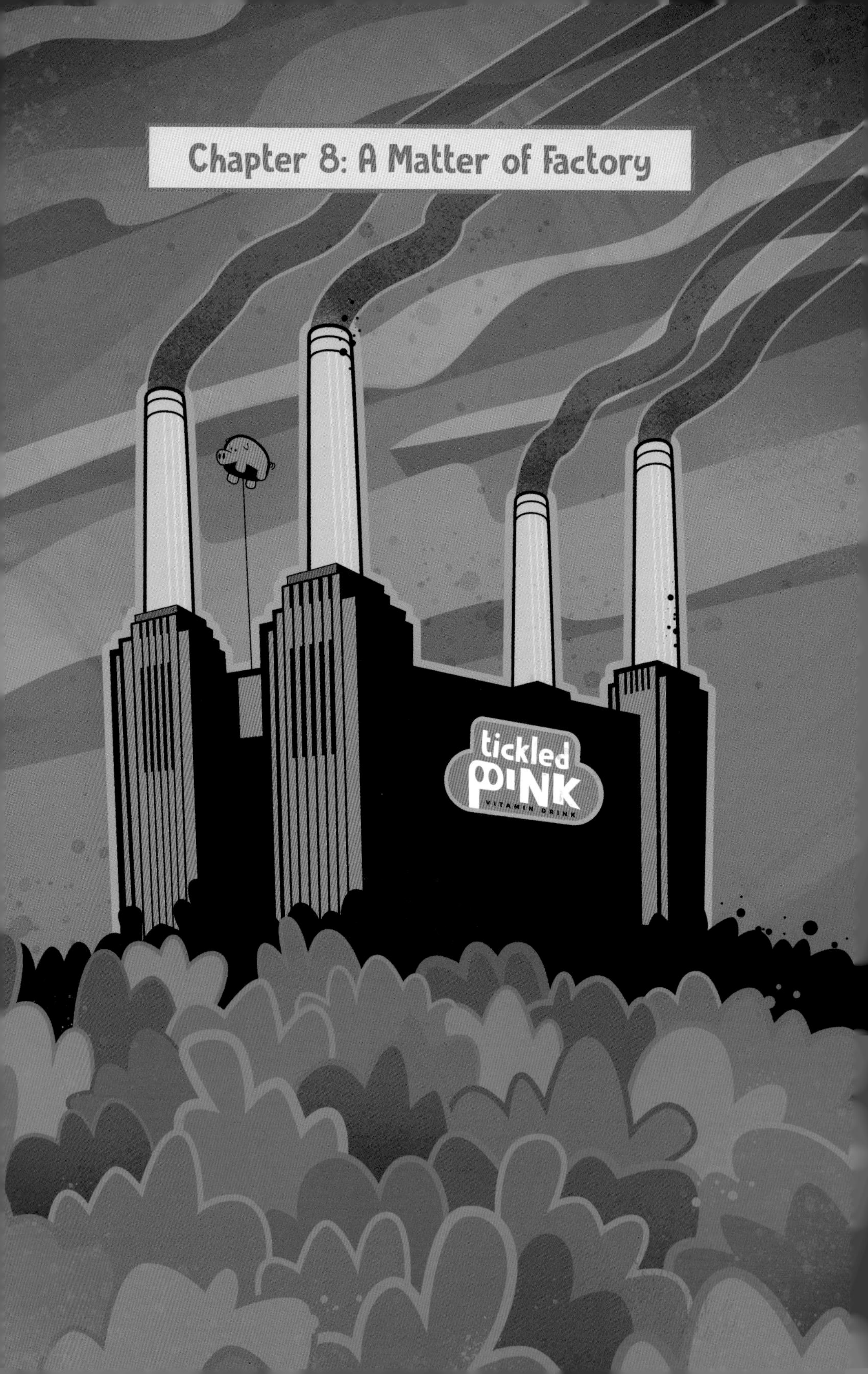
tickled
PINK
VITAMIN DRINK

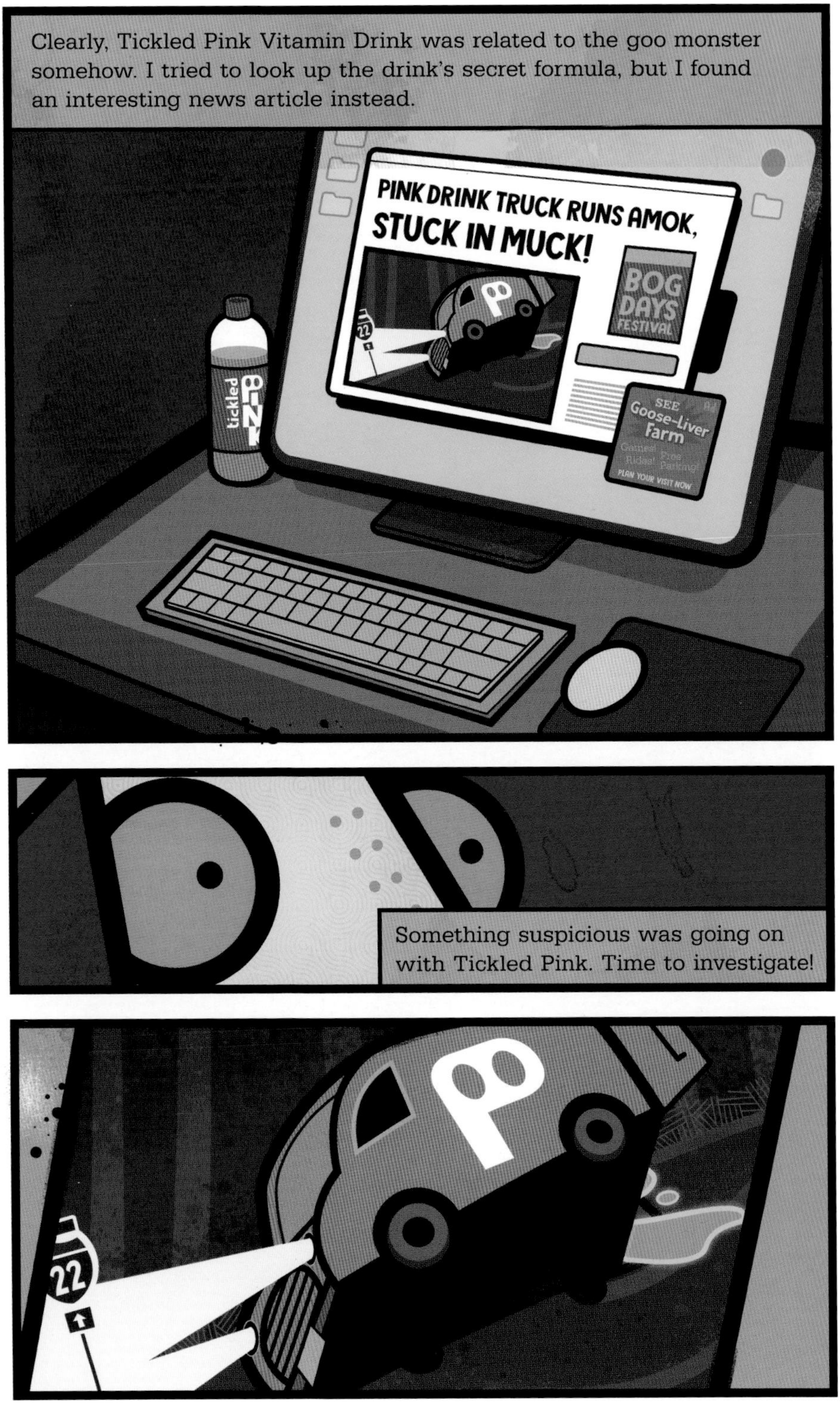
Clearly, Tickled Pink Vitamin Drink was related to the goo monster somehow. I tried to look up the drink's secret formula, but I found an interesting news article instead.
PINK DRINK TRUCK RUNS AMOK, STUCK IN MUCK!
BOG DAYS FESTIVAL
SEE Goose-Liver Farm
PLAN YOUR VISIT NOW
tickled PINK
22
Something suspicious was going on with Tickled Pink. Time to investigate!
22

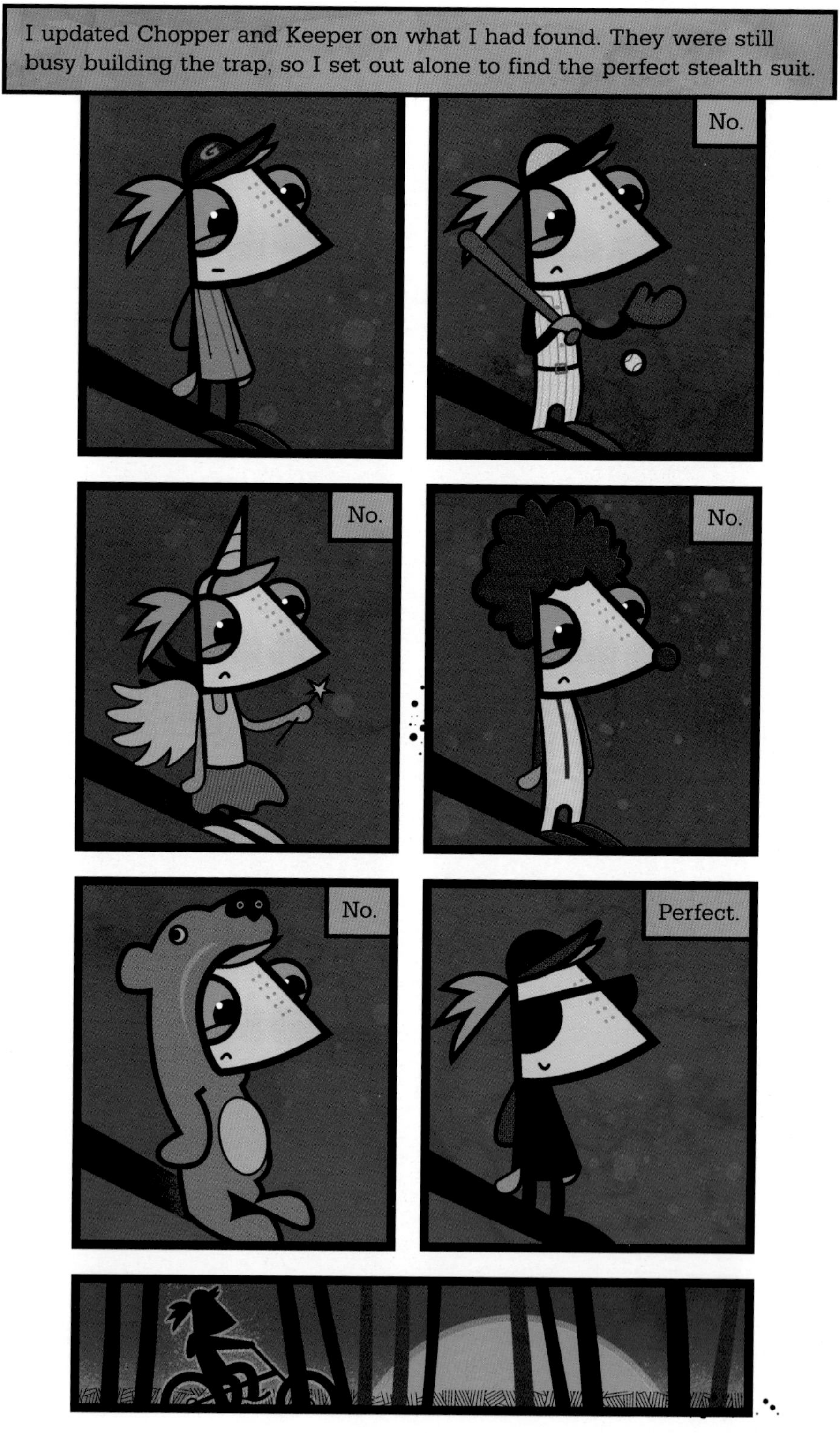
I updated Chopper and Keeper on what I had found. They were still busy building the trap, so I set out alone to find the perfect stealth suit.
No.
No.
No.
No.
Perfect.

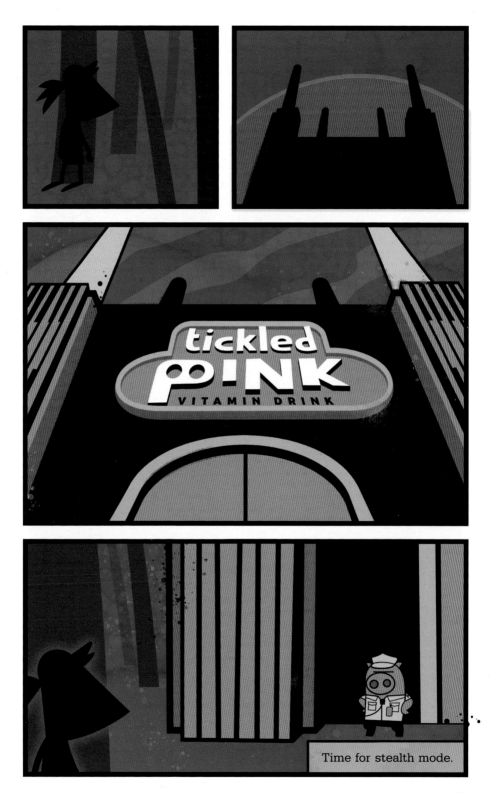

tickled **PINK**
VITAMIN DRINK

Time for stealth mode.

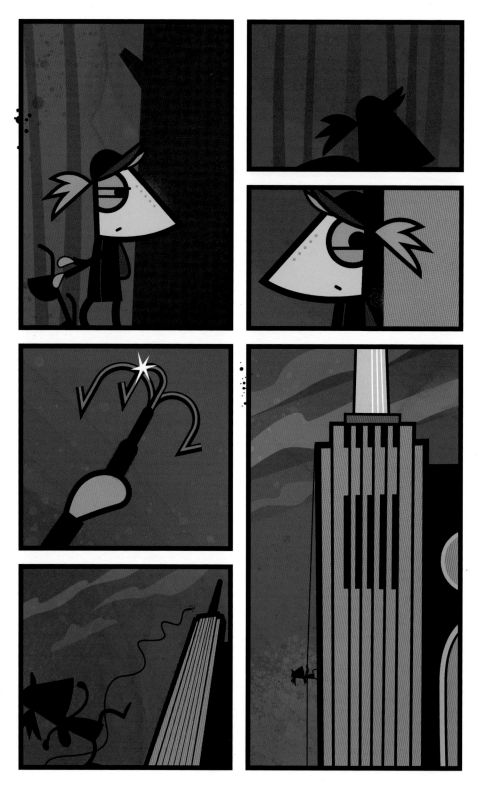

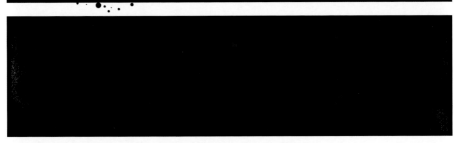

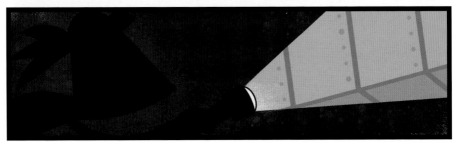

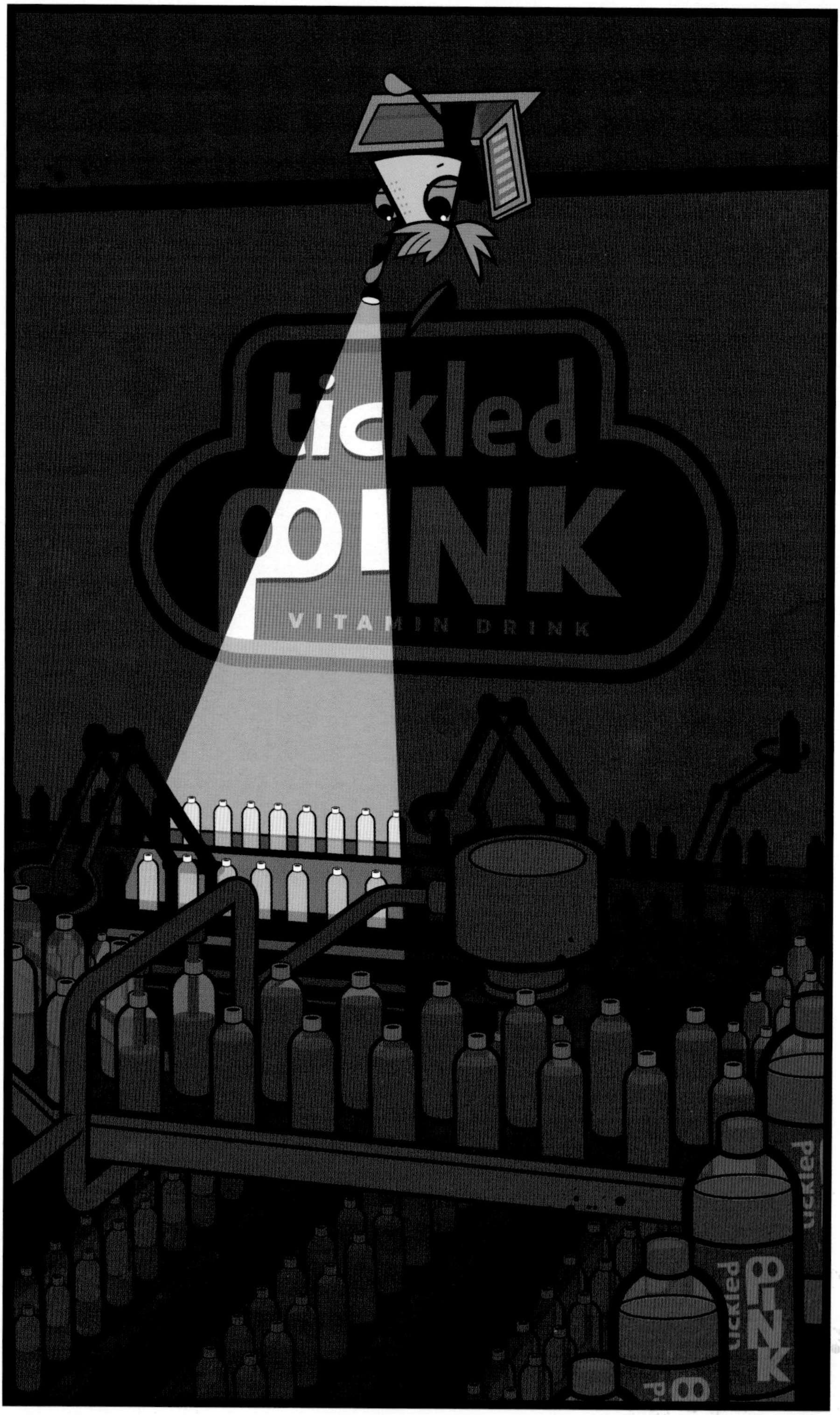
tickled
PINK
VITAMIN DRINK
tickled
PINK

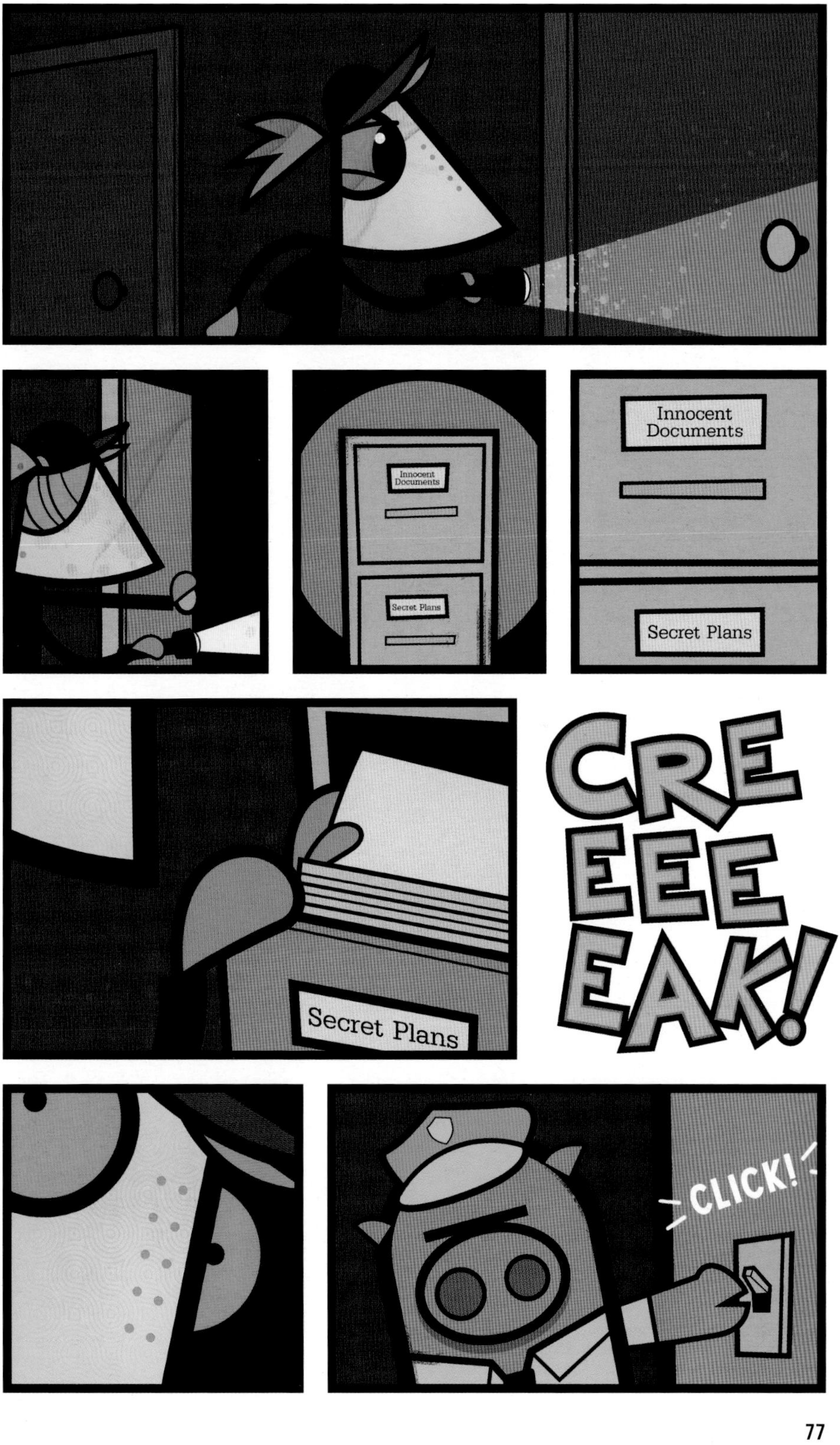
Innocent Documents
Secret Plans
Innocent Documents
Secret Plans
Secret Plans
CREEEEEAK!
CLICK!

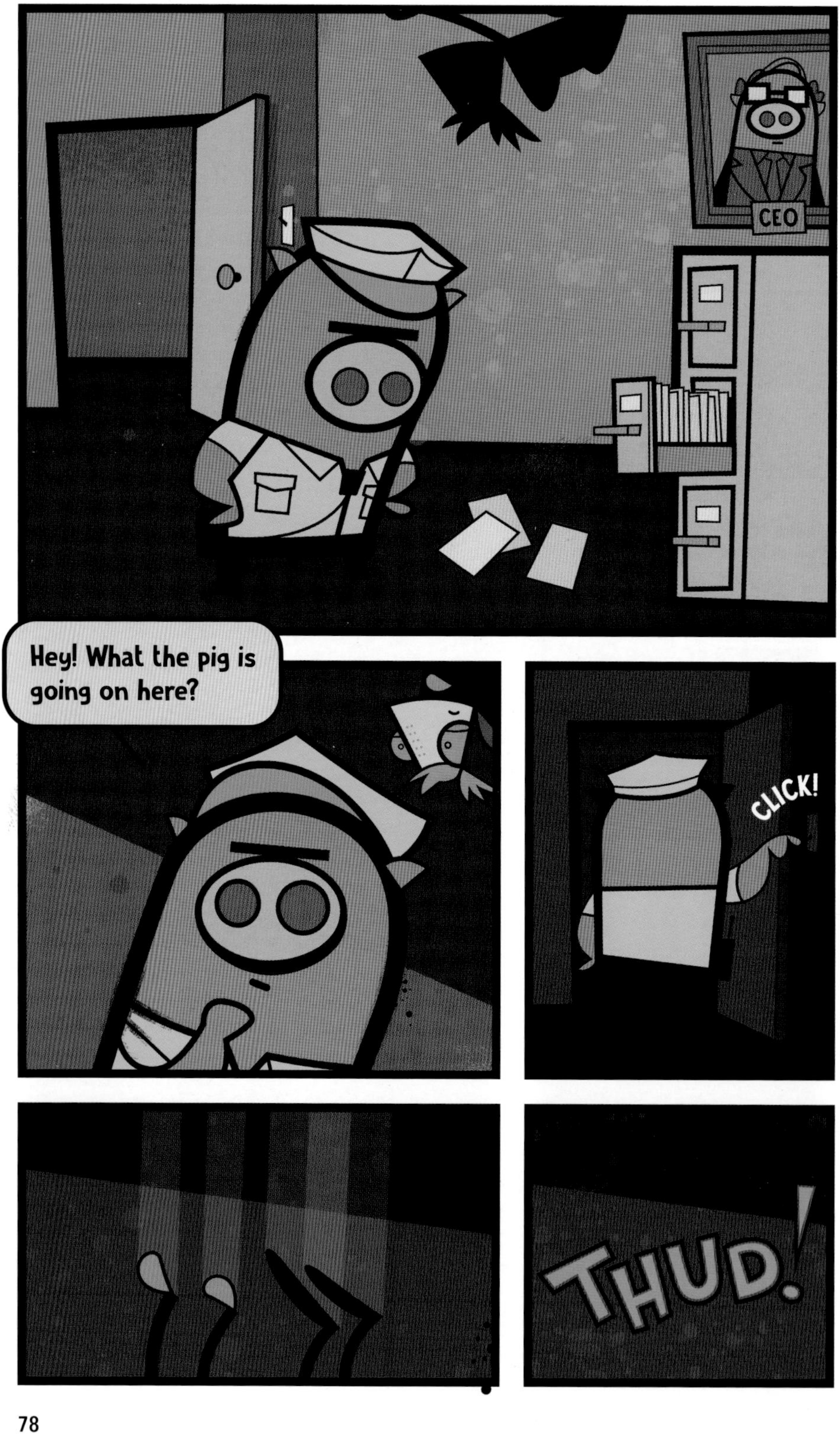
CEO
Hey! What the pig is going on here?
CLICK!
THUD!

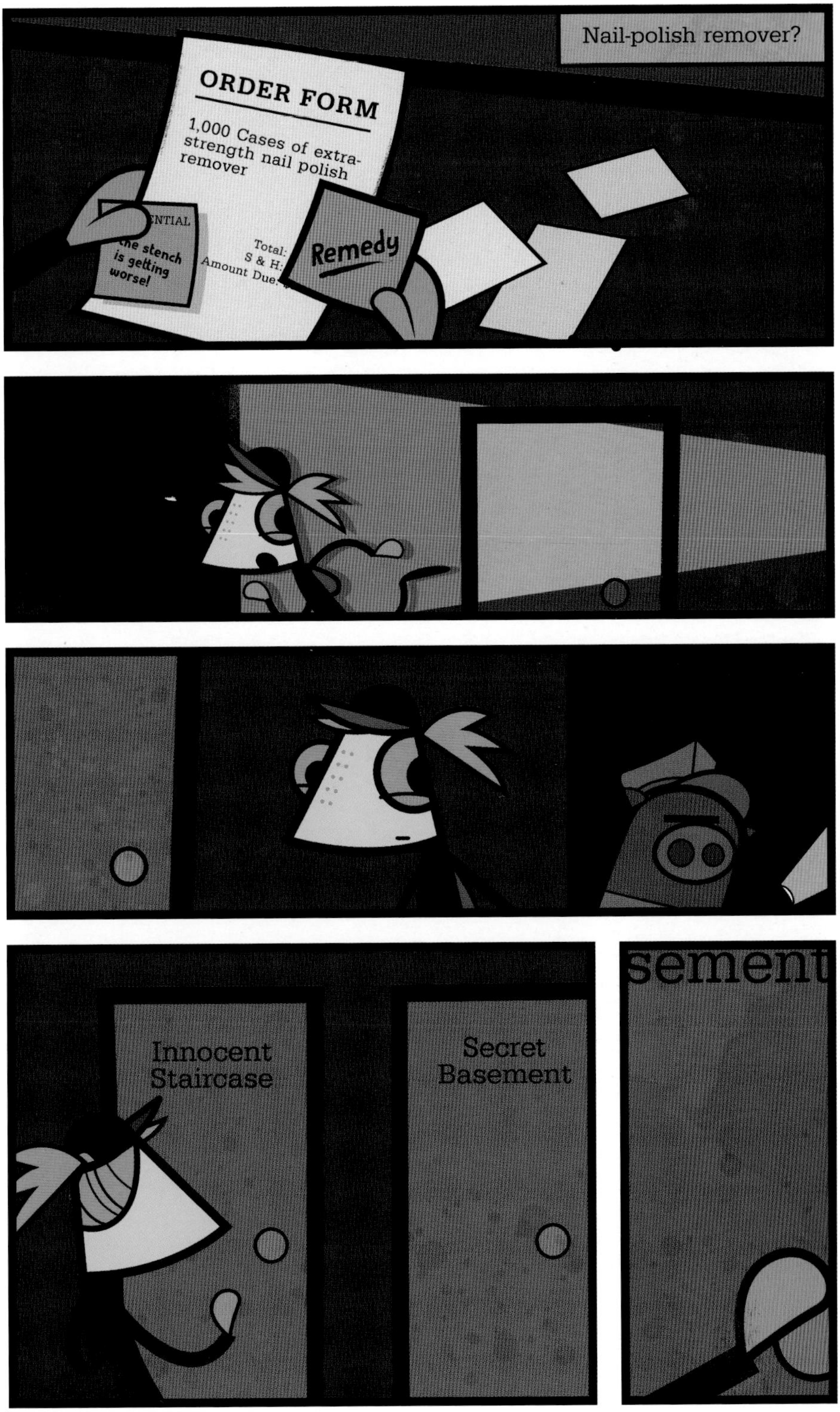
Nail-polish remover?
ORDER FORM
1,000 Cases of extra-strength nail polish remover
Total:
S & H:
Amount Due:
the stench is getting worse!
Remedy
Innocent Staircase
Secret Basement
sement

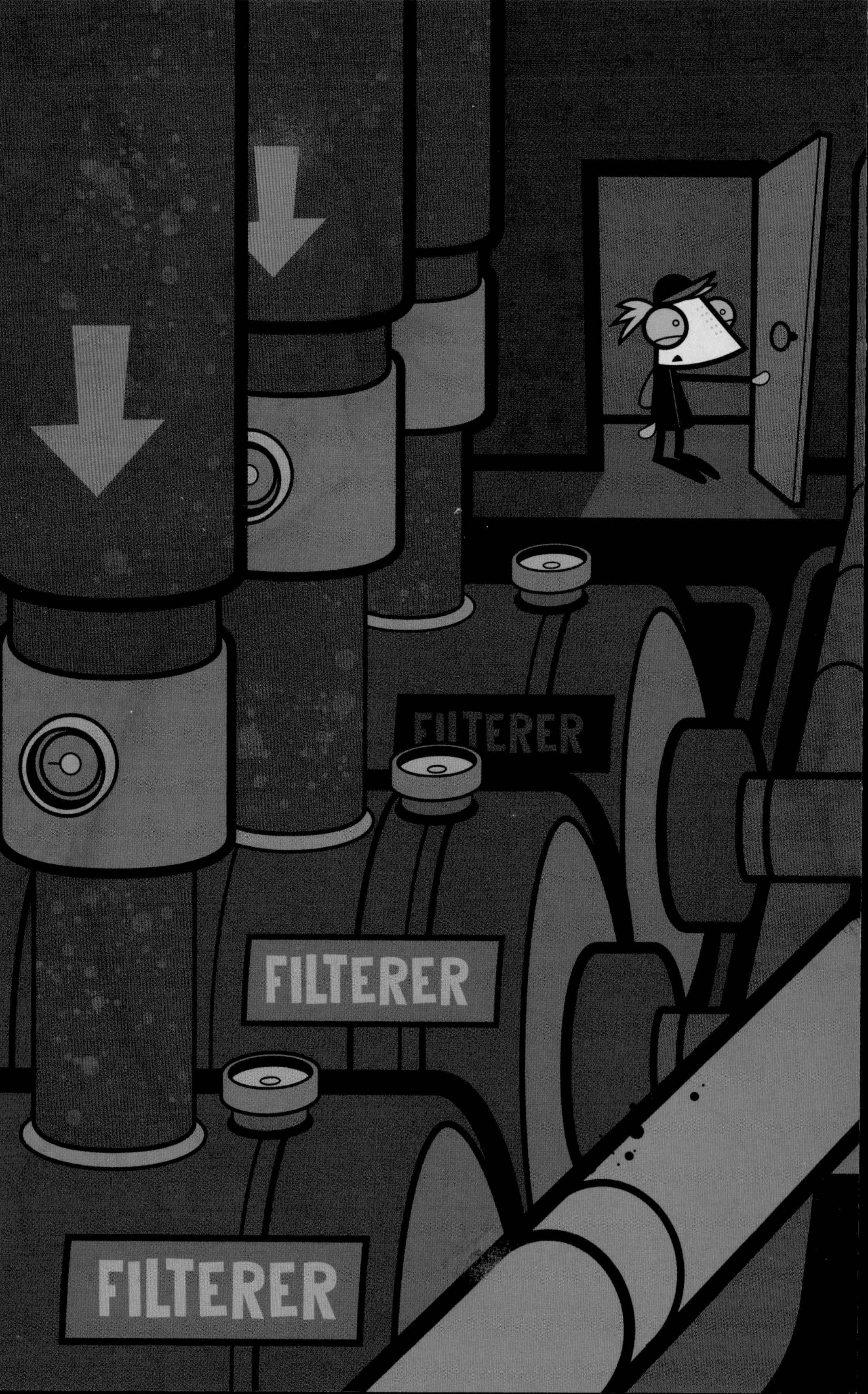
FILTERER
FILTERER

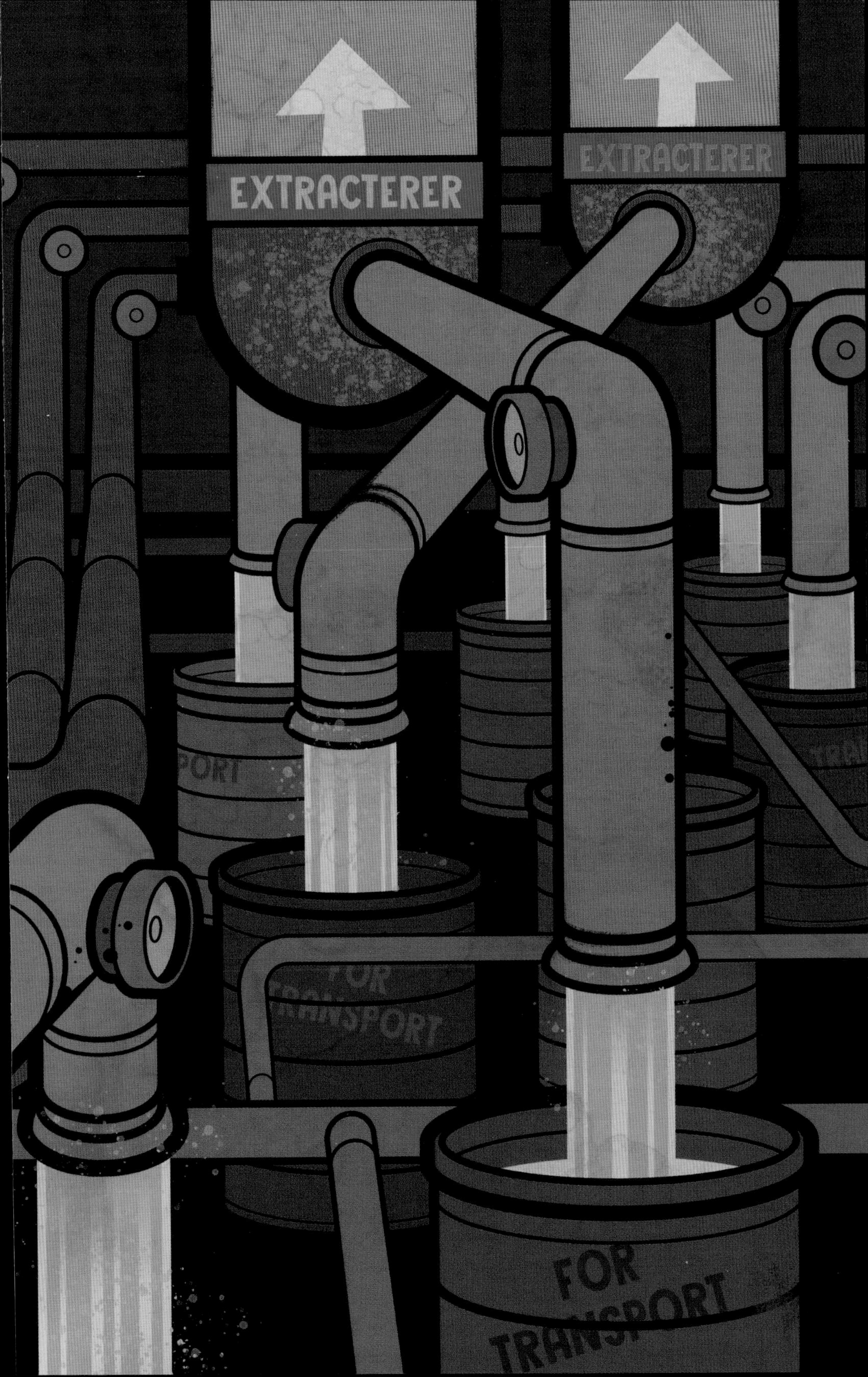
EXTRACTERER
EXTRACTERER
FOR TRANSPORT
FOR TRANSPORT

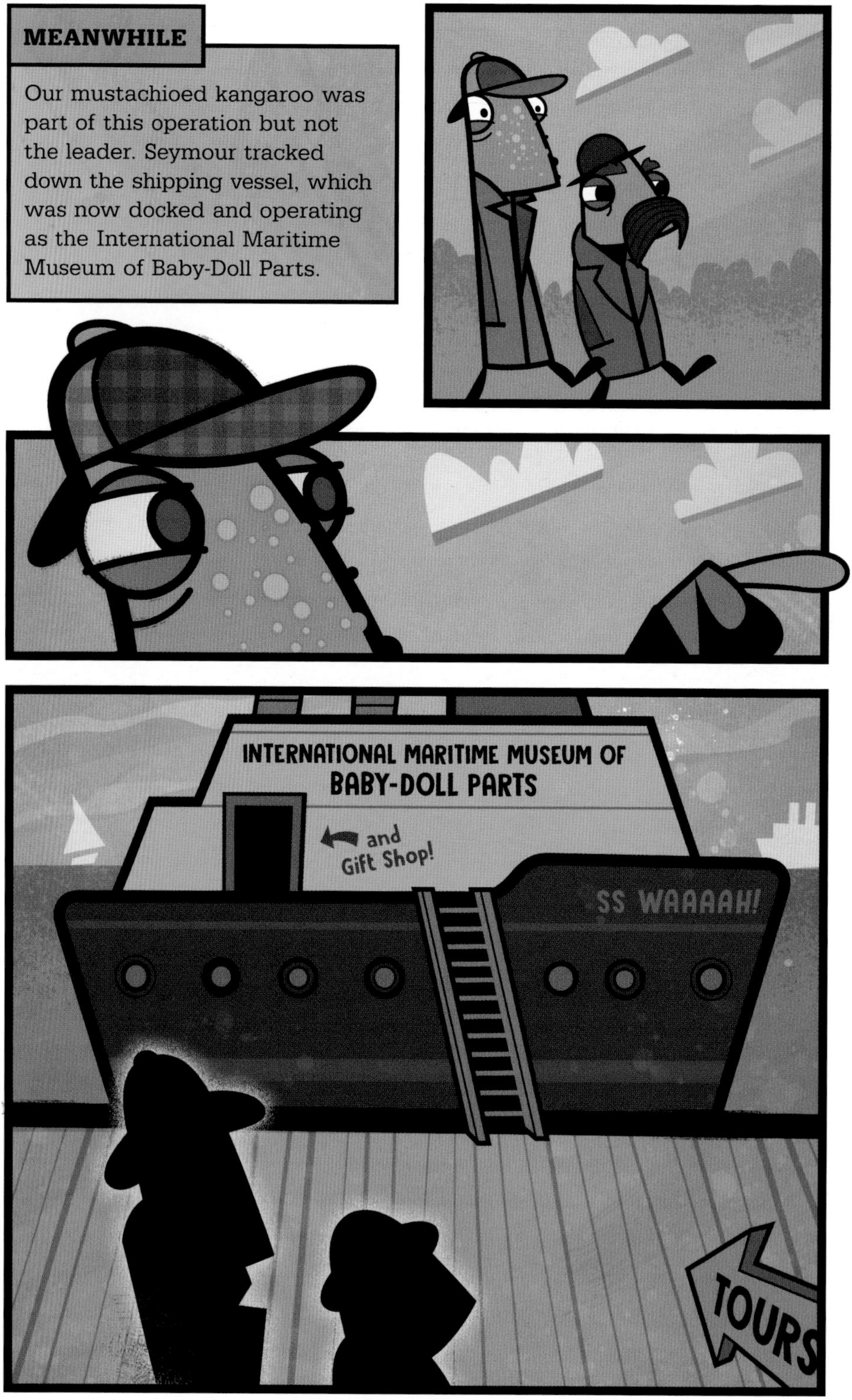
MEANWHILE
Our mustachioed kangaroo was part of this operation but not the leader. Seymour tracked down the shipping vessel, which was now docked and operating as the International Maritime Museum of Baby-Doll Parts.
INTERNATIONAL MARITIME MUSEUM OF BABY-DOLL PARTS
and Gift Shop!
SS WAAAAH!
TOURS

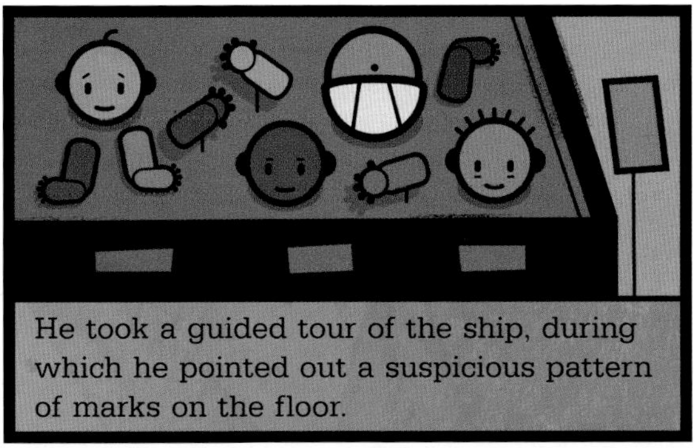
He took a guided tour of the ship, during which he pointed out a suspicious pattern of marks on the floor.

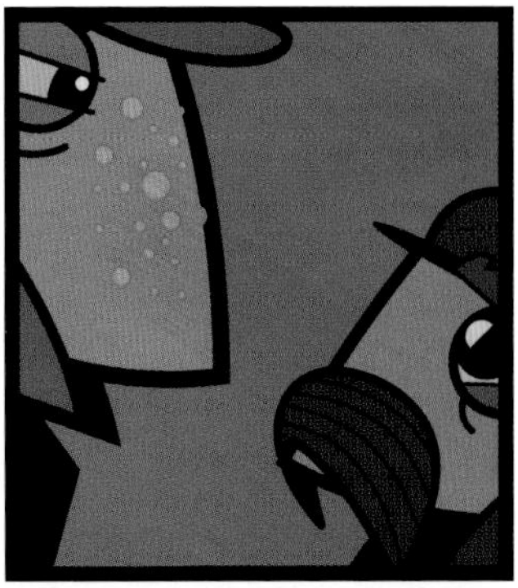

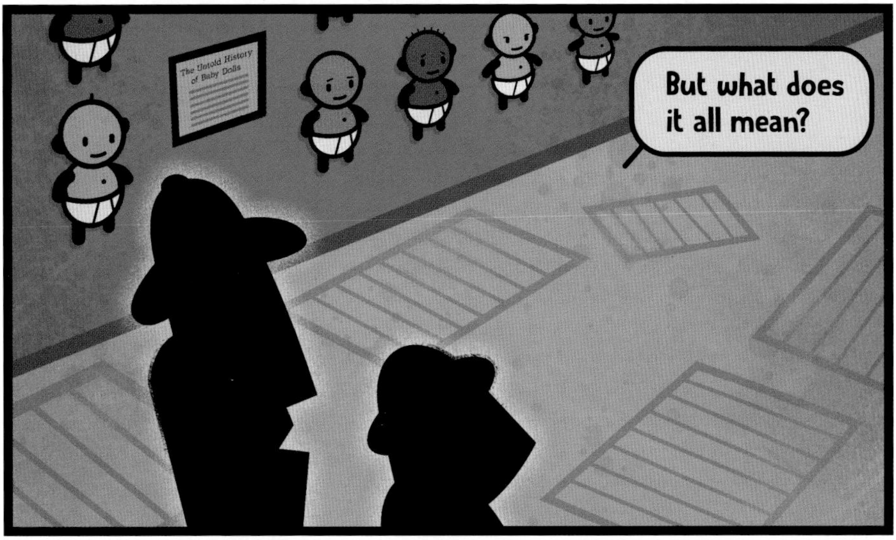
The Untold History of Baby Dolls
But what does it all mean?

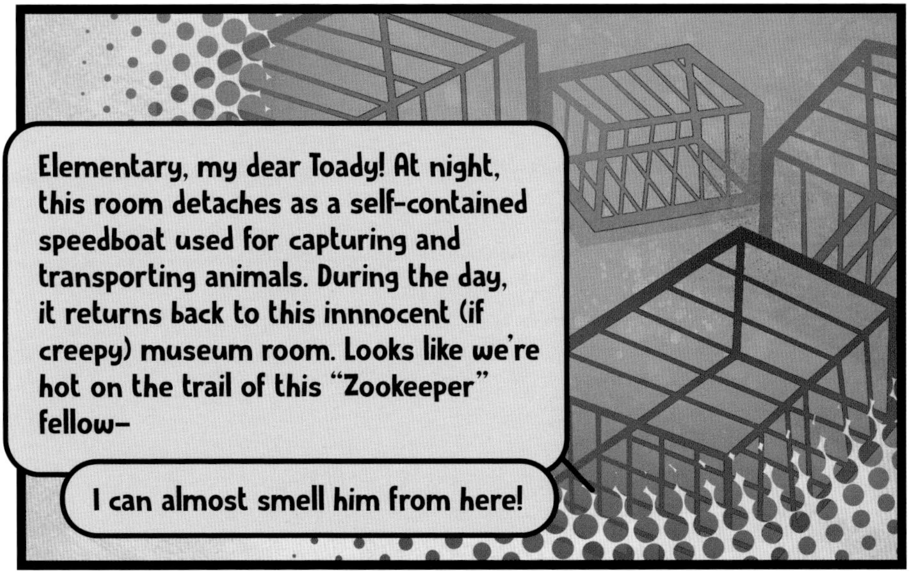
Elementary, my dear Toady! At night, this room detaches as a self-contained speedboat used for capturing and transporting animals. During the day, it returns back to this innnocent (if creepy) museum room. Looks like we're hot on the trail of this "Zookeeper" fellow–
I can almost smell him from here!

Chapter 9: What Goes Up

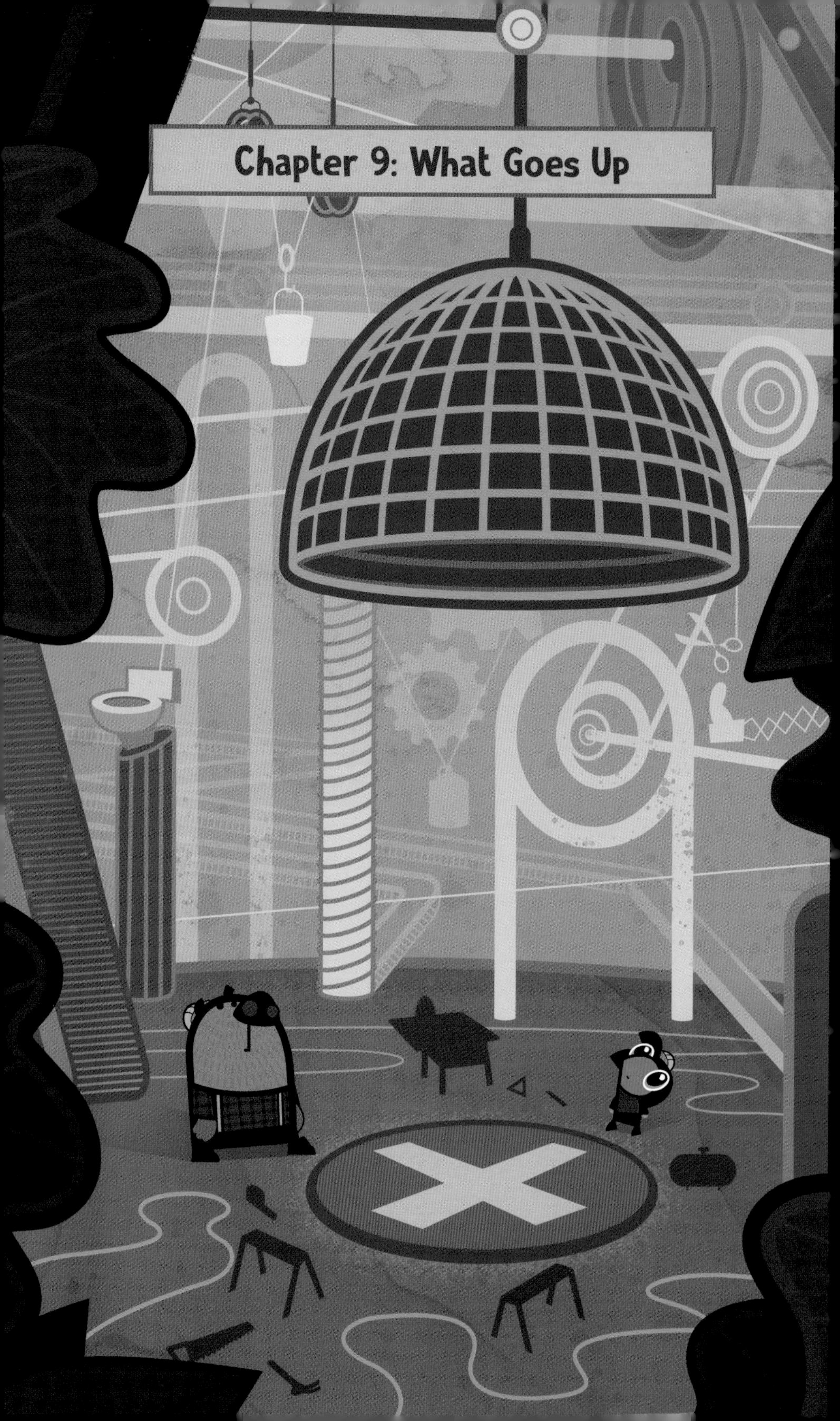

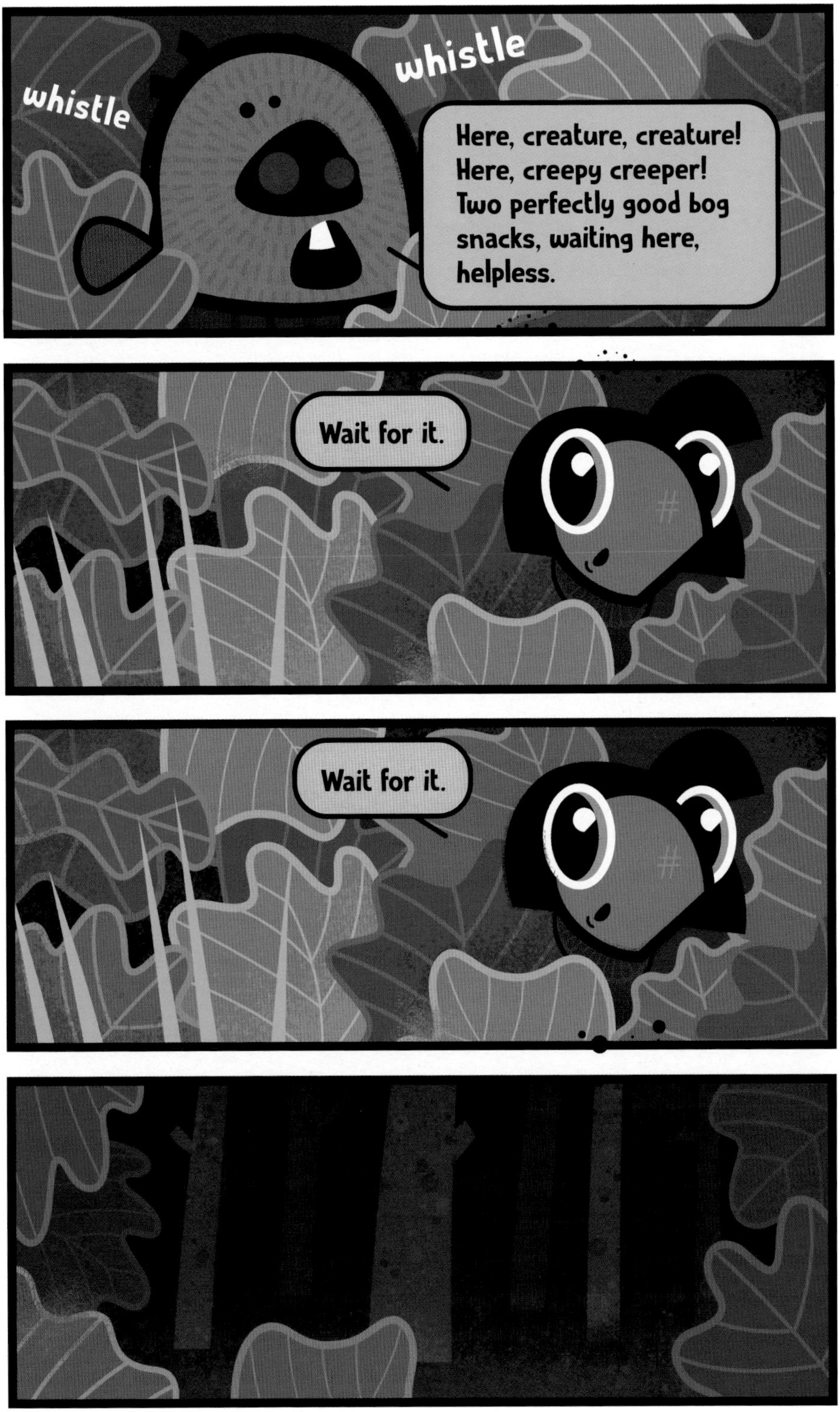
whistle
whistle
Here, creature, creature! Here, creepy creeper! Two perfectly good bog snacks, waiting here, helpless.
Wait for it.
Wait for it.

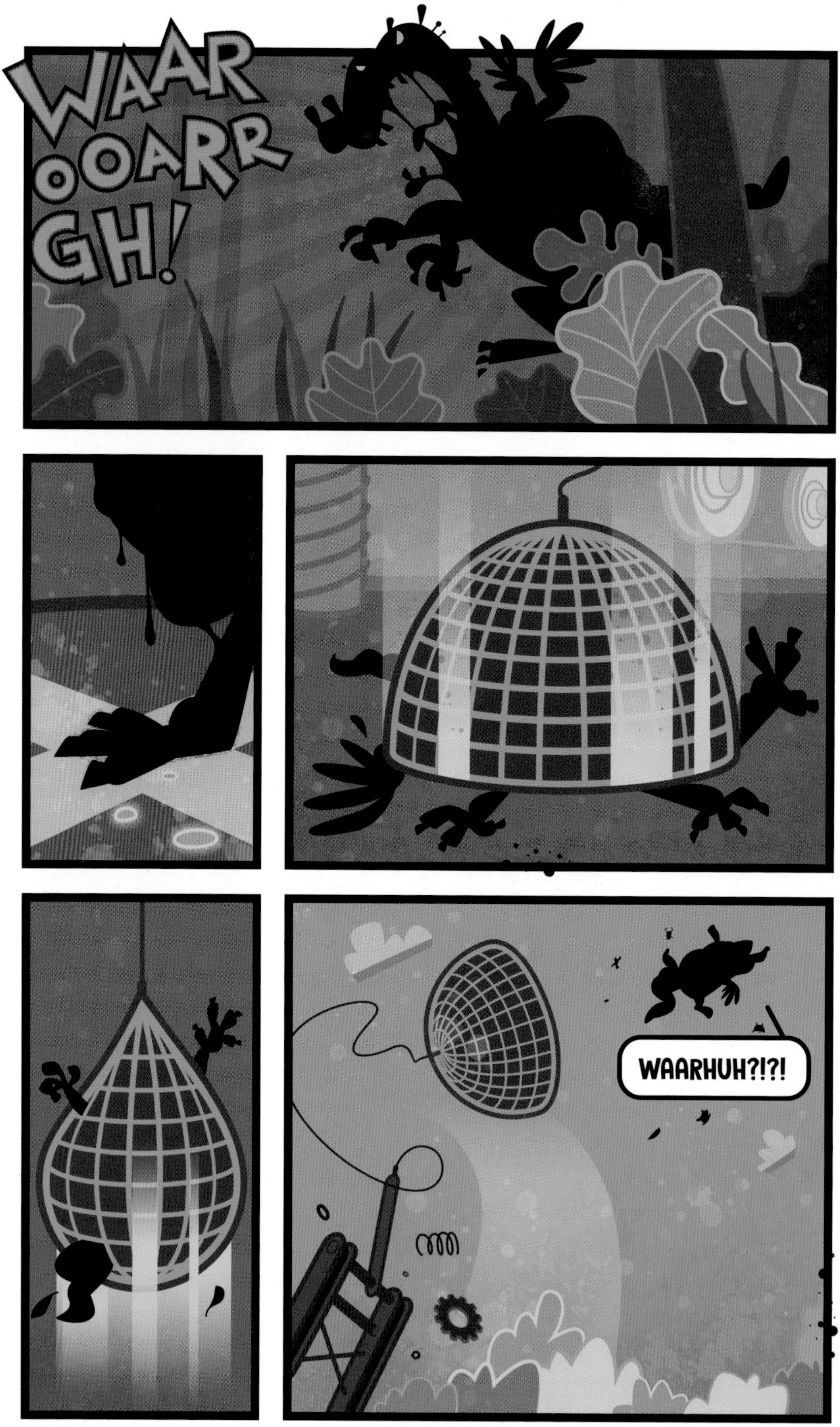
WAAR
OOARR
GH!
WAARHUH?!?!

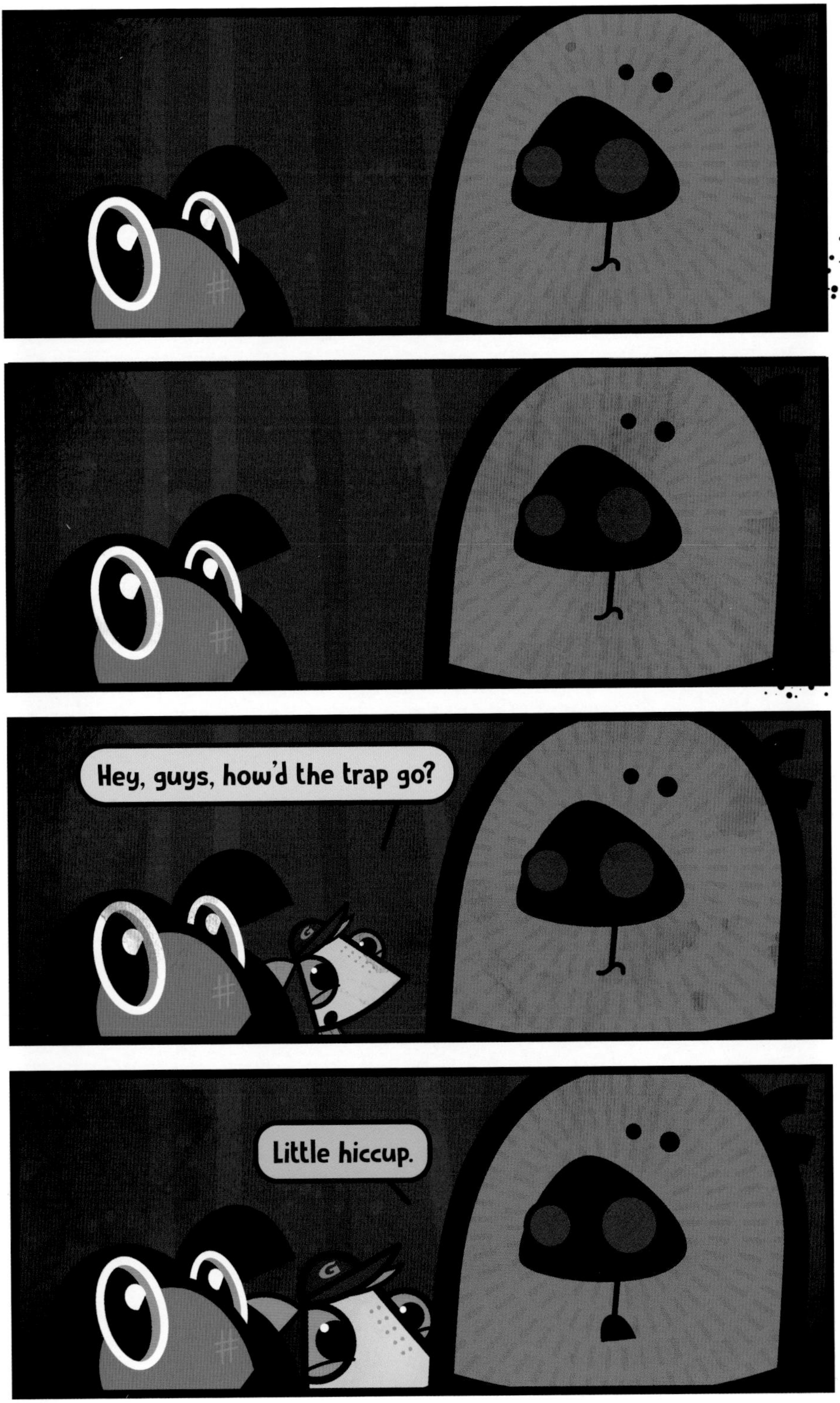
Hey, guys, how'd the trap go?
Little hiccup.

Chapter 10: A Hole in the Wall

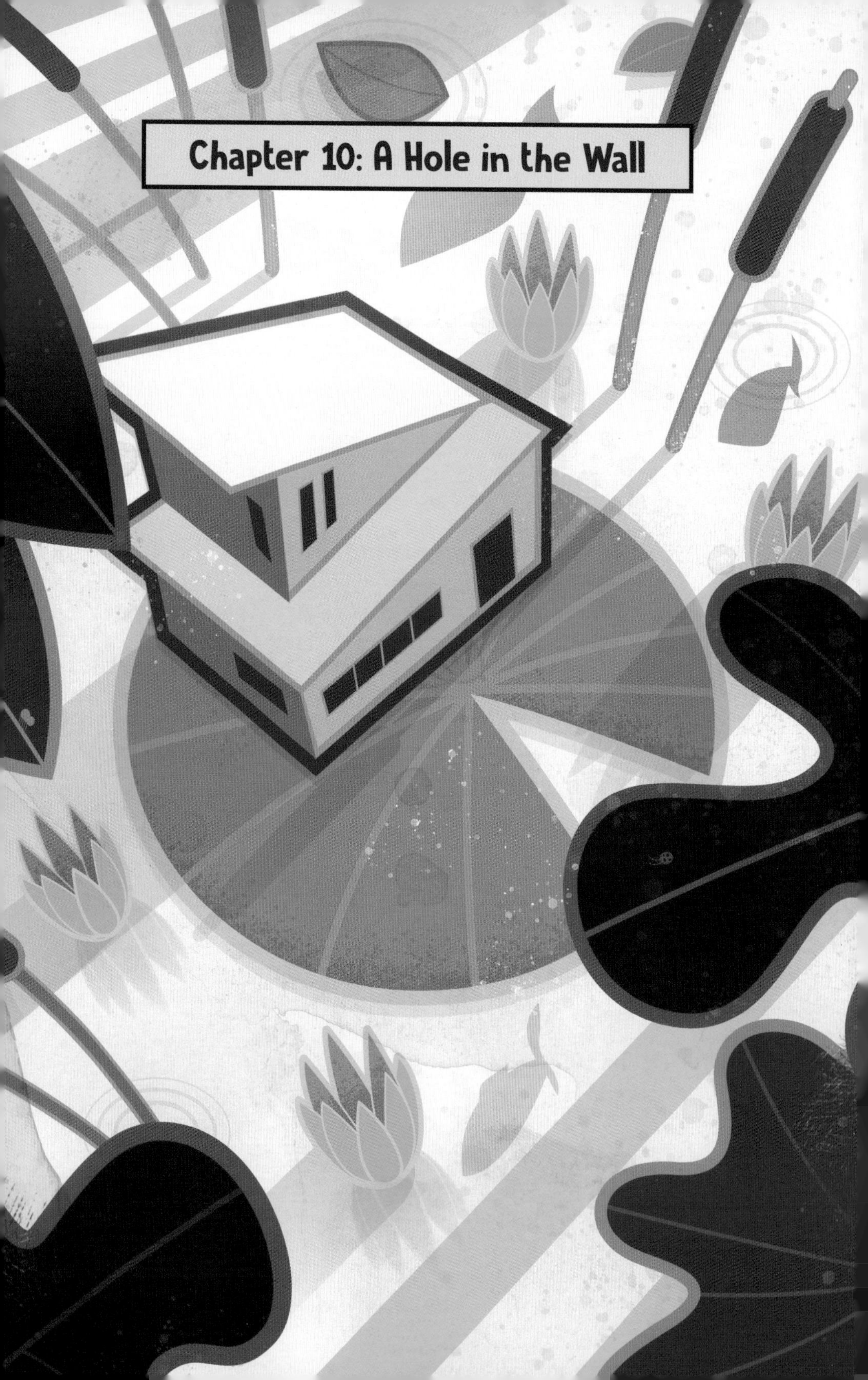

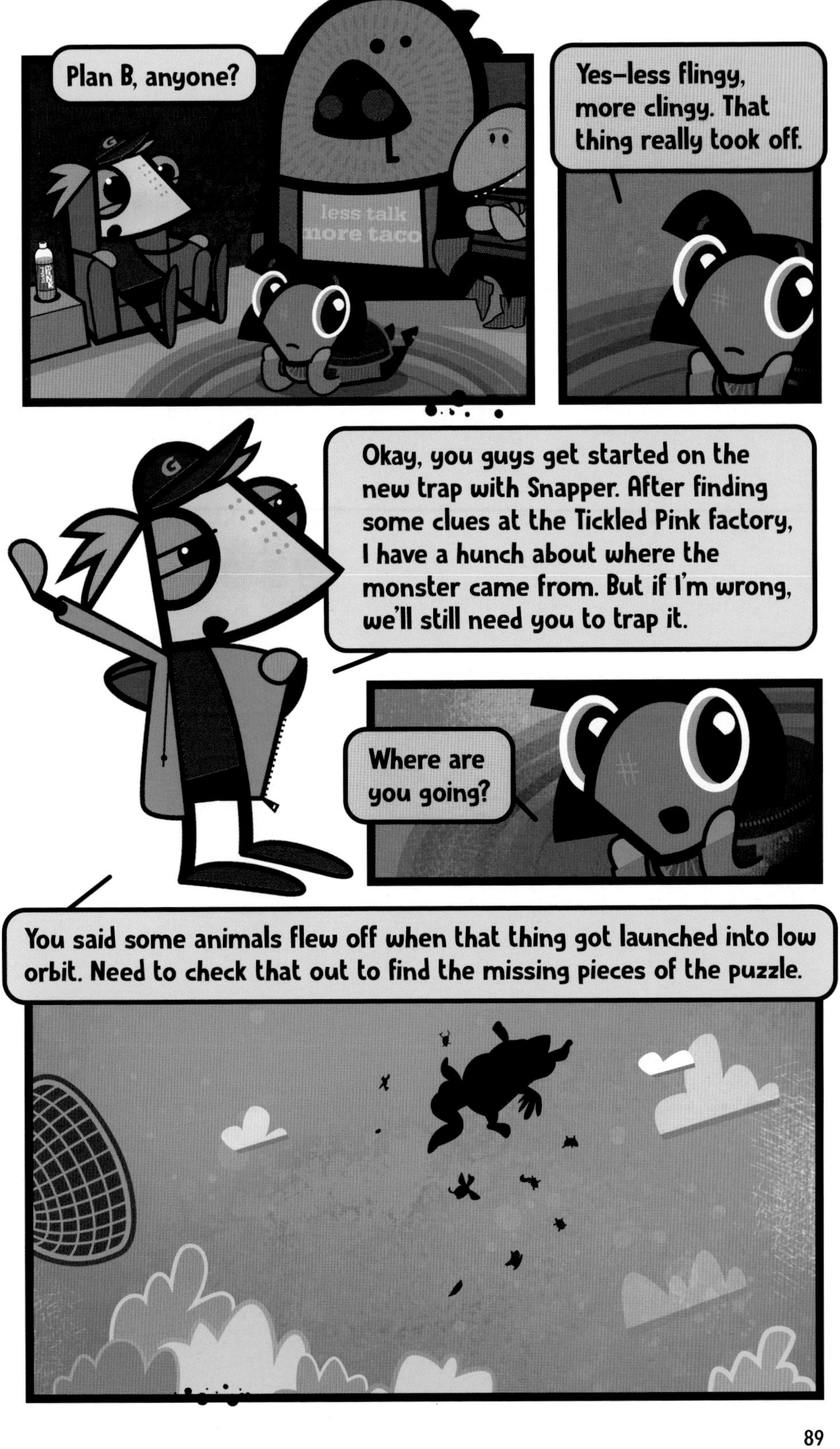
Plan B, anyone?
less talk
more taco
Yes—less flingy, more clingy. That thing really took off.
Okay, you guys get started on the new trap with Snapper. After finding some clues at the Tickled Pink factory, I have a hunch about where the monster came from. But if I'm wrong, we'll still need you to trap it.
Where are you going?
You said some animals flew off when that thing got launched into low orbit. Need to check that out to find the missing pieces of the puzzle.

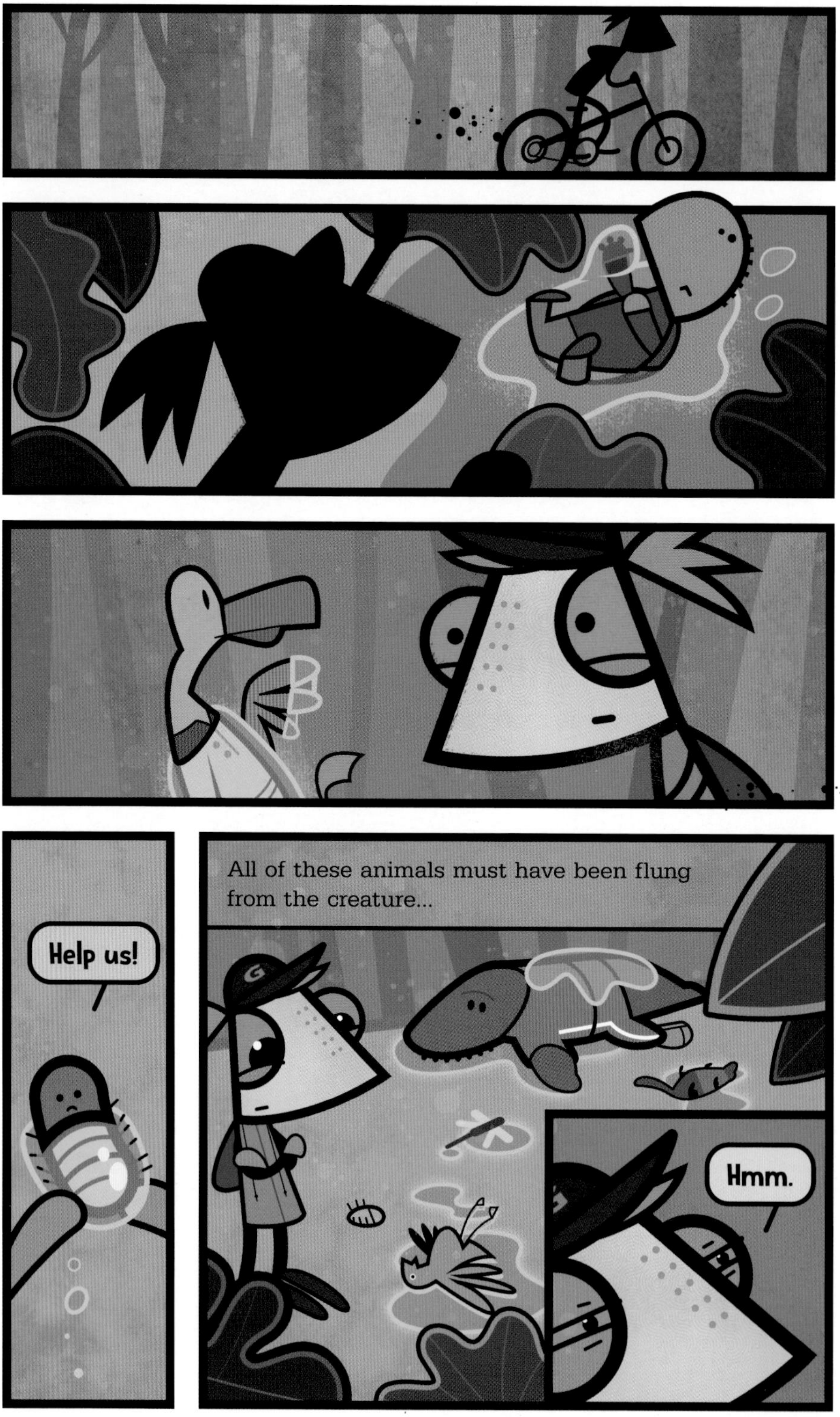
Help us!
All of these animals must have been flung from the creature...
Hmm.

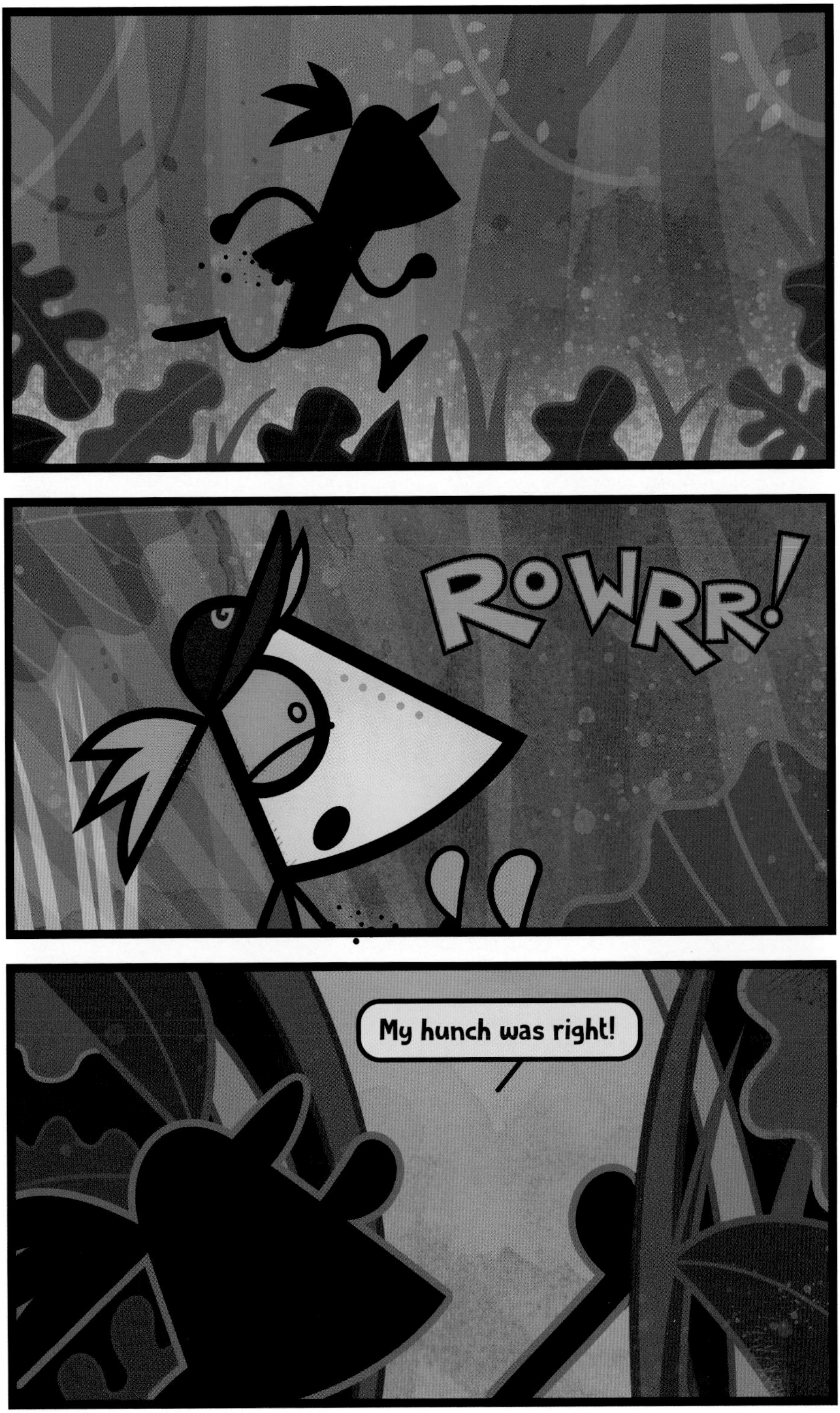
ROWRR!
My hunch was right!

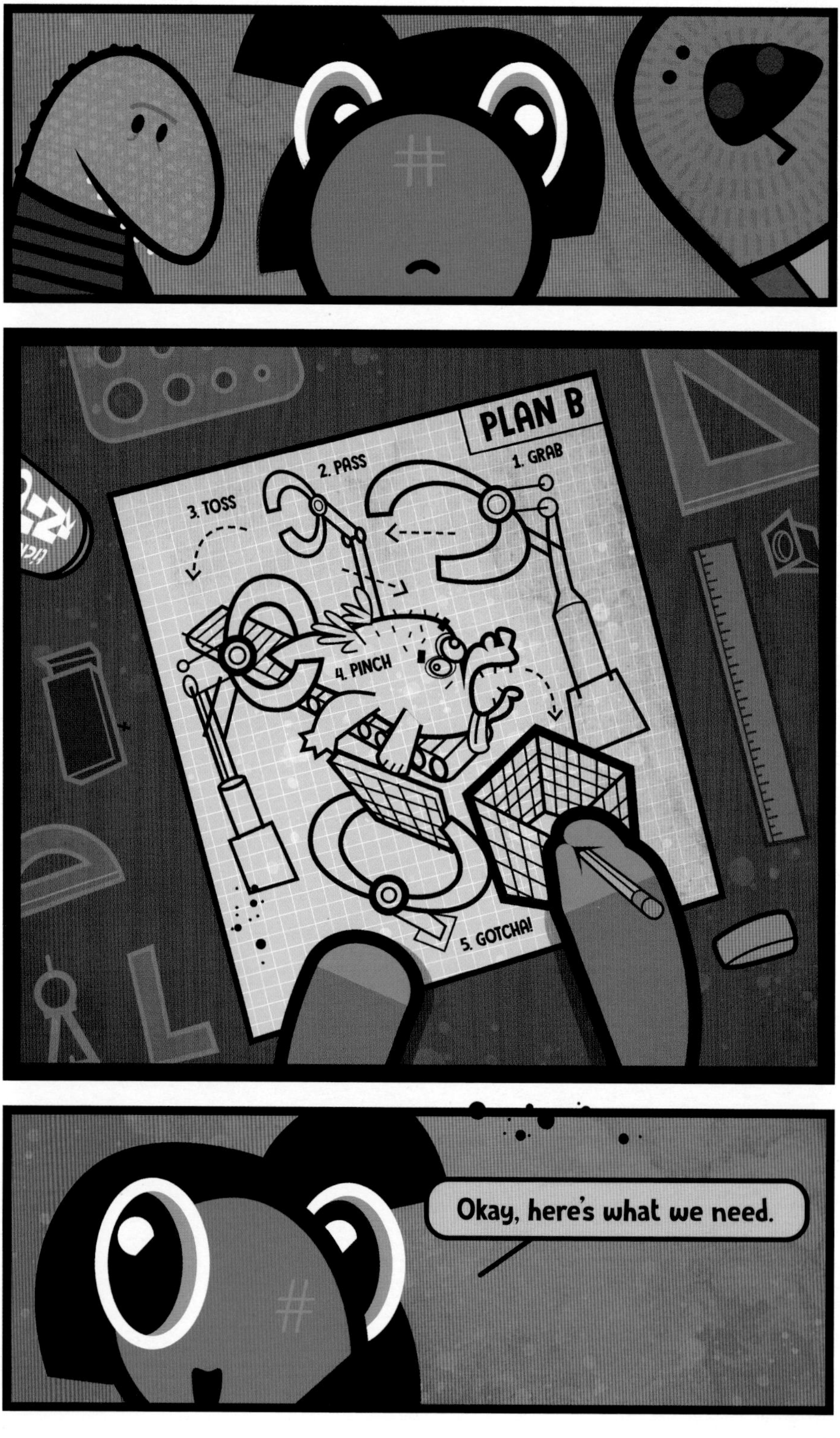
PLAN B
1. GRAB
2. PASS
3. TOSS
4. PINCH
5. GOTCHA!
Okay, here's what we need.

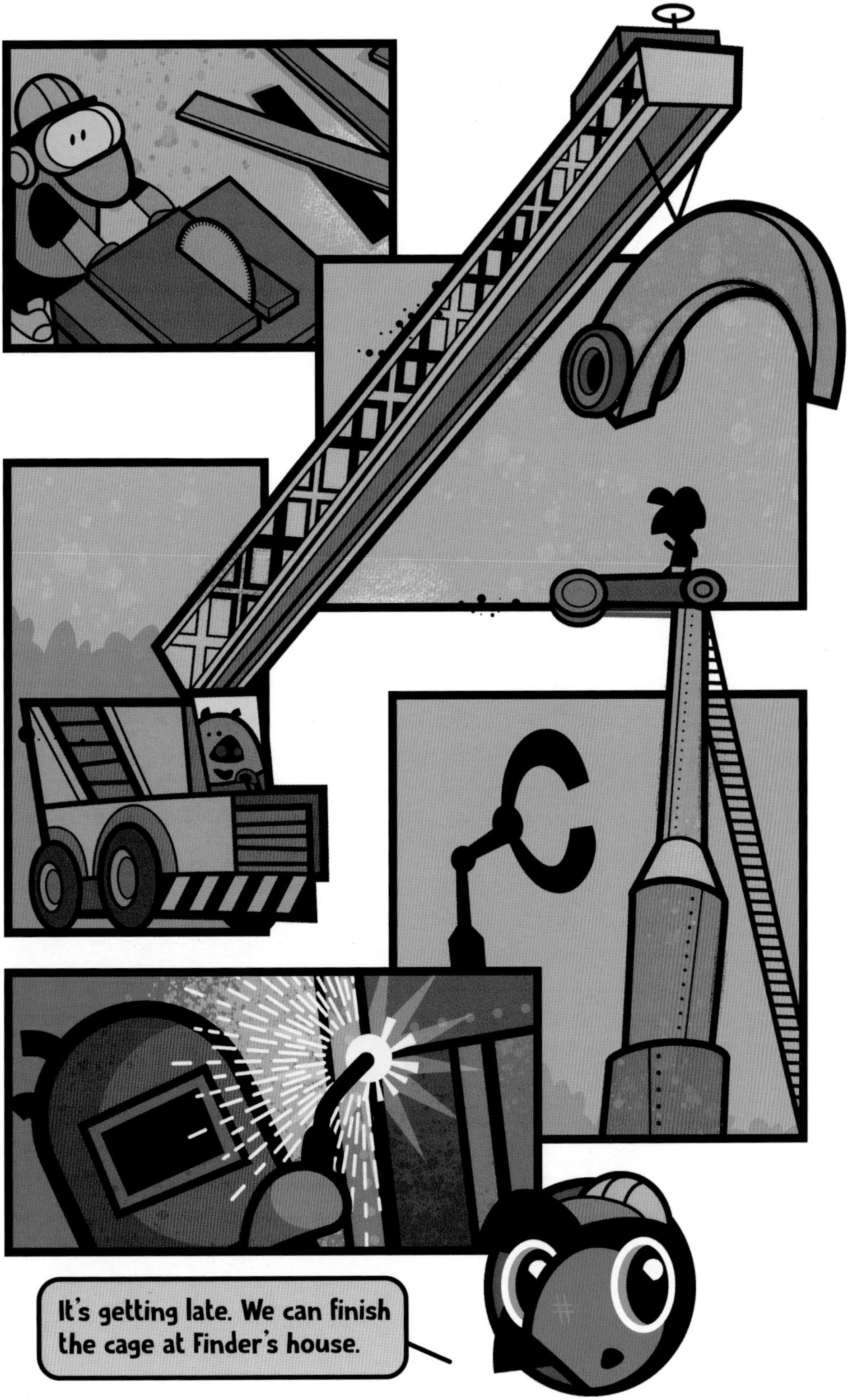
C
It's getting late. We can finish the cage at Finder's house.

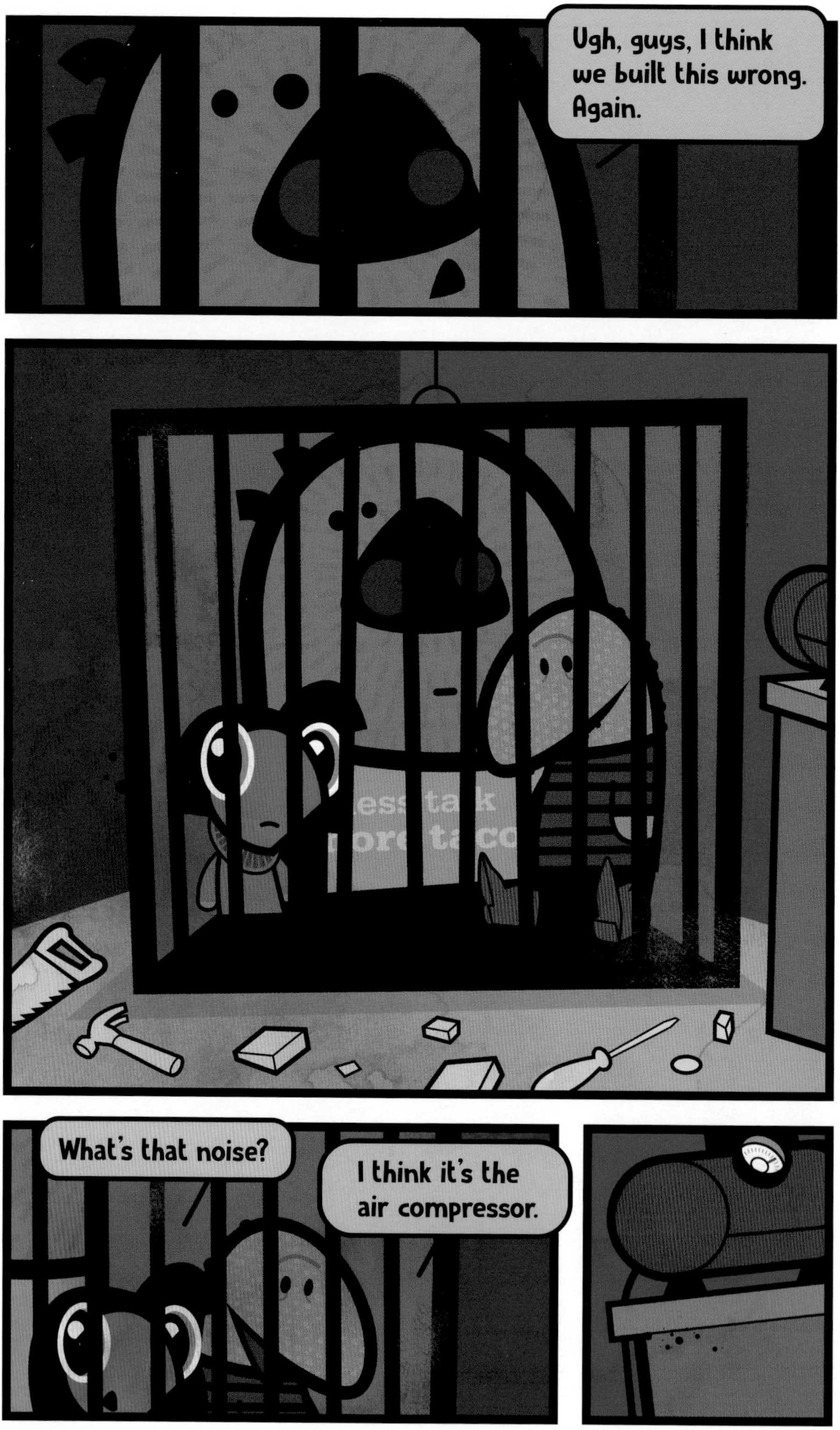
Ugh, guys, I think we built this wrong. Again.
What's that noise?
I think it's the air compressor.

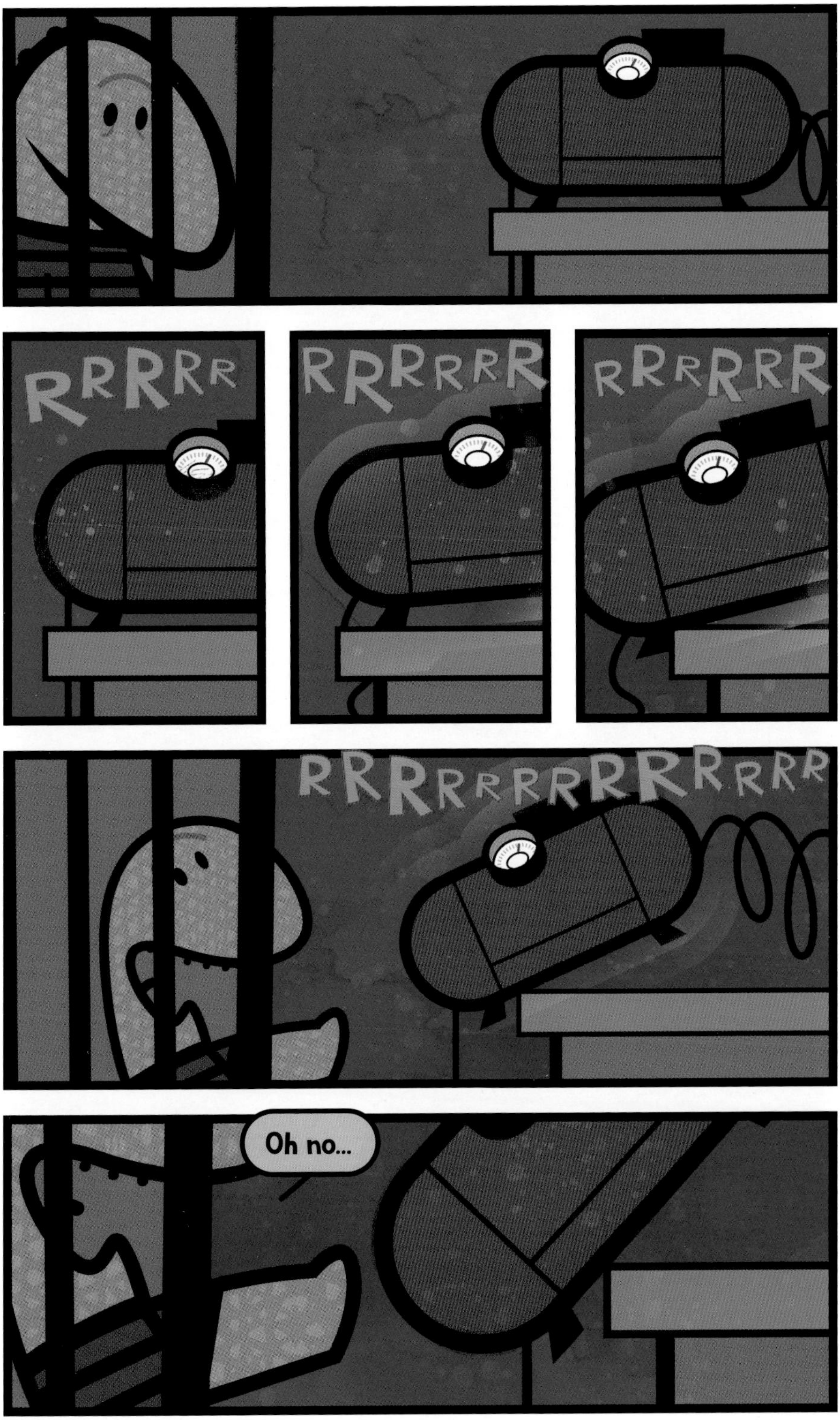
RRRRR
RRRRRR
RRRRRRR
RRRRRRRRRRRRRR
Oh no...

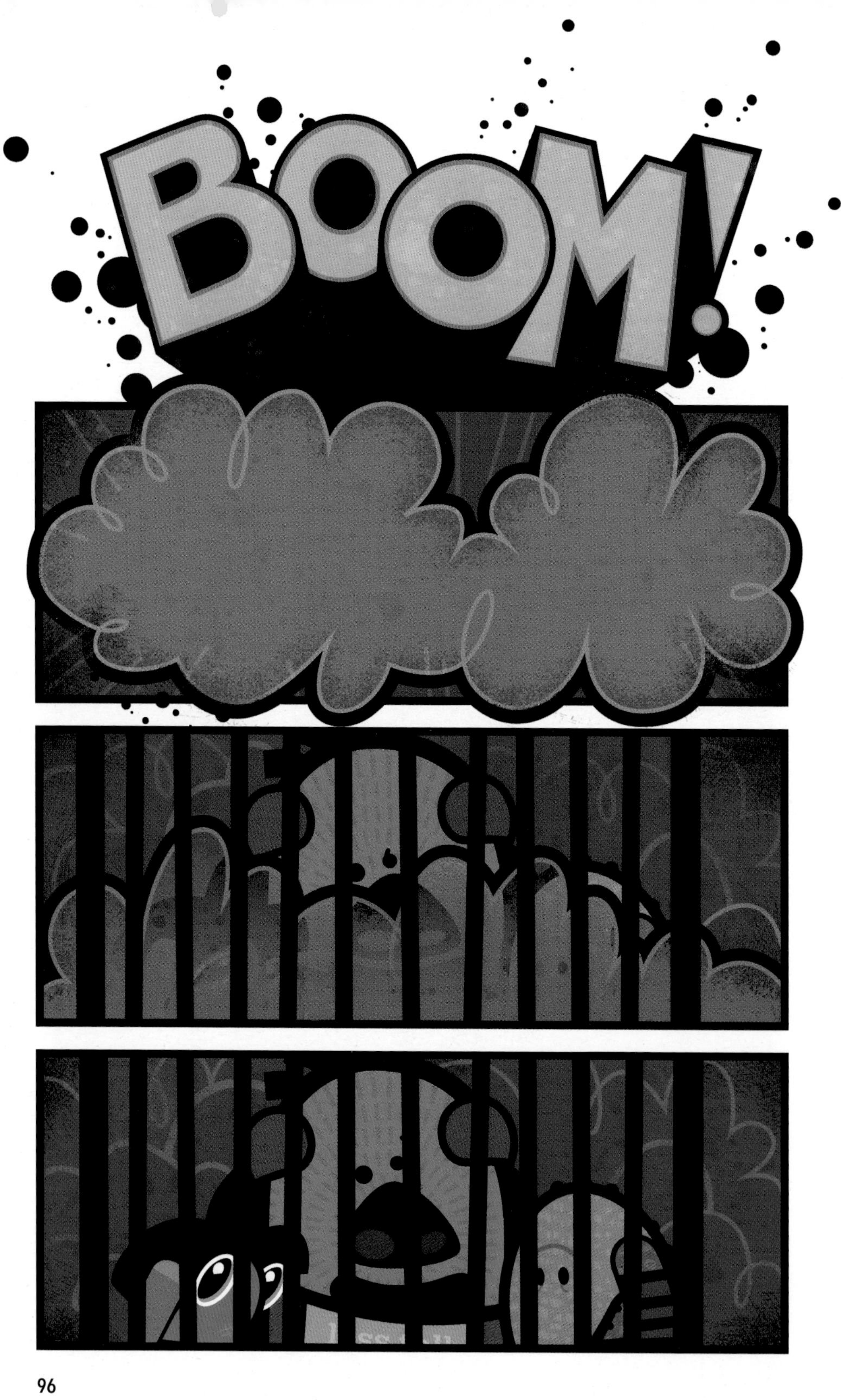
BOOM!

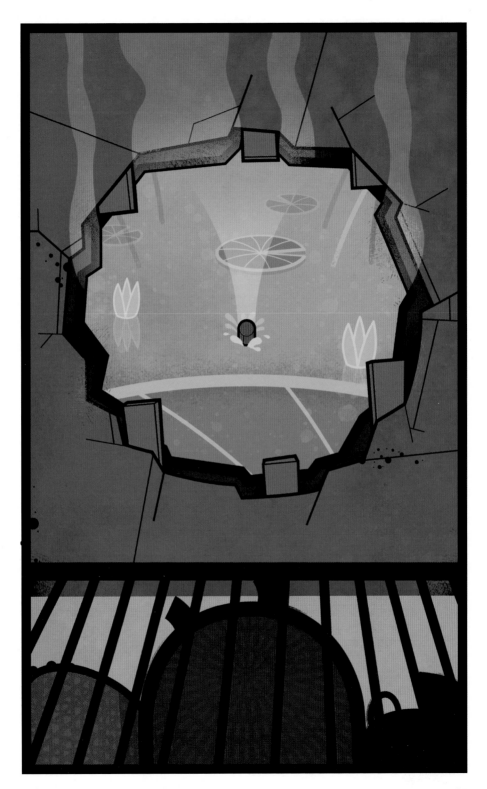

MEANWHILE

From the positioning of this particular porthole in the hull, whoever is in the control room has a perfect view of the lighthouse across the harbor.

Maybe it will shed some light on our current situation.

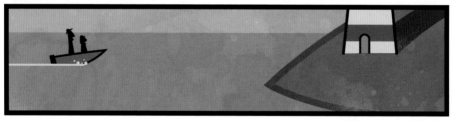

Good sir, please do me the courtesy of allowing me to ask but one question.

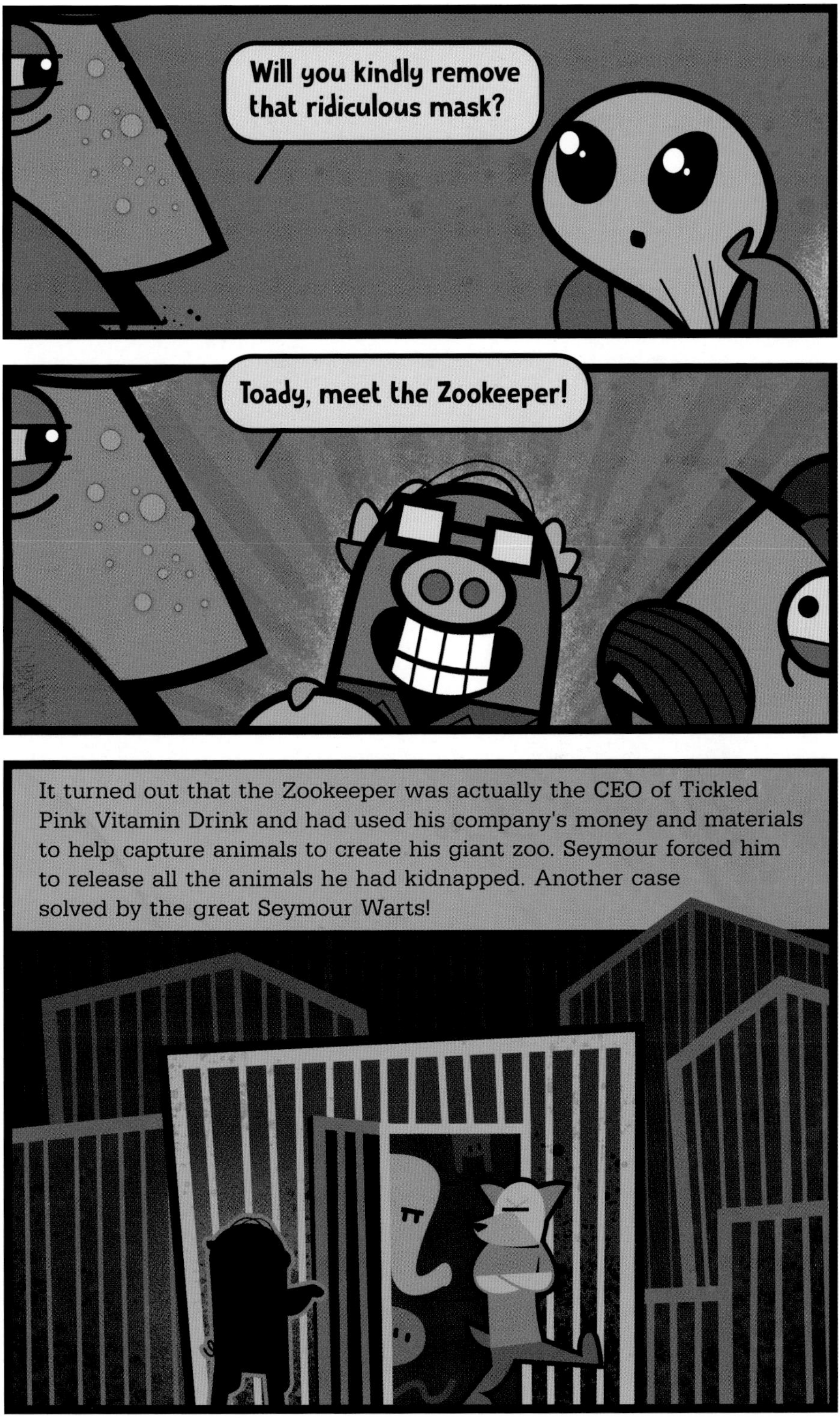
Will you kindly remove that ridiculous mask?
Toady, meet the Zookeeper!
It turned out that the Zookeeper was actually the CEO of Tickled Pink Vitamin Drink and had used his company's money and materials to help capture animals to create his giant zoo. Seymour forced him to release all the animals he had kidnapped. Another case solved by the great Seymour Warts!

Chapter 11: The End. (Almost.)

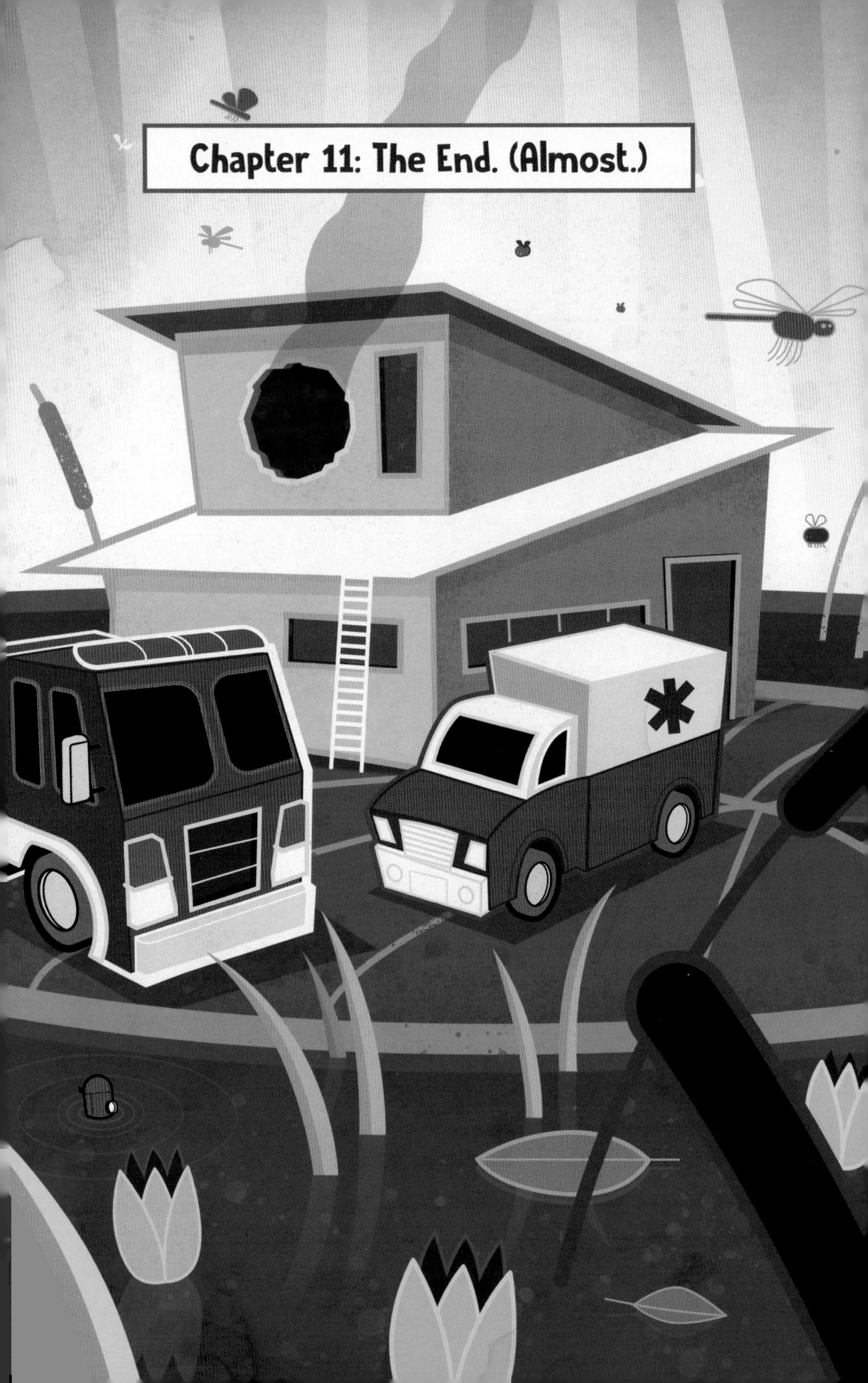

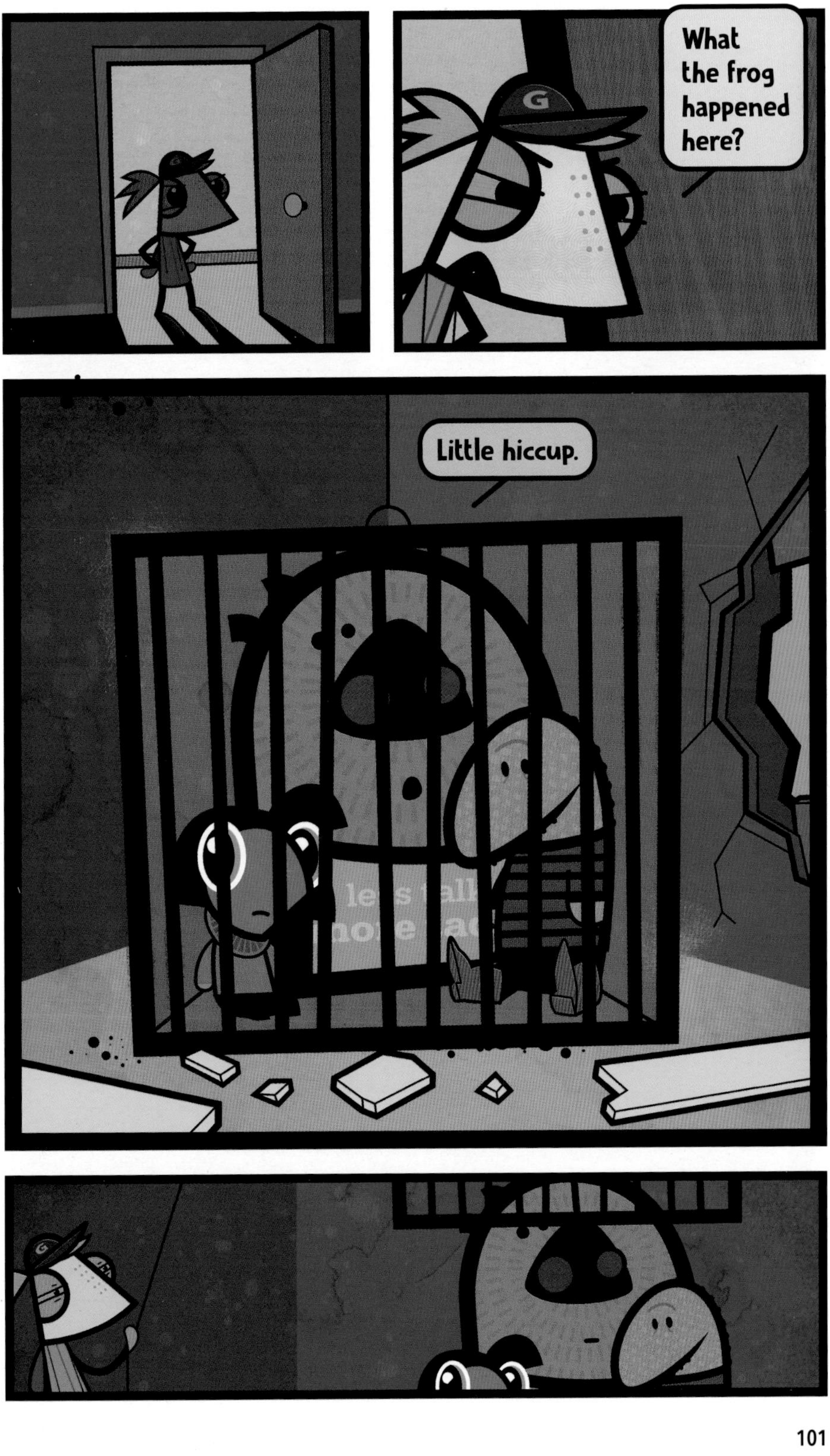
What the frog happened here?
Little hiccup.

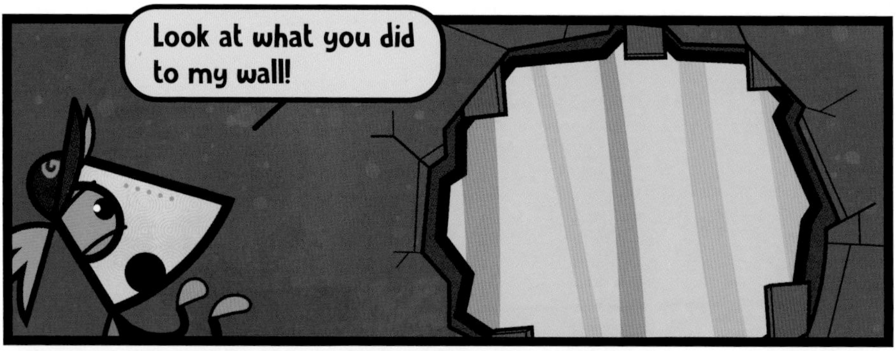
Look at what you did
to my wall!

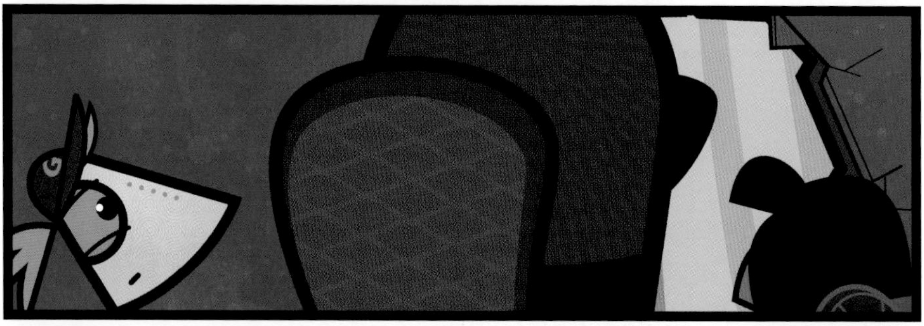

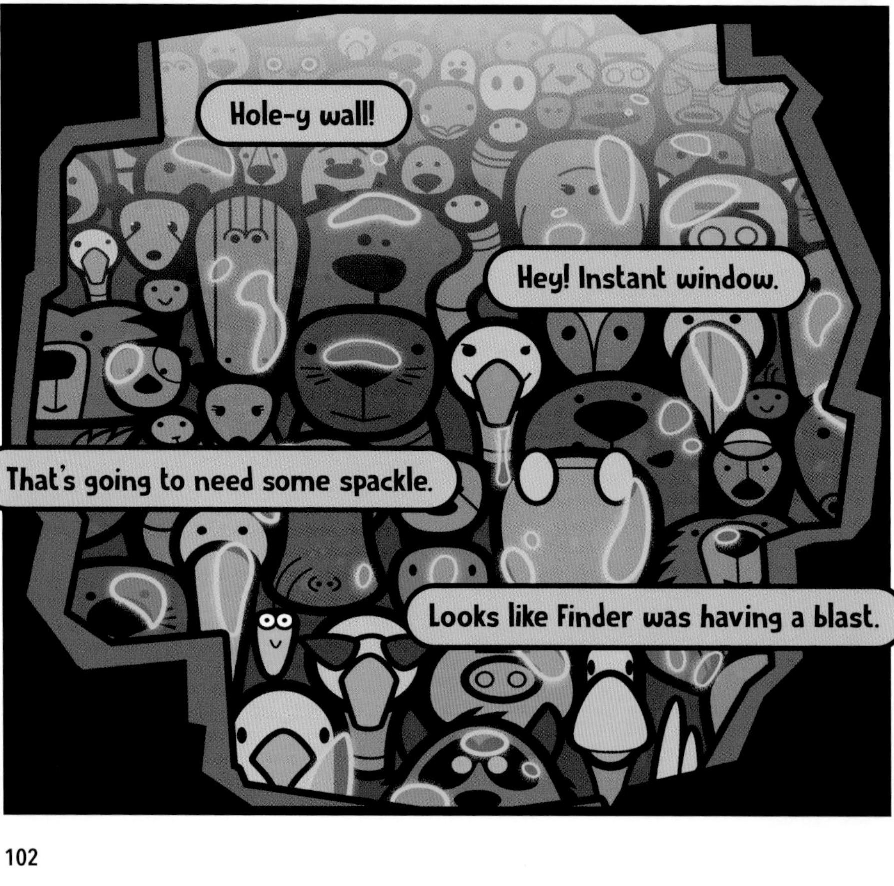
Hole-y wall!
Hey! Instant window.
That's going to need some spackle.
Looks like Finder was having a blast.

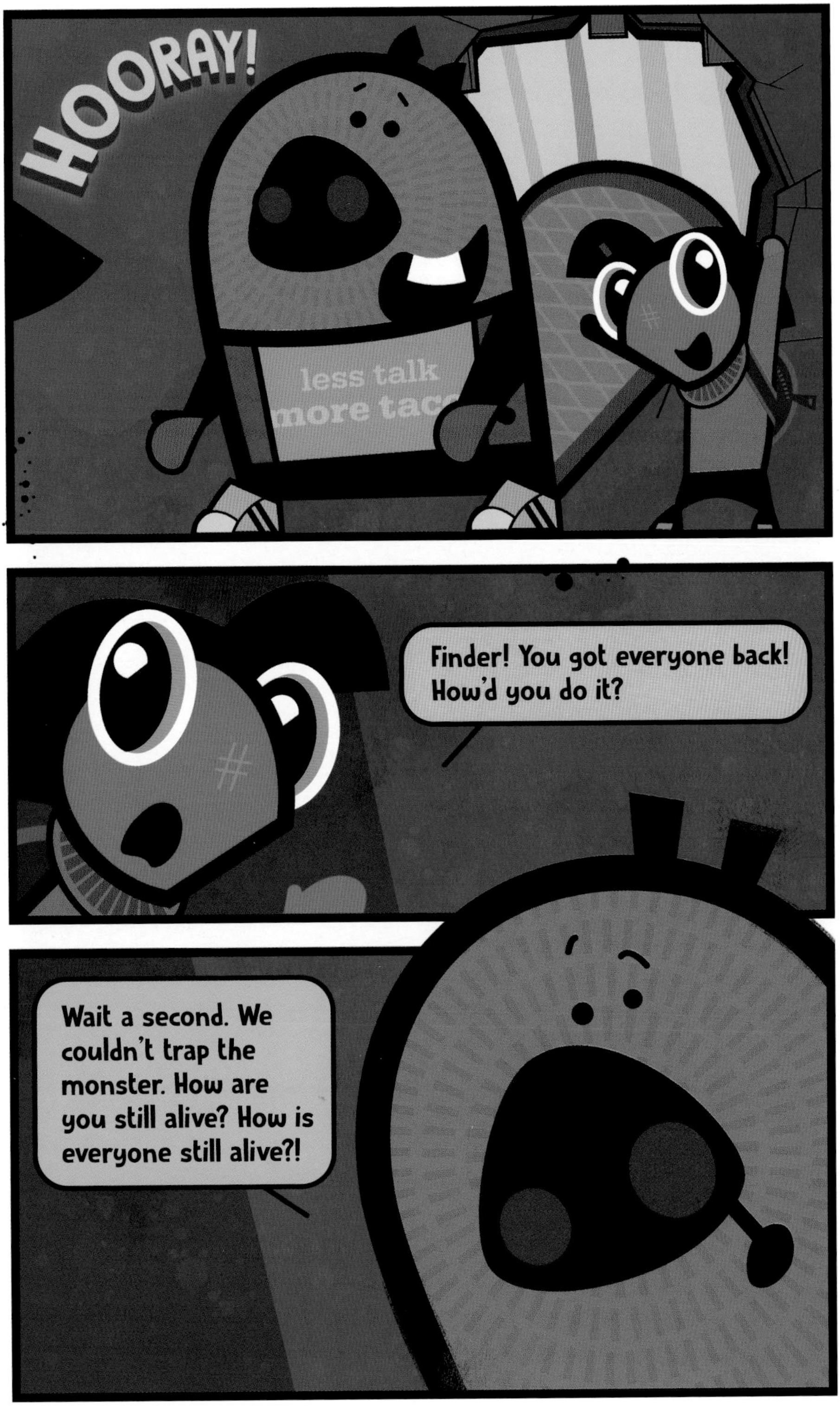
HOORAY!
less talk more tac
Finder! You got everyone back! How'd you do it?
Wait a second. We couldn't trap the monster. How are you still alive? How is everyone still alive?!

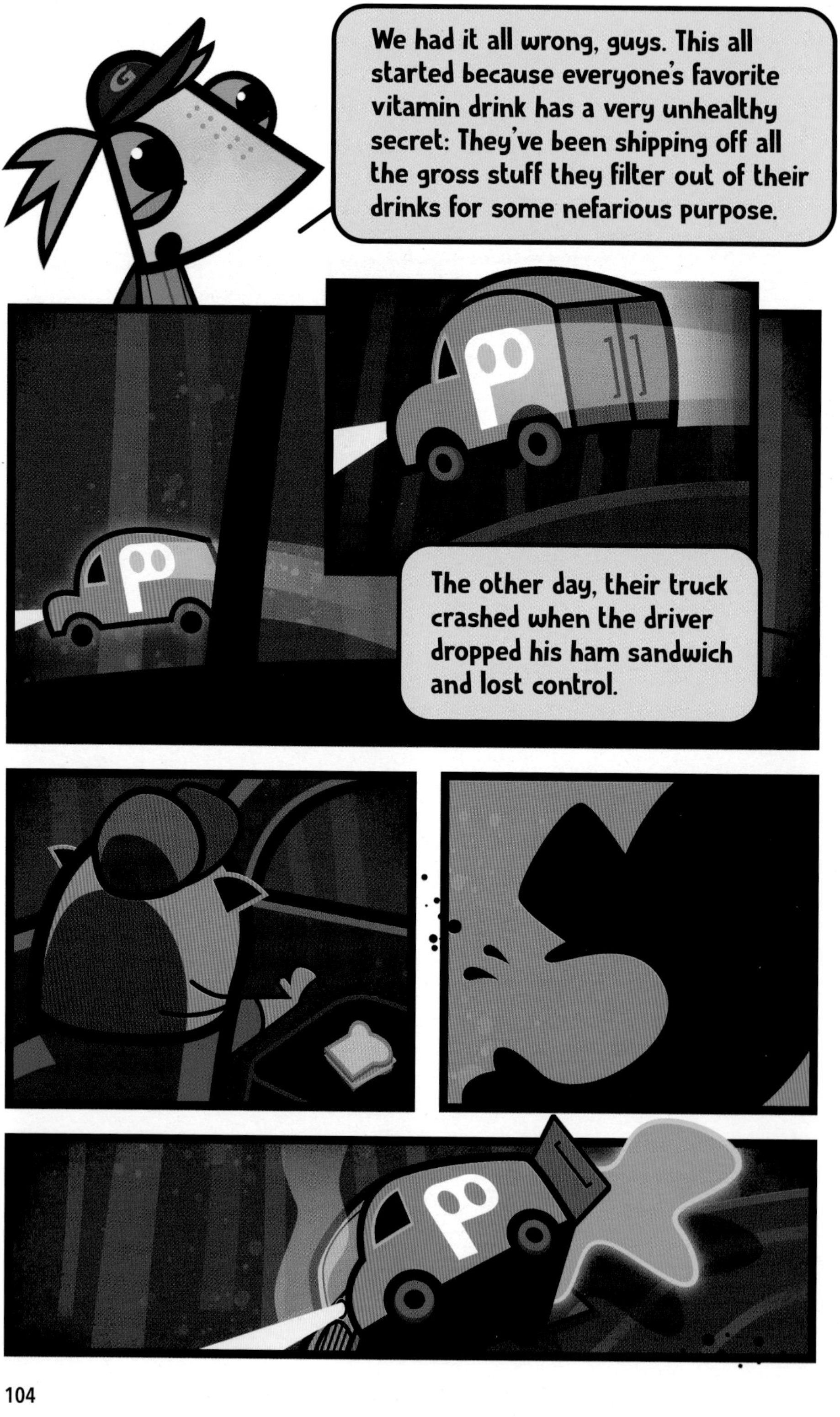
We had it all wrong, guys. This all started because everyone's favorite vitamin drink has a very unhealthy secret: They've been shipping off all the gross stuff they filter out of their drinks for some nefarious purpose.
The other day, their truck crashed when the driver dropped his ham sandwich and lost control.

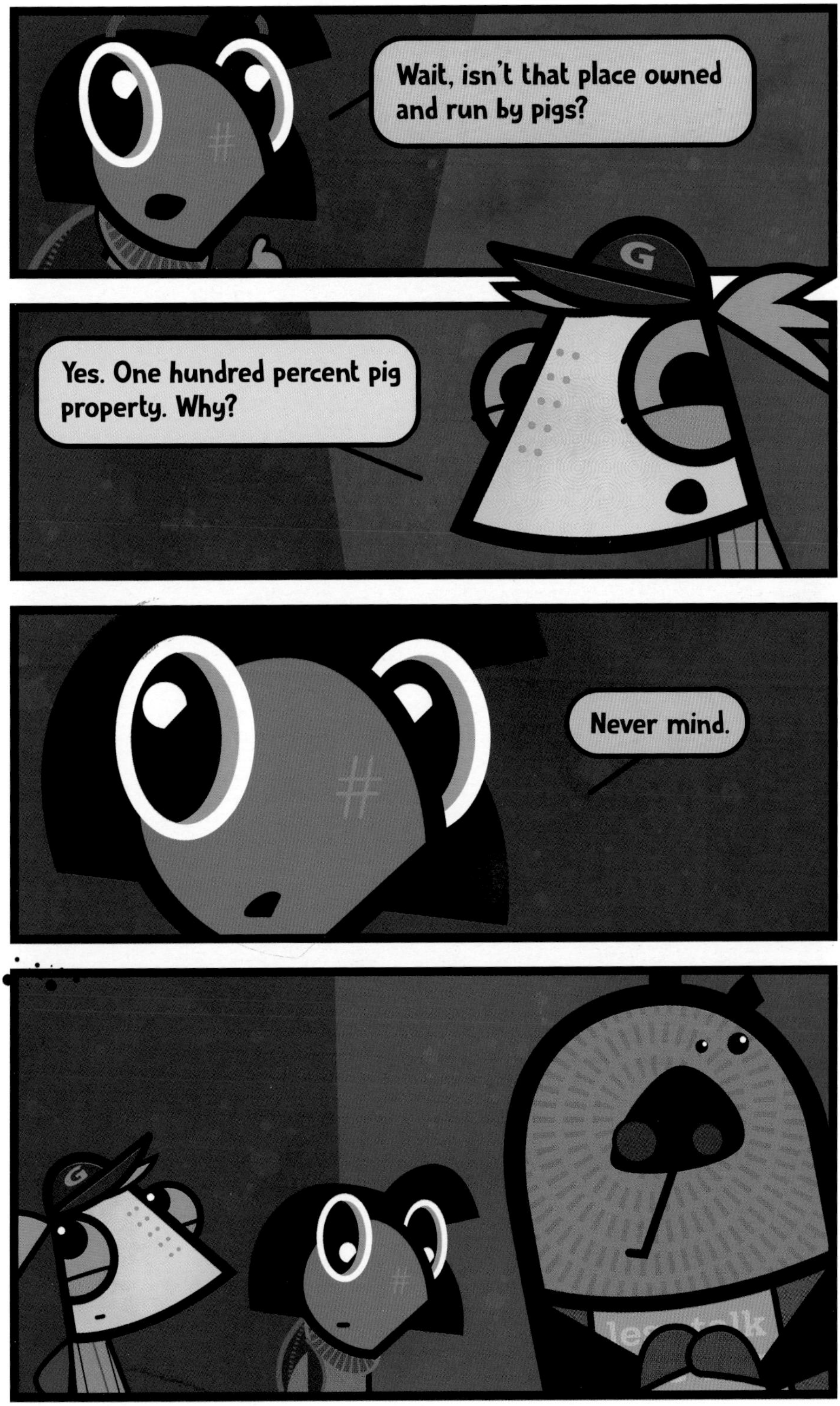
Wait, isn't that place owned and run by pigs?
Yes. One hundred percent pig property. Why?
Never mind.

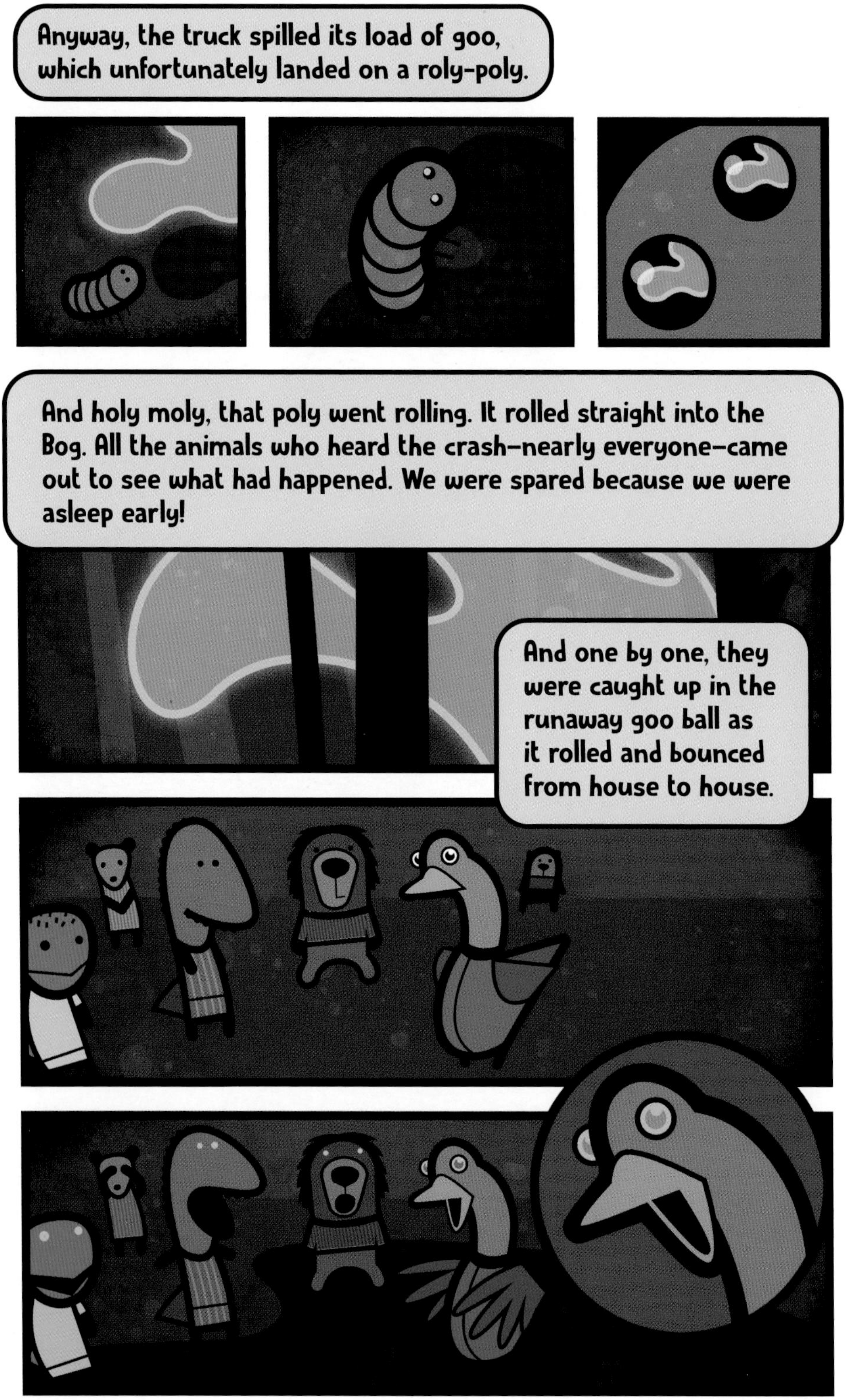
Anyway, the truck spilled its load of goo, which unfortunately landed on a roly-poly.
And holy moly, that poly went rolling. It rolled straight into the Bog. All the animals who heard the crash–nearly everyone–came out to see what had happened. We were spared because we were asleep early!
And one by one, they were caught up in the runaway goo ball as it rolled and bounced from house to house.

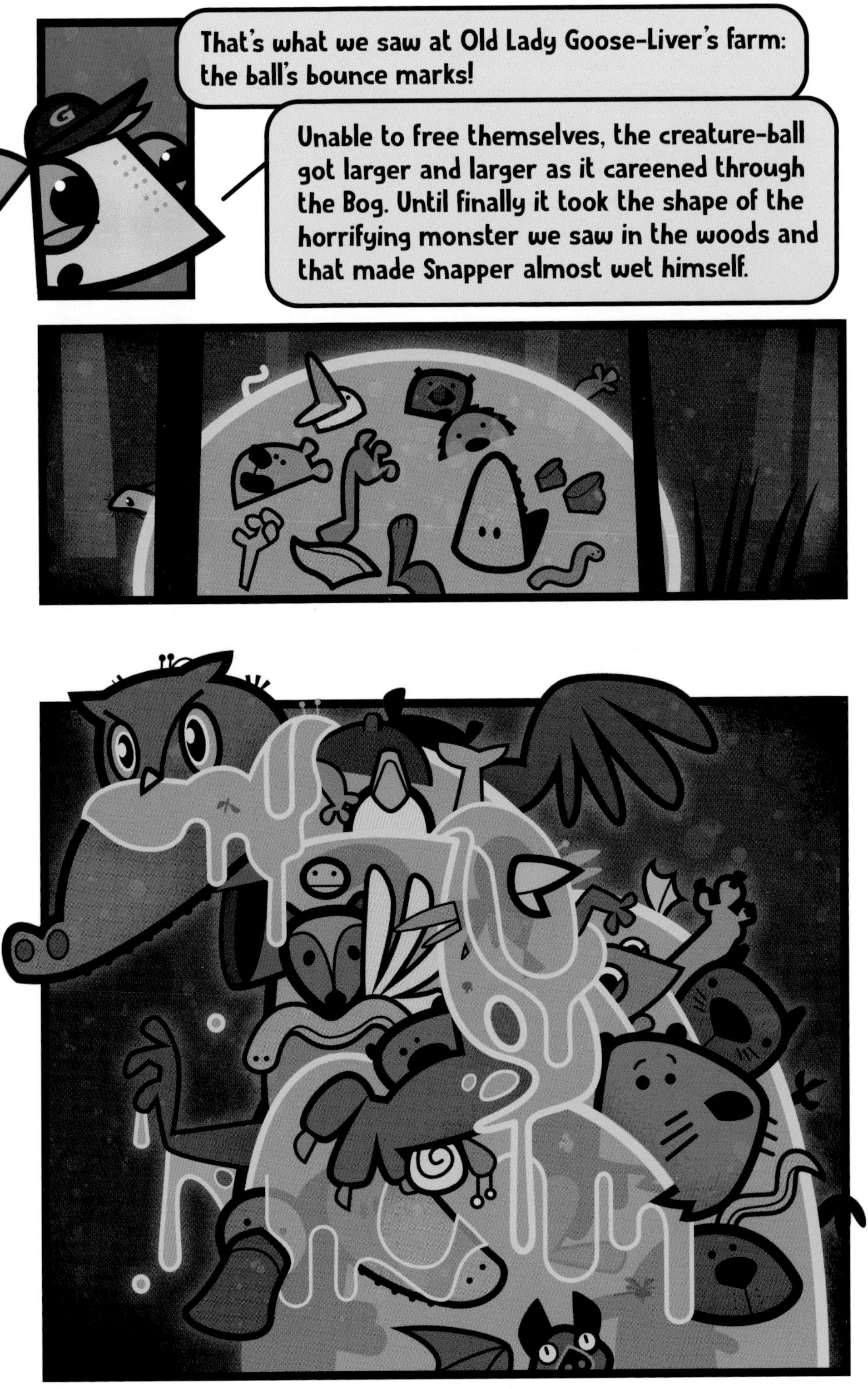
That's what we saw at Old Lady Goose-Liver's farm: the ball's bounce marks!
Unable to free themselves, the creature-ball got larger and larger as it careened through the Bog. Until finally it took the shape of the horrifying monster we saw in the woods and that made Snapper almost wet himself.

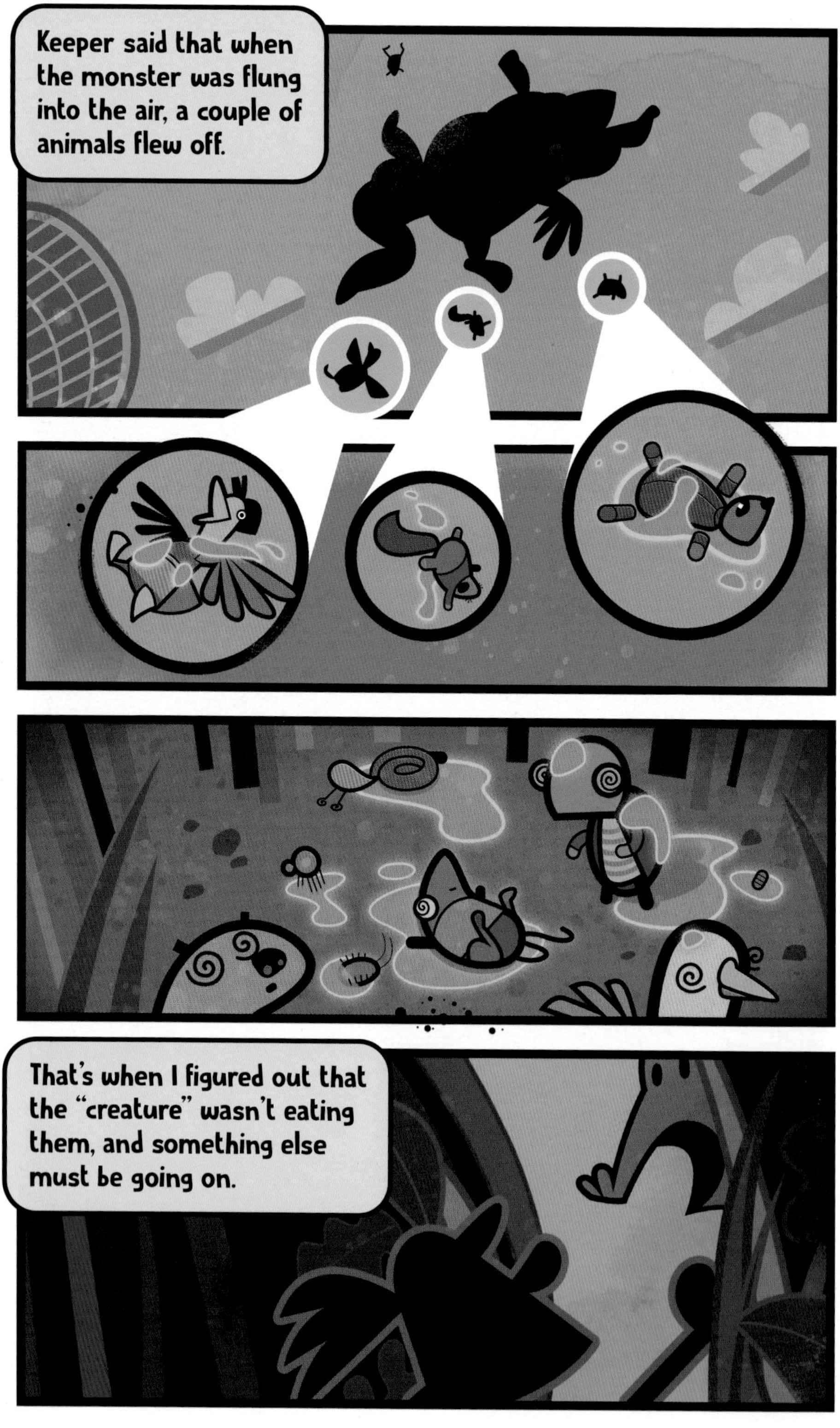
Keeper said that when the monster was flung into the air, a couple of animals flew off.
That's when I figured out that the "creature" wasn't eating them, and something else must be going on.

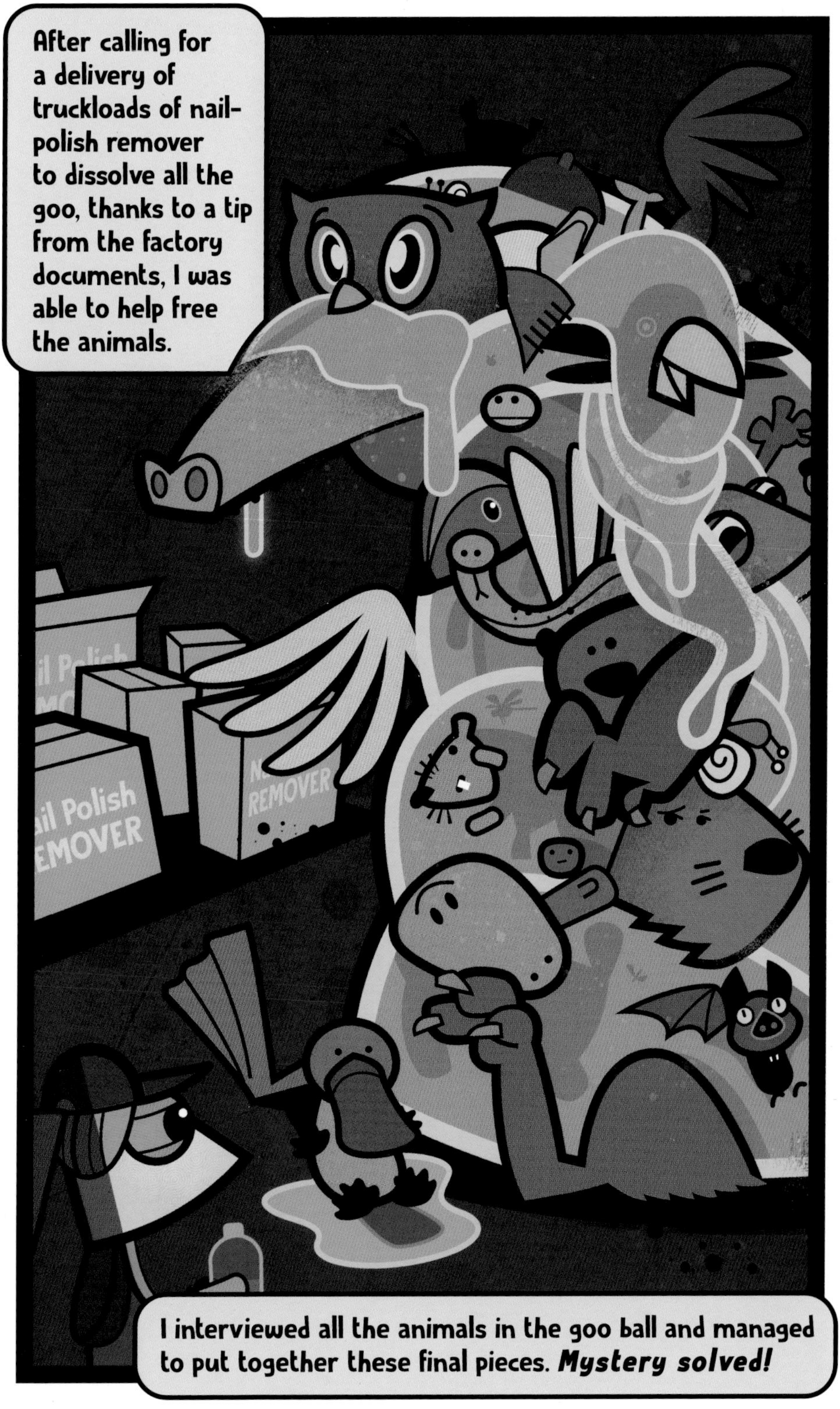
After calling for a delivery of truckloads of nail-polish remover to dissolve all the goo, thanks to a tip from the factory documents, I was able to help free the animals.
ail Polish
EMOVER
REMOVER
I interviewed all the animals in the goo ball and managed to put together these final pieces. Mystery solved!

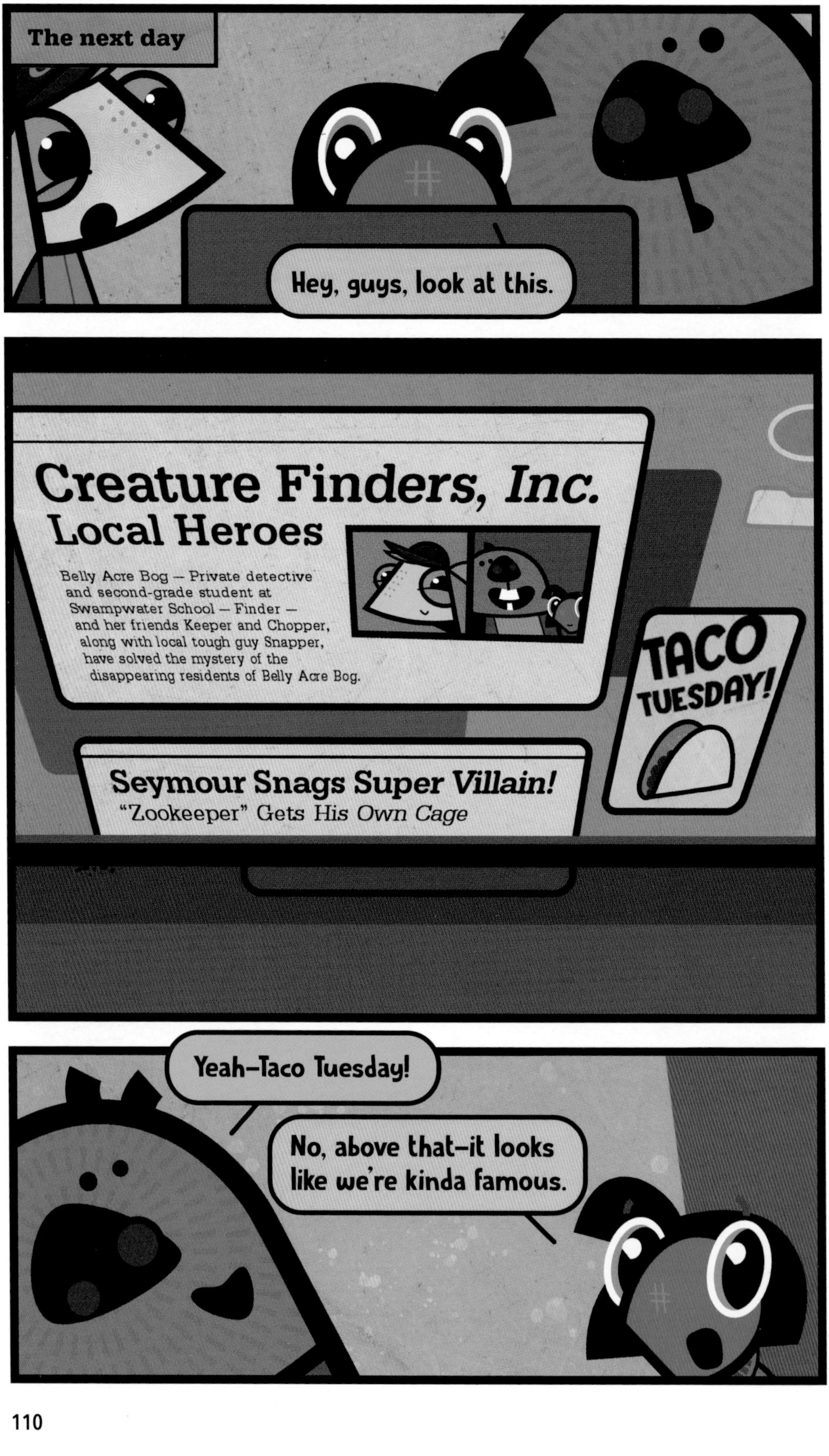

The next day
Hey, guys, look at this.
Creature Finders, Inc.
Local Heroes
Belly Acre Bog — Private detective and second-grade student at Swampwater School — Finder — and her friends Keeper and Chopper, along with local tough guy Snapper, have solved the mystery of the disappearing residents of Belly Acre Bog.
TACO TUESDAY!
Seymour Snags Super Villain!
"Zookeeper" Gets His Own Cage
Yeah–Taco Tuesday!
No, above that–it looks like we're kinda famous.

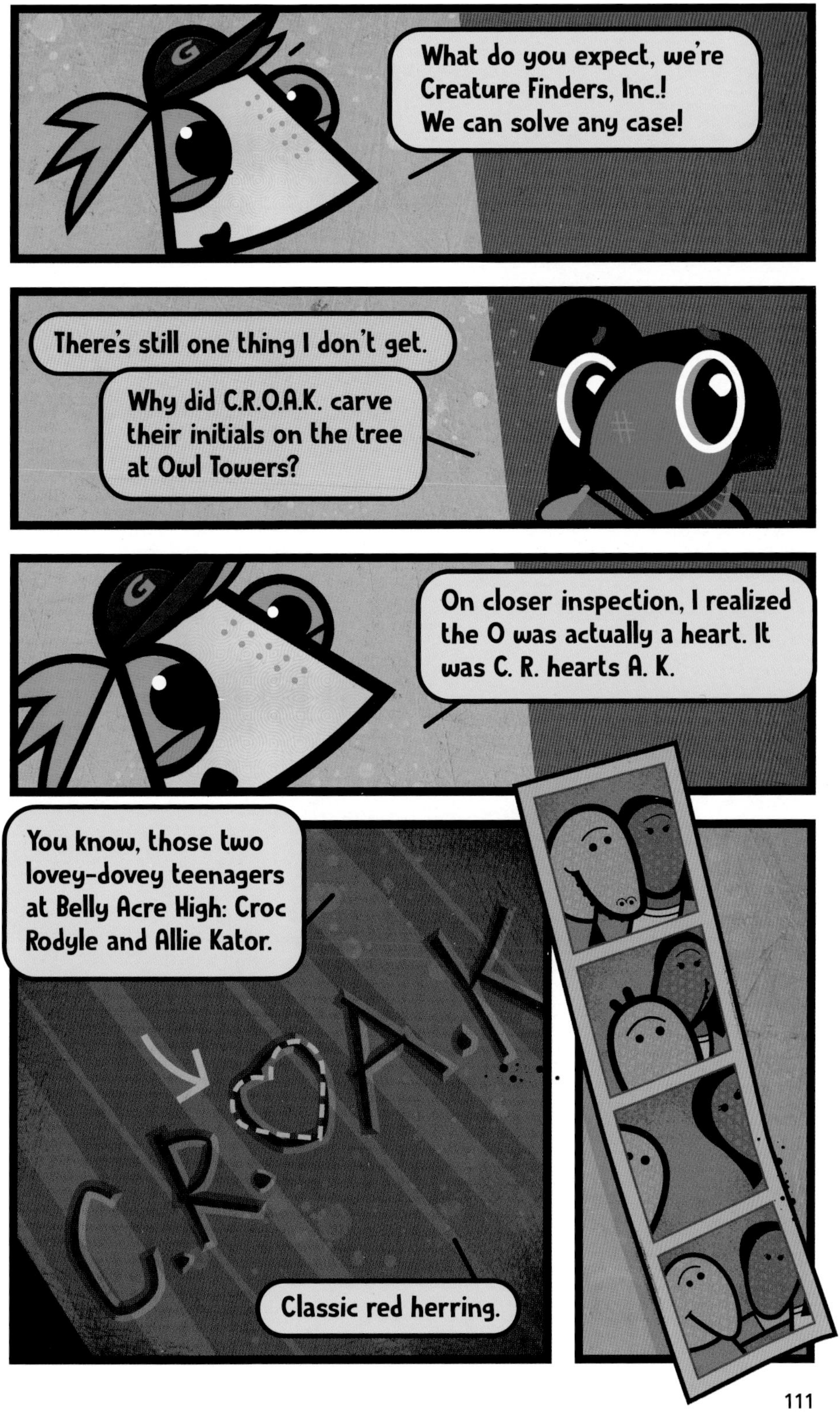
What do you expect, we're Creature Finders, Inc.! We can solve any case!
There's still one thing I don't get.
Why did C.R.O.A.K. carve their initials on the tree at Owl Towers?
On closer inspection, I realized the O was actually a heart. It was C. R. hearts A. K.
You know, those two lovey-dovey teenagers at Belly Acre High: Croc Rodyle and Allie Kator.
C.R.
A.K.
Classic red herring.

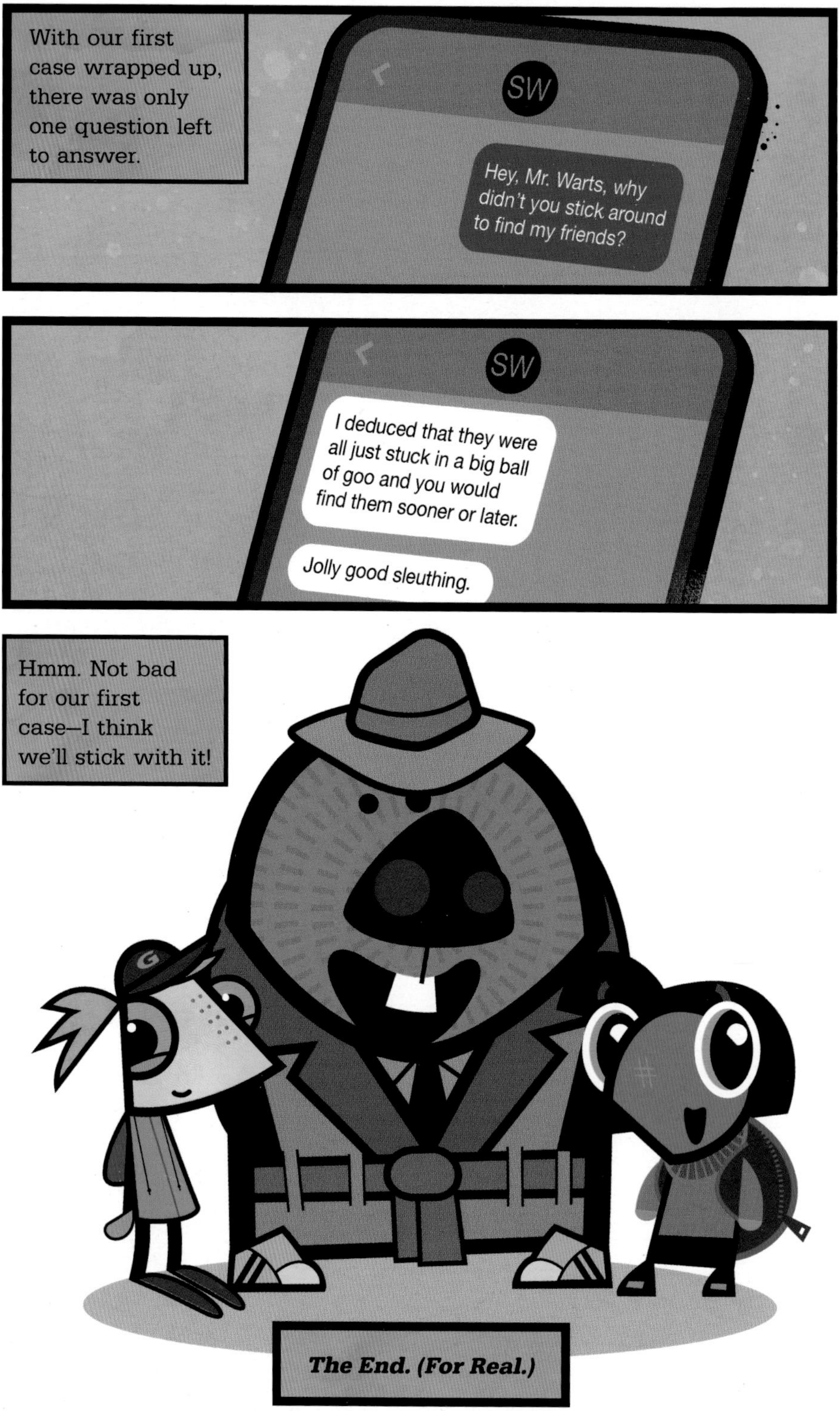
With our first case wrapped up, there was only one question left to answer.
SW
Hey, Mr. Warts, why didn't you stick around to find my friends?
SW
I deduced that they were all just stuck in a big ball of goo and you would find them sooner or later.
Jolly good sleuthing.
Hmm. Not bad for our first case—I think we'll stick with it!
G
The End. (For Real.)